KENNETH GILES
Death Among the Stars

WALKER AND COMPANY · NEW YORK

Copyright © 1968 by Kenneth Giles

All rights reserved. No part of this book may be reproduced or transmitted in any form or by any means, electric or mechanical, including photocopying, recording, or by any information storage and retrieval system, without permission in writing from the Publisher.

All the characters and events portrayed in this story are fictitious.

First published in the United States of America in 1969 by the Walker Publishing Company, Inc.

This paperback edition first published in 1985.

ISBN: 0-8027-3112-0

Library of Congress Catalog Card Number: 70-81069

Printed in the United States of America

10 9 8 7 6 5 4 3 2 1

THE DAILY BULLETIN

Founded as a daily paper by a Temperance Society in 1890, its masthead proclaiming 'the paper that any English Rose may read without a blush', a statement which was, however, abandoned during the exceptionally hot August of 1891.

In order of importance:

Proprietor:	Sir Peregrine (created Knight for social services: enthusiastic endorsement of the Munich Agreement). Years of relentlessly chasing mickles have made him a great muckle.
Managing Editor:	John Jolly, Esquire. About all one can say is that he is a proper s.o.b.
Head Porter:	Robert Walpole Bocker, elderly but with a wealth of experience.
Assistant Editor:	Peter Leeming, a patient wheel-horse.
Editor:	A very clean and obedient man, although obese.
Fashion Editress:	Miss Wasey Tump, a lady with an unfortunately kind heart. Her Assistant is young Miss Mabel Snowberry, slightly overweight and with a tendency to shirk work by retiring to the loo.
Astrologer:	Percy Button, a man of dubious antecedents.
Sports Sub-editor:	Archer McClout, ex-Sydney, N.S.W.

Author's note: The *Daily Bulletin* is pure fiction: as a newspaper it could hardly exist. An author must produce reasonable names, but he should emphasise that the *Sydney Bulletin*, a weekly with a very long and admirable history, ably managed and going strong, was not in the author's mind. Newspaper proprietors are in the author's experience kindly men and certainly not prototypes of Sir Peregrine. His many friends in the newspaper world are not depicted, with the exception of the Managing Editor, John Jolly, who anyone who worked with the author will recognise as an accurate self portrait.

"RETRENCH ALL OUTSIDE contributors," Sir Peregrine had snapped almost exactly a year ago before taking his grey Rolls-Royce to the Board of Empire Consolidated Paint. Of late City interests were taking up an increasing amount of his time. The lethal cut-and-thrust of newspaper politics, the cigarette-smoke festooning the whisky bottles in crowded little side rooms on the fourth floor were things of the past, largely because Sir Peregrine and a cold-eyed fat man of equally lethal potential controlled everything popular between them.

As usual Sir Peregrine was right. The nature correspondent, a retired stockbroker, had written an abusive letter from his Shropshire estate, but the bi-weekly three hundred words were now penned by a sub-editor, an elderly man and hence unable to protest, who had long bored everybody about his Surbiton allotment. Science was sent up by an unpleasant, pimpled youth in the library who had done it at school and read a lot of science fiction. The ex-stable boys who were special course correspondents and who were reputed to get up at five and spy on training gallops through powerful binoculars had gone. Not that it made any difference, thought John Jolly, staring at the caps of his tan shoes. A level pound on Happy Man's daily nap was currently fifty-six pounds five shillings and fourpence in the red as opposed to seventy-nine pounds six shillings and eightpence the previous year and his vis-à-vis Tishy now returned a profit of nineteen shillings and eightpence as against the sixty-seven pounds of loss incurred when the telegrams had poured in from Epsom and Newmarket.

But the astrologer, Percy Button, who had lived at Margate, or rather in the refinement of Cliftonville, had presented a minor problem. The name, Dr. Ali Hassan, was the registered property of the company. John Jolly had found to his surprise that his quite reputable American Encyclopaedia—dated 1912, most of the *Daily Bulletin*'s library being vintage—devoted seven pages to explaining the matter. He had almost made his mind up to give the task to the fashion editress—he didn't like the way she looked at him when she thought he could not see, as if observing out of the corner of your eye was not something he had learned thirty years ago on the old *Swansea Echo*: sometimes he really believed that he and Dylan used to get slopped together. Out of the blue this fellow Button proposed that he should join the staff at half his freelance earnings. He should have smelled a rat, thought Jolly. Who would exchange the briny joys of East Kent for London? And didn't some of these astrologers make a packet through small ads? Same as the stable boys. He had heard that one picked up fifty nicker per week by selling to the public the same info that he had been grateful to receive thirteen quid for from the *Bully*, as the staff called it.

Jolly became conscious that his spine had drooped and there was a silence. Leonine Leadership—a phrase coined in the *Tribune*—was his trade mark and he threw back the immense head, crowned by a mop of small grey curls, lately so familiar to commercial TV viewers.

"Fetch the police," said John Jolly quietly, his small eyes dwelling momentarily upon Percy Button who, blue in the face, lay on top of the desk with what appeared to be a bootlace tightly embedded in his neck above the rose-coloured nylon shirt. A most unpleasant colour combination, thought Jolly.

"I 'ave, sir, ten minutes ago when the boy phoned down. On their way, sir."

John Jolly loathed the superciliousness of Bocker, the elderly, stooped Head Porter, who made no bones about his superiority over everybody except the composing room foreman, a snarling wretch feared even by John Jolly. Yet Bocker was invaluable. If inside information was required, the editors found it better to have a discreet word with Bocker, whose contacts were strange and variegated, than brief a reporter who would retire to some remote pub and return with a large expense sheet.

And there were people who somehow got in and became threatening; one's secretary phoned Bocker and a large man named Alf quickly appeared to do what was necessary.

'The Wretched Boy', galley proofs dangling in his hands, was goggling adenoidally at the corpse.

"Get along, boy, and no talking," said Jolly, leonine.

"These 'ere proofs, sir, 'e carn't read 'em now."

"Give them to the Sports Editor with my orders to do what is necessary."

John Jolly and Bocker looked at the small bookshelf, containing what seemed to be a collection of Victorian sermons. Could there really have been a Dean Hole and a Prebendary Snook, thought Jolly, wishing that somehow he could rid himself of the impassive Bocker. A sly thought, product of all the affiliation cases he had taken down in Gregg at Swansea, reminded him to retain a witness. And very soon there were noises. A big man with waxed moustaches who was clad in a crumpled serge suit looked in. "Police here."

"Superintendent, glad to see you." Jolly extended a hand in greeting.

"Sergeant Honeybody," said the big man. "We've got the ambulance, the doctor, three photographers, two fingerprint blokes, and, oh, yes, here's Mr. James."

"Superintendent!" Jolly prepared for his two-handed shake, which gave the impression of some kind of spiritual rape.

"Inspector James, sir."

Jolly withdrew his hands. The man was mousy and not imposing. How dare they?

"This is a preliminary," said James, a trifle wearily. "The garbage truck. Eventually you will get top brass around."

"I see," said Jolly, uneasily, because Sir Peregrine would not like it on the score of prestige, the deadly rival having had a superintendent when he had slipped on some decayed fish whilst boarding the Brighton Flyer.

A small doctor had entered and looked dispassionately.

"Anything up to two hours." He did things with a thermometer.

"That is from two p.m. until now?" said Inspector James.

"More definitely, around three o'clock; my own opinion, but it's over to Path. Probably a blow producing unconsciousness, then strangulation."

"Won't keep you, Doc," said the self-effacing Inspector, "but definitely strangling?"

"Twenty to one on. Could be poison dressed up and disguised, but why the hell? Sir Plunkett will tell you in twenty-four hours, plus fancy theories." The doctor bustled out.

The large, fat sergeant was nursing a notebook. "You'd be the Editor, sir," he said to Bocker.

"'Ead Porter, guv, and bin for nineteen year. This is the Managing Editor."

"John Jolly, Inspector." The Editor ignored the Sergeant. "The corpse is our astrologer. The copy boy—he goes to press early as a standing feature, or did," Jolly massaged his large, hooked nose and thought of tomorrow... "discovered him."

"Perhaps we can talk elsewhere," said the Inspector. "There will be the technical stuff, photographs etcetera."

"Could we publish one?" asked Jolly, keenly.

"I cannot see why not." Inspector James tweaked his chin. "Not contempt or anything, but see that your man just flashes it through the open doorway so there can be no allegation of meddling."

"Bocker, tell Mr. Wilkinson to get here pronto with a camera to flash deceased."

Two lifts with attendants were flanked by a smaller one with purple doors which was self-operated and air-conditioned. John Jolly looked faintly startled when, after having ushered Inspector Harry James into its deodorised interior—Sir Peregrine had been hooked by Lifebuoy Soap advertisements when he was making his second fortune in the 1930s organising boiling-down and glue-making—Sergeant Honeybody's bulk jammed him against the back wall.

"What button, sir?" asked the Sergeant.

"Four," said Jolly, "that's the executive floor. Accountants and things."

"We have the staff canteen and the ladies' toilets up there back at work," said Honeybody with careless affability, as he stuck a large forefinger on to the appropriate button.

Sir Peregrine discouraged luxury and always took his current mistress tourist on their trips to Bermuda, so Jolly's personal office, which he was rarely in, was small and had plastic tiles which exuded a kind of rubbery smell when it got warm.

They sat down, with Honeybody's notebook balanced on a vast palm.

"When did you know it happened?" asked Inspector James.

"I get in at two, the cackle reached me at, oh, say fourish. I have a conference at five."

"Now, about deceased," said the Inspector.

"A Percy Button who wrote the astrology column. One minute." John Jolly's massive forefinger poked a telephone dial. "Jolly. Full details re Percy Button." He doodled on a scratch pad.

"Aged fifty-one, born in Bridlington. Used to live at Margate and freelance. On January thirteen last year he joined us full time. Unmarried. Lived not far away at 14 Quaker's Court."

"Seems kind of anonymous."

"He opted out of the non-contributory pension fund—it would have been difficult on account of his age—and, well, there was nothing much we needed to know."

"Special friends?"

"Well really, I think the Assistant Editor, Mr. Leeming, would be the best person to see...."

"And you know of nobody who might have wanted to..." Inspector James made a small apologetic gesture.

"Good God, no!"

The small intercom—the Inspector noted it had only six channels—buzzed.

"Bocker, sir, speaking from the 'all. Two uniformed police officers are with me. Is it all right if I give them the day's egress sheets?"

The Inspector cocked an eyebrow.

"Anybody entering this building, except for the purpose of delivery, is required to sign a form, name, address and nature of visit. Bocker or his assistant time-stamps it. This is to ensure that an important name cannot be lost."

The Inspector thought he detected a slight shiftiness on Jolly's broad Irish chops.

"By all means give them to the police. How many?"

"A quiet day, sir, twenty-three and them mostly from the trade."

The Inspector interposed. "Mr. Bocker, did any stranger leave a bit after three?"

"One Joe Milk, sir, on about oil."

"Oil!" said John Jolly.

"Under the nave of St. Paul's, a huge deposit, but the Dean won't let him dig it up."

"Why was he let in?"

"Oh," said Bocker comfortingly, "if you start ejecting too many people spiteful tongues start to wag.... I remember a drunken rugby team and all the bother we 'ad, before your time o' course. He calls on all the offices once a month. Here the senior boy—wants to be a journalist—gives him twenty minutes, then he trots off happy as a little king. Used to work a fruit barrer until 'is brain got water on it. Nice little old fellow 'oo lives off Seven Dials. 'Is son has done nice in the sweetie line."

"Thank you," John Jolly flicked the switch. "There are times when talking to Mr. Bocker I realise the meaning of 'floodgates'."

"Seems to know his job."

"He left the *Mail* when Lord Northcliffe died—said it wasn't the same—and came here."

"Sounds oldish."

"Over retiring age, but he appealed to Sir Peregrine...."

Inspector James made a mental note that perhaps there were certain under-currents.

Jolly had creased his brows and flicked up the switch again. "Oh, Bocker, do you know of an astrologer that can put in a few hours part-time until we, er, make, um, other arrangements?"

"There's a bloke who drinks in the Grapes, sir. 'E gambles real 'eavy and is partial to brandy, so he needs money all the time."

"Try to get him in tomorrow." Jolly switched off. "Sorry, Inspector, but—I find I have to deal with each situation as it occurs and before it's buried. Which brings me," he directed a sepulchral glance to the floor, "the Staff Manager and the Assistant Chief Accountant are always there in the case of working journalists. And, of course, the flowers to be arranged by Bocker."

"We'd better await the Inquest, sir."

"Quite. I don't know what Sir Peregrine will say, he abominates unpleasantness."

"Dare say so did the late Mr. Button."

Jolly's eyes could become very cold.

"What is important," said Inspector James, "is to establish who last saw him."

"And that I can do." Jolly's large freckled paw opened what appeared to be a small box of cigars and produced a microphone. "This operates a hailer in every room of this building including toilets. In case of fire, bombs, or insurrections, I can take full charge." He stretched his head back so that the flaps around his throat straightened. "Hear this, hear this."

Jolly uttered a Welsh obscenity—the accent was rather bad, thought the Inspector who had spent boyhood time on a desolate hill farm—"this bloody little light is supposed to go on at the side of this effing microphone. Curse the maintenance staff. Curse them...."

"The light went on at my desk, sir, on account that lifting that thing actuates one, but as I didn't hear no noise I took the liberty of riding up in the private lift." The door had opened noiselessly and Bocker's grey head drooped obsequiously. He carried a flashy combination screwdriver in one hand.

Bocker dexterously removed the microphone from Jolly's hand—'nerveless hand' was the cliché, thought the Inspector—

and fiddled. "Just one of the wires come loose, Mr. Jolly, sir."

In the distance Inspector James heard a booming travesty of Bocker's soft tones.

"Hear me, hear me," said Jolly, a red flush on his cheeks. "The astrologer, Mr. um, Mr...."

"Percy Button, sir," said Bocker as the speakers echoed him.

"As I was saying, Mr. Button. Anyone seeing or communicating with him between two and four, or even earlier, should communicate with me. Repeat, anybody seeing Mr. Button, particularly between two and four."

Jolly magisterially replaced the microphone.

"He came back from 'is lunch at one fifteen as was his custom, sir," said Bocker, putting the screwdriver in his breast pocket, "same as usual."

"You saw him?" asked the Inspector.

"It's between twelve and three that 'they'—the daft 'uns—try to come in, sir, so for fifty years, man and boy, it's been corned-beef-and-pickle sandwiches and an eye on the doorway for yours truly, assistant head porter and then head. Always the same with Mr. Button, out at twelve, then a Baby's Head and Chips, a Kit-Kat bar and white coffee at the A.B.C. Back here sharp."

"How do you know this?" asked the Inspector.

"You get to know, sir," said Bocker. "Now the Sports Editor, in the line of duty, goes into a few licensed premises. At the moment," Bocker consulted an elaborate watch, "he would be in the Pindar of Wakefield. Mr. Muffitt—Features—is a recently married man and takes a taxi home to Brixton for a late lunch hour. And so on."

"Quite! Quite!" said Jolly, as the telephone rang, and he listened, briefly.

He replaced the receiver.

"That was Miss Tump—she's Fashion Editress. The odds and ends are on the third floor: syndication, sports stastistics, I mean statistics, the library, personnel, the nurse, etcetera. Tump and her girl are next to this, er..."

"Button, sir," prompted Bocker.

"Yes," said Jolly with an evil look. "And how I'm to explain it to Sir Peregrine I don't know. Button had obtained a box of one hundred ball-point refills from Stores. The rule is that the appropriation for each one must be made out on the form provided, okayed by the departmental head—in his case the General Features Editor—and taken to Stores on the sixth floor."

"They all do it, sir," soothed Bocker.

"I'll take them apart," said Jolly. "I will have rules obeyed...."

"About Miss Tump," said the Inspector.

"At about five past three the old hag wandered into, er, Button's office to cadge a refill. Too effing lazy to go to the sixth floor. There's no lift—Sir Peregrine had it removed; it was just encouraging them to indent for copy paper to take home. The canteen's up there and the printers' bog. You'd be surprised how long they can hold it rather than walk up a couple of hundred stairs. Of course they try to make keys to the staff lavatories, but Bocker keeps an eye on that."

"I've been meaning to talk to you about the sinks in the dark rooms, sir," said Bocker, "just next door to the composing room and..."

"Get me Wilkinson," snarled Jolly. "Get him!"

"He's superintending photographing the Scene of the Crime, sir," said Bocker, "and as a matter of fact, sir, he did tell me that it—revives was his expression—the developer. Less is used than it was..."

"It's saving us money?"

"Yes, sir, and the men work better when they're not extended, if you know what I mean."

"Perhaps Mr. Bocker could take us to see Miss Tump," said the Inspector.

"Carry on, Bocker!" said Jolly.

"A pretty how-d'you-do, this," said Bocker in the lift, "they're upsettable people, all nerves unless steadied with the drink, mostly."

"Perhaps you and the Sergeant could have a brief wet," said

the Inspector, "on H.M. I dare say your assistant is coping."

"There's a nice little place I know down the road, the one with the corned-beef sandwiches and good bitter," said Honeybody. "I used to take the pornographic magazine blokes there quite regular."

"I know it." Bocker looked at his watch as the lift jolted to a standstill. "My deputy can carry on."

The Inspector tapped at the door of the office next to the late Button's. What transpired to be Miss Wasey Tump was a tall, thin, rangy woman with buck teeth who looked as though she might gallop off.

"I must get back to me dooty," said Bocker, thirsty, "unless..."

"As we said," said Sergeant Honeybody, "a pot at the Hen and Feathers never hurt no one."

"Encouraging Bocker to drink," said Miss Tump, "is like encouraging Niagara Falls to pass water."

She had a pleasant voice. Her office was rather larger than the late Percy Button's, but also contained a young fat girl peering through spectacles at a page of type and photographs attached to a kind of lectern.

"Perhaps we might discuss things in a more salubrious atmosphere," said Harry. "My Sergeant is public by temperament, so mayhap the saloon. All oak and discretion."

"Be back at seven, Mabel," said Miss Tump, "but put the stuff away."

Few but the initiated knew of the Hen and Feathers, 'the Old Hen', as the crazy little seventeenth-century building, with its blackened wood and incomprehensible little judas window set in every door, was known to *aficionados*. Its landlord was a large shaggy old Irishman who was famous for his malapropisms—the Inspector always swore they were rehearsed.

"I found a lovely old bottle of pork wine in the back of the cellar. Before my time, Superintendent."

"Inspector, but a small one, and Miss Tump?" asked Harry.

"Half of bitter. Thanks! I suppose you're on about poor old Button?"

Harry nodded.

"At approximately three ten I entered, said, 'Give us one of those pen refills, please, Percy'. He got out the box, very deliberate as was his wont. I took one and that was that."

"How was he?"

"The same. Fit, fattish, always giving the impression of having rapidly concealed something in his desk drawer. I often wondered about dirty photos."

"Like that?"

"My dear policeman, nobody was purer in speech than deceased. But if he was typing anything he always took it out of the machine and placed it face downwards. That, actually, is a phobia some of us have, but Percy, moon-faced Percy, did rather seem to itch a bit."

"How well did you know him?"

"I do not think anybody knew him well. He wrote the stuff, the copy boy took it to the comps, Features would bark anything about space over his phone. He was like that milk-dispensing machine old Peregrine put in on the ground floor, except as far as I know Button doesn't, didn't, give short measure." Miss Tump paused and sipped. She seemed to be deliberating, then came to a decision. "I do not think he was British by birth."

"What!"

"In journalism, Inspector, it is often advisable to take an odd name. That frightful bastard Jolly was born Brown—I happened to meet a retired Swansea journalist who described him as a vile boy who amply fulfilled his early promise. You surely do not imagine anybody could be named Tump?"

"Well..." said the Inspector.

"Oh, the really brainy girls, Whitehorn *et al.*, don't need a gimmick. But I'm just very competent and don't ask for more money, which is why Jolly keeps me on. My father was half Lithuanian, half German, my mother was Polish Hungarian. I speak seven languages."

"You sound English."

"My father had the perspicacity to realise that both Stalin

and Hitler meant exactly what they said at a time when Mr. Chamberlain was vetting the receipts from the Birmingham public lavatories. So we came here."

"Had this man Button an accent?"

"You'll find journalists drive you mad, raconteurs to the backbone. We never listen to each other, but, boy, a captive civilian audience! I think he was a Hungarian. Inside Jolly's bonhomie lurks a very small, spiteful person and he specialises in snide remarks. I was walking towards the lift alongside Button about four months ago, and there hoves Jolly, fresh from his snooping activities. He says something or other and as I neared the lift I muttered something in Magyar which is an excellent tongue to be vulgar in. I must say it was apposite and funny, and I was just wondering if it would shock my father when I saw Button's face. Suppressed laughter! I'm not kidding. And when you have the key, it's easy. There were slight Magyar intonations in Percy's voice."

"What did he say when you asked?"

"My parents," said Miss Tump, "inevitably gave their time to various refugee organisations. I did a little stamp-licking. One thing you learned was not to pry. If Button had something to forget, why should I pick at him? If I want to talk Magyar I can in plenty of places outside the *Bully*."

"To tell you the truth, the *Bulletin* is not on my list of required reading."

"If you want to know anything about the rag, the Assistant Editor, one Peter Leeming, has been there twenty-five years, stupendous for this neck of the woods, long before old Peregrine added it to his empire. Leeming, for what it's worth..." she drained her glass and Harry followed suit.

"Another pork, please, and...?"

"Small pink gin."

The landlord looked baleful as he always did when his mispronunciations were echoed back, but he filled the glasses.

"I was saying that Leeming stumbled on the format. We're mostly syndicated magazine stuff, heavily worked over. News agencies provide the news, a minimum of reporting, some exposé stories. The *Mirror, Sun Express* etcetera have a large quota of straight news. We have bloody little. We cater strictly for mindless monsters, of whom there are enough to keep Sir Peregrine in expensive blonde women. I joined because with the languages and four years on local papers I thought like a sucker I might get a foreign appointment. But they don't have foreign correspondents—why should they when there's Reuter, so says Sir Peregrine? And my job: I revamp the agency fashion stuff. The only trip I get to Paris is at my own expense come holidays. And then I don't go near the rag trade."

The Inspector savoured the dryness of the port and made a note to keep on the right side of the publican.

"As good a drop of port as I've tasted these long years, Mr. Ryan."

"Ar," the publican was half placated. "You fellers don't know how lucky you are. The wife and I took this Christmas tour to the Greek islands on account of you could pay in sterling, with three perfessors and a folk dancer. Resinous wine, purple wine, they kept on about it... made you sick. And the little feller, something at Oxford, told my wife he'd press her to a mazurka. When we came back I looked it up. Some kind of indecent dance. I nearly wrote to the shipping line. But here you get decent English liquor and grub." He looked righteous.

"Comedian," thought Harry. A surmise struck him. The man was rehearsing. "Tell me, Mr. Ryan," he said, "are you a Savage?"

"I have the honour." A trifle chap-fallen, the publican went back to polishing some glasses.

"He's a professional wag," said Miss Tump, "life and sole—fishy stories—of the club."

"You don't do too bad," said Harry.

"Pro stuff; we hate amateurs. All comedians have sad little people inside."

Harry watched her drain her glass.

"Our masters await," he said.

Indeed Honeybody's large face had momentarily craned round the partition which masked the public bar from the presumably higher taxed denizens of the saloon. Outside the Inspector and Miss Tump were joined by the Sergeant and Bocker, the latter insisting on a respectful two paces to the rear.

"When do you knock off?" Harry asked Miss Tump.

"Sevenish. There's an occasional with-it thing at night, but mostly I've got the photographs and copy in hand by two-ish."

"And you, Mr. Bocker?" The Inspector glanced back.

"Around twelve, sir. The sons are grown up and in practice. I live with a younger sister whose husband I disapprove of on political grounds. Me old friends are in this street. A bit of a wet, a good dressed steak as we used to say, and regular look-ins to the foyer to keep an eye on the night staff. People only cause trouble, sir, with a full belly, so I keep an eye on seven—pre-theatre—and eleven-thirty. If they cut all this foreign aid out and there weren't full bellies you wouldn't get the trouble abroad."

The foyer of the *Daily Bulletin* seemed filled with police. A broad stout man, Superintendent Porterman, had commandeered a small desk on which droves of plain clothes men periodically converged. Harry groaned, for they liked each other not in the least and Porterman leaned heavily towards paper work which generally meant unpaid overtime.

"Goodnight," said the Inspector to Miss Tump and Bocker, who was looking aghast at the invasion of his realm. "Come with me, Sergeant."

The liftman was all of eighteen and inclined to be uppity until the Inspector waved his warrant card. "Mr. Peter Leeming and get a bloody move-on before I kick your arse to Charing Cross."

Leeming sat at the back of the long news room, with its steady pulsation. The copy tasters, green eye-shaded, spiked, vetted, and passed on the pounds of flimsy paper. Leeming had the harassed expression of a man who had spent the years waiting to hear the worst. He was very tall, thin in a delicate and rather decorative manner, with hair so blond that it was difficult to tell if it was going white, and a skin the texture of dried, skinned cod. He was listening to the telephone.

"Yes, Mr. H., I know, sir. Sir P.'s very conscious of it. . . . If it's parlour pink they want, we can't with due respect swim against the stream and tell them it should be green. No, no, sir, Sir P. has the shareholders to consider, sir. We have public money invested and a responsibility. Believe me, sir, Sir P. has instructed us all to do everything we can. Good night, sir.

"God!" he said, replacing the handset, and gazing at Harry's warrant, "I've heard of you, Inspector. You can't do right in this business. You tell the Tories it concerns shareholders and they shut up; tell Labour it's public interest and they crawl in. But then, God help me, you've got the Liberals and town councillors. About Percy Button, I suppose."

Leeming told a fat man that page two would not do for the Home Counties and sighed. "I looked it up. Twelve years ago we had the usual four-inch astrology. At that time I was in charge of Features. A Percy Button wrote from Margate with a new idea. A witty astrology column, with samples. It *was* witty—little pungent jokes. Altogether something new. Whether he saw the stars majestically and in clear, Inspector, cuts no ice with me. But it got its readership. When Sir P. decided to cut outside freelance work, Mr. Jolly, in his wisdom, took Button on the staff. We will find him difficult to replace. Mr. Jolly has an idea of a female astrologer with pin-up girls."

"Who is in line for the job?"

Leeming's eyes were small and shrewd. "No motive there, no promotion that side of the astral ocean. The job will be thrust on to some poor devil of a staff writer. Jolly mentioned Miss Tump. And at no increase in pay."

"Curiously, nothing much is known about him," murmured the Inspector.

Leeming shrugged. "The old Fleet Street with Chesterton waving tankards and hard doers catching the six o'clock trams over the river has been gone for some years. We're just steady pros doing a technical job. Button wrote a column and kept six days ahead with emergency stuff to be used if he was ever ill, which staff records record he never was, and I had no other interest in him."

"Was he foreign?" Inspector James snapped the question.

"He spoke and wrote like an Englishman, flat London accent. His copy was a little American, I thought, which added a touch of salt, but a lot of journalists assume it."

"Thanks, Mr. Leeming." They left him to four men who were exercised in their minds concerning the rival attraction of rape in Fulham and rude words on a synagogue in Balham.

The foyer was bedlam. Reporters from other papers were trying to get in and being repelled by Bocker and two gigantic assistants.

"Be calm, gentlemen," Superintendent Porterman was intoning, a bishop among cops.

"'S'news ennit?" screamed a dirty little man in a green pork-pie hat. "Freedom of the press, ennit? All the horgans should 'ave admittance."

"I'll 'ave your ears framed," rumbled one of the large men.

"Gentlemen," threatened Porterman, "I'll have you all cleared out."

"You try," said a dignified man who looked like a bogus company director. "The Press Council will have the uniform off your back."

"Don't give me your bloody clichés," shouted the Superintendent, stung.

Harry James and Sergeant Honeybody slipped out as somebody swung a punch.

Quaker's Court was down a small street—Pepper Lane—where you could smell the stench of Thames mud at low tide.

Honeybody sniffed. "Good for the lungs, they say."

"I'd rather a double Haig for mine," grunted the Inspector, reflecting on the inevitability which always placed the number you looked for at the extreme end of any thoroughfare.

Number fourteen did look rather as if it had been washed up at high tide. The Inspector, who disliked small boats on principle, could never remember which was port and which was starboard, but number fourteen had a definite list to one or the other. There was a faintly rotted quality about it, the ancient bricks, scarred by sulphurous fumes and pigeon dung, might have been driftwood. It could not be at this time of the year, but the Inspector thought he detected the faint lingering stench of fog in the air. But when they went up three grimy steps and pulled a wire bell the door opened and there wafted out stale cabbage odours.

Harry James was familiar with London lodging-house-keepers, falsely smiling, trying to eke out a living of sorts from tenants who loathed them, rack-rented by landlords, everlastingly tormented by antique plumbing and complaints about horse-hair mattresses. The woman who ran number fourteen was a cut above the usual run, a pleasant middle-aged blonde who whitened under her make-up as the Inspector explained his errand.

Percy Button had occupied two rooms on the second floor, a bedroom and a sitting-room, both rather chintzy but pleasant and obviously recently decorated. The living-room was lined with bookcases, of the extending type. Harry shook his head. He had never seen so many current reference books, town council reports included.

"A bit of a crease here, Harry," said the Sergeant, for a moment unbending. He addressed the Inspector by his Christian name around four times a year, excluding parties.

The wall-to-wall synthetic carpet showed a bend in the corner of the room. The Sergeant dropped ponderously to his knees.

"The tacks have been removed." The corner of the carpet flipped up and over. Honeybody removed a floorboard. Inside was a leather box.

"Steel underneath and a combination lock." Honeybody caressed it.

"Leave it," said Harry, a memory of one of his police courses flickering in his mind. "We carry it tenderly back to the lab."

He glanced around, noting a very elaborate radio. Of American make, he saw from the name plate, and probably the best—certainly the most expensive—in the world.

"I discourteously forgot to ask your name." He addressed the landlady.

"Mrs.—I'm a widow—Ethel Curl."

"Had Mr. Button been here long?"

"He was here when I moved in two years ago. My impression was that he was a very old tenant. We have mostly old tenants, bachelors working in the City who find it comfortable."

"Many visitors?"

"None at the door that I can ever recall; but of course the gents often bring other gents home for a convivial glass. I am willing to provide snacks like toasted cheese. All I worry about, frankly, is noise. No noise, no packdrill."

"Who owns the place?"

"I do. My husband was a builder; he left me enough to buy it. This street will be worth a lot of money one day."

"We are taking this box." The Inspector scribbled in his notebook and tore off the sheet. "This receipt will cover you. And I shall seal the door, pending a thorough examination of these rooms. Any pecuniary loss to you will be compensated in due course."

"Of course, Inspector, I should not dream of troubling you."

"He had no relatives?"

She shrugged. "None that I knew of. It was 'good morning Mr. Button, good morning Mrs. Curl'."

They moved out. Harry got the tiny can out of his wallet, lit a thimbleful of surgical spirit, applied the adhesive paper over the crack between door and lintel, doled out heated sealing wax and applied his thumb to both ends.

"There will be some men around tomorrow. Sorry to be a nuisance."

"A pint, sir, frankly I need oiling. When you get to my age it's the knees and they have good beer in this area." Honeybody's moustaches waggled as he supplicated.

"Just one," the Inspector saw by his watch that it was nearing seven. He shook Mrs. Curl's hard, capable hand.

In fact they had two and it was eight before Harry tapped at the door of his superior officer, Superintendent Hawker.

Strange grunting sounds seemed to come through the worn oak panels, squeaking and, the Inspector could have sworn, foul language. Hawker was ancient for bodily offences and was in any case afraid of women, so Harry turned the handle and burst in, stopping as he saw Hawker's Harris-tweed-clad legs—the old gentleman was meditating rearing pigs and cashing in on the Common Market—wildly gyrating in the air.

"Turn off the effing current," howled Hawker.

The Inspector saw that the aged Superintendent was apparently anchored to some kind of apparatus, itself umbilicular to an electric plug. This he removed, and he saw Hawker's face scarlet with indignation and high blood pressure.

"A health seat," panted the Superintendent, "wouldn't it be just like a Yank to send a poor old man like me an electric chair?"

"A Yank?"

"A Miss Olga Hadden. I had occasion to observe that the salts didn't stir me like they did, so this arrived with a note saying it got rid of her daddy's wind."

It looked expensive, chromium, plastic, pulleys, and a powerful electric motor at the back.

Harry peered. "There's a bloody great sign, 'Caution, always consult instruction book'."

Hawker was being extricated by Sergeant Honeybody. "Careful, man," he snarled, "my vitals are like a map of Europe." To the Inspector, he said, sulkily, "I don't read instruction books; once I nearly cut my thumb off in a fan as the result of looking at one."

Harry saw a fattish manual on the desk. He picked it up and riffled through. "From a brief peering, sir, sedentary workers should start with number one, a gentle, rocking massaging movement apparently endorsed by Dean Rusk. You were on nine, apparently favoured by heavyweight boxers and President Johnson. Try it again tomorrow. It says that it soothes, brings up wind, regularises the bowels and has the same effect on the liver as a twenty-mile ride." Hawker peered malevolently over the big desk. His gaze alighted upon the small case deposited by the Sergeant.

"Christmas," he whispered, "you spotted it?"

"Never saw one but the manual has a photo. Under the wall-to-wall in Percy Button's flat."

As though to marshal his own thoughts, the Superintendent addressed Honeybody. "Meddle with one of these and something inside—there's a choice of four chemicals—develops white heat in a few seconds. When you get it open, there's a fused mass of what-not."

"Does it explode?"

"God, no, the people who use these are professionals. They don't want a public outcry; just fifteen years and exchanged for a British bod within two years. We'll open it; two fellows in asbestos armour with laser beams, if they're lucky!"

"Oh, God!" said Harry. Every policeman hates espionage work.

"His prints," said Hawker gloomily, "belong to a Percival Bretton, with the inevitable Canadian passport—it must be an industry there—who operated a shop in Washington selling books on the occult in 1947. There was a mad typist in the State Department who wanted to communicate with the Devil. Quite a bad leak. The F.B.I. were about eight hours too late. Hoover told me over the phone that he thought one of his operatives got a bit too close to Bretton alias Button. Trouble was that this Bretton didn't *look* very smart. Hoover thinks he might have been middle echelon—communications etcetera—and I'd accept his word about anything."

"We'd better take his flat apart. Fourteen Quaker's Court, Pepper Lane," said Harry.

Hawker spoke rapidly over the intercom. "They'll be there in ten minutes. You dictate your report here and now. God alone knows what top priority calls I'll be getting. I'd like to get the Home Secretary in that chair and turn him on!"

Harry reached down and switched on to tape. Occasionally he paused to allow space for Honeybody's basso.

"Hm," said Hawker at last. "I can only hope that Porterman

gets it by attrition; who was where at what time."

His green telephone rang and he listened almost without comment for ten minutes.

"Carry on. Get in immediate touch with Mr. Porterman. Carte blanche for this one."

Hawker belched as he replaced the handset. "Perhaps it does bring up the wind at that, but there comes a time when you prefer wind. I remember my old mother and the laxatives they used to have...no matter." He drummed his fingers on the desk, a sure sign of worry. "The bird has flown the coop. No Mrs. Ethel Curl, but an incinerator with nicely sifted ashes, a right professional effort. Your seal on Mr. Button's room broken, the bookshelves higgledy-piggledy. On a quick check Mrs. Curl kept herself to herself. It is not a giving-out district, but she did not shop locally. None of the local banks carried her account. The rest of the tenants seem old city clerks of the superior brand."

"Prints?" asked Harry.

"None at all in her private flat in the sub-basement. Quick sponge job. We'll move the latest equipment in tomorrow. Too bad you didn't spot her as a fake."

"She was as English as I am, apparently."

"And you an offensive little Welshman! I'd report you for this, James, but for the fact you're lucky. Never saw a man who dropped so many catches only for them to alight in his trouser pocket. You, Sergeant, get down to Identikit and build this old bitch's picture up."

"Hardly that, sir," said Harry stiffly, as the Sergeant left, leaving a kind of conspiratorial leer, "attractive, spent money on her appearance."

"They're always the worst," groaned Hawker, "but between you and me, Mr. James, did you have a wet?"

"About thirty-five minutes, sir, two pints."

"That'll look good in the Report, now that feller in the House is always on about morality."

"Nothing wrong with two pints, about four bob between us into the Exchequer."

"I suppose there was a barmaid?"

"Three fat girls."

"You see," groaned Hawker, "when this whatsisname tells it it'll be you and Honeybody rolling them the other side of the bar among the empties. Nasty tongue he's got."

"Not when the Press see the girls and Honeybody," said Harry, with a slight inward doubt about the latter. Whilst the girls were chaste, heavily stayed English roses, Honeybody did look a bit on the libidinous side, come to think of it.

"Twelve minutes before you got here," said Hawker, "a fast ship, Latvian register, took off down the Thames. She specialises in perishable, semi-refrigerated stuff and she had half loaded when the captain told the agent he was taking off."

"Can't we have her boarded?"

"My God," said Hawker, "we're not living in Palmerston's time. *Board her* and the P.M. denounced as a fascist tyrant? You're joking. In any case she'll be beyond the Limit by now, one of the fastest ships afloat, despite the rust. It's pretty well established that she carries elaborate instruments under the Polish ham."

"I thought we jammed them," said the Inspector.

"Of course; half the barges along the river are filled with Military Intelligence, and frogmen attach things underneath foreign hulls. Ah, well, get home, Inspector. No point in you staying. Tomorrow we should have *some* facts."

The Inspector went and found Honeybody in the lab. The Sergeant was good on Identikit, although in the case of women he fell foul of busts.

"Now, Honeybody," said Harry, "your imagination has given her at least a forty-five-inch bust. She was at most thirty-two."

"I remember looking at it," said the Sergeant doubtfully, but the technician leered at Harry and reduced the measurement on the board.

"Legs, now," said Harry. "She had a mini-skirt and had those rather muscular, slightly bandy legs that are so sexy."

"Ah," said the technician, "rare to find a leg man these days; the American influence, I always say."

"Get a move on," said Harry. "I think the nose is too large."

"Her bust I may have exaggerated," said Honeybody, "but that great conk, no. I remember thinking she'd be a prime bint but for the conk."

Eventually they went up in the lift to the ground floor. The Sergeant's daughter had married and flown the coop seven months before and Mrs. Honeybody, on the formidable side, was paying the happy couple a visit of inspection, although not before arranging for the neighbour, her dearest friend, to keep a diary reporting Honeybody's comings and goings. The Sergeant had not dealt with hardened criminals for many years for nothing and his counter-move was to approach Elizabeth, the Inspector's wife, who had a soft spot for the Sergeant. His wife owned, surreptitiously because shop-keeping is not encouraged in the Force, a fish-and-chip shop, so in return for cut-price hake—Elizabeth had an economy campaign on—plus the firm understanding that he provided his own drink—the Sergeant was allowed free victuals and an armchair in the Inspector's living-room until he reared his monstrous bulk erect and with alarming solemnity went down to his taxi. Elizabeth, by request, kept a notebook listing Honeybody's arrivals and departures which, with a solemn declaration as to sobriety, was destined to confound Mrs. Honeybody on her return.

Harry had whined about ethics and perjury.

"Don't be absurd, Harry," his wife had snapped.

The Sergeant, carrying an old Gladstone bag which clinked, insisted on paying for a cab, leaving the Inspector to gloomy thoughts about income tax and the amount of cash you could pocket if you sold fried fish.

As he kissed his wife he noted with alarm that one floury hand clutched the paperback edition of Doctor Spock. There was wafted to him the faint, offensive smell of nappies drying on a clothes-horse before the gas fire. The Inspector frequently despaired of a changing world. His wife's young, earnest, bespectacled lady gynaecologist was against nappy-wash services, and disposable ones. Indeed if she had had her way Elizabeth would have been delivered in the flat instead of in a huge

Government-supported midwifery factory where Amanda, at the Inspector's insistence, had come to light at the statutory Welfare State six pounds avoirdupois.

"Dr. Hollybotham is out on a caesarean," Elizabeth wailed, "does dog food hurt them?"

"Now, now," Honeybody's sheer weight impelled Elizabeth backwards down the hall, "no panic and we'll get it straight."

"It's the play pen," said Elizabeth. "Mr. Bones gets in."

Mr. Bones was an enormous dog of doubtful antecedents.

"She won't nosh her Heinz food unless he eats his grub in it at nights. I went out to do the potatoes and when I came back Bones was eating the Heinz and she had her face down in his dog food."

"What the bloody hell was the Heinz doing in her play pen?" The Inspector felt the warmth of blood in his neck. He never remembered the sensation occurring before he married.

"I put it down to cool because of the potatoes."

"Curse the goddamned potatoes." The Inspector flung his hat on to the ugly little table inside the door. It bounced and he had to stoop to pick it up with lack of dignity. "Anyway," he said sullenly, "it's only dried horse meat. They give it to foxhounds."

"Harry James," flared his wife, "you are the biggest..."

"Now," said Honeybody, "let's have a look at the little imp. I'm the father of six."

By the light of Honeybody's pencil torch Amanda slept cherubically, a small fist doubled under her chin.

The Sergeant—his bulk, Harry often surmised, was so filled with gases created by fish and alcohol that he floated lightly on his enormous feet—led the way to the living-room, his temperament somehow swathing Mr. and Mrs. James with calm.

The Sergeant sat in his armchair and removed his boots, revealing stretch socks extended to a dimension that surely neither a Marks nor a Spencer ever envisaged. He opened the Gladstone bag.

"To celebrate my old lady's eigntn day away—she's rearranging the happy couple's furniture—I brought a nice bit of turbot and a bottle of gin. As to Amanda, my youngest, now an inspector up north, used to eat snails."

Elizabeth shuddered.

"Cracked 'em with his teeth and sucked 'em out. First time my Dodo phoned the lodge doctor, and did 'e go for her scone-hot! He said if the lad swallowed ballbearings or screws—a lot of them lying around during the Depression—she had to seize him by the ankles and shake. If he was to turn blue she had to phone the quack again. Don't worry, love!"

With the curious change of pace which Harry had observed, perplexed, among women—his mother could still annoy him at will—Elizabeth was delving among the cookery books.

"Now, Mrs. J.," said the Sergeant with the comfort that Harry was conscious he could never emulate, "just egg, breadcrumb, crisply fry, with tartare sauce—though I'm partial to the bottled tomato—and chips, nicely done. You young girls over-do it, if I may say."

Elizabeth, by some strange alchemy, accepted the statement, and the Inspector lay back comfortably as Sergeant Honeybody opened gin and snapped ginger ale tops.

2

THE FISH HAD been wonderful, but there was a knocking at the Inspector's temples when, at seven, his wife tugged his ears.

"Pancakes cut in slices, mixed with ham, cheese and white sauce. Amanda wishes to get into bed with you."

Amanda was fascinated by things on the bed head which she thrust into the Inspector's mouth. Removing the toe-nail clippers she made a thrust towards his left eye. She had her mother's curly hair and enormous eyes. Some poor devil was going to inherit trouble, thought Harry, as his daughter took hold of the ointment which he used for a rheumatic left wrist. He met Honeybody coming out of the bathroom.

"You here?"

The Sergeant was not at his best. "The gin, sir, perhaps you 'collect imploring me to use the guest."

The Inspector, having a dim memory of the late hour when he would willingly guarantee anybody's bank overdraft, grunted and went into the shower, faintly hearing the squeals of delight which accompanied Amanda's greeting of the Sergeant.

"What a joy it is to be a pa," exclaimed Honeybody, who was bouncing Amanda at the breakfast table and periodically removing pieces of egg from his plate into the bird-like, pursed mouth, a process which Harry realised, had he employed it, would have raised anguished shrieks from his wife and telephone calls from Dr. Hollybotham. He ate morosely.

"Are you bruised?" asked Elizabeth, sweetly.

"Bruised? What are you talking about?"

"Well, you did trip over your shoes and fall heavily into bed. You should thank me for forcing the Alka-Seltzer down your gullet."

Amanda was dancing merrily on the Sergeant's broad thigh as Honeybody looked at the ceiling and ate toast and cherry jam. He would end up in a minority, thought Harry, unless he got a boy—or did not they notoriously side with the female parent in such matters as drinking and women?

He ate a rather heavy breakfast in silence.

Finally Harry kissed the nape of Elizabeth's neck under its shower of tawny hair. She hardly noticed him as she potted Amanda. "'Bye, dear," she said absently.

"After she has several, sir," said Honeybody as they boarded a bus—Elizabeth was set on St. Hilda's after a good private school and the Inspector, in a moment of despair, had sold his car and the small country hideaway—"she'll settle down. Interest her in a business, Mr. James, second-hand clothes was what I thought, but Dodo opted for the fried fish, having a mind of her own."

"Chuck it!" said Harry, paying the fare to a morose Jamaican.

"You got trouble, sir?" the conductor enquired.

"Heavy."

"You got no idea what I got," said the man, making change from two shillings. He looked rather pleased.

"Sit down," said Superintendent Hawker, eventually. Porterman flanked him, plus several sergeants and a small man named Peating.

"This box, from deceased's lodging, contained a wobbler," Hawker stabbed a finger at a small object like a sieve. "Attach this to a tape recorder and set it—as a safe—and record what you will. About a million permutations, all erased if you set the wrong keys. You then put over it whatever music you wish. Also there was this micro-dot apparatus—it boils down a document to the dot over a full stop—plus a device which will give you a thin sliver through the skin producing death within two minutes. Nice."

Hawker had a carton of yoghourt on the desk. "Sir Bradbury says it helps the stomach," he explained.

"I think nothing touches Milk of Magnesia," said Porterman, subsiding to a glare.

Mr. Peating proved to be a cryptographer with an aura of dedication.

"Not to bore you," he said eagerly, his small mouth wrinkled, "but the old figure systems can easily be broken by grid plus computer investigation, which means..."

Half an hour later Hawker stared uneasily at the carton of yoghourt which was beginning to sweat small globules of strawberry-coloured liquid.

"So you broke it," he cut through the small torrent of words.

"Oh, no!" said Mr. Peating. "I thought I had explained. It is an arbitrary code. Twenty years ago we could not have spotted it, but the computers broke down a number code, based I am afraid on a book. You cannot translate this kind of thing; all these publishers pouring out their books. I recommended the Home Secretary to have it stopped, but..." Mr. Peating shook a mournful head... "for instance the fellow we got last week who used to get there early to open the private vault used a guide book to Portugal published in 1896. The Boss wanted to proceed against the publisher, but the firm had gone out of existence in 1907. No, sir, this presumably instructs agents to do certain things at certain times. There is a definite pattern, every fourth word. Take this, 'Sagittarius : Beware of incurring debt. Be prudent but if you cannot be lucky. Don't joke with strangers. A good day for shopping.' Now, the words *incurring, but, be, joke* etcetera means something; we do not know what; but over four years—the period of our present scrutiny—it means something."

"Do you mean that every goddamned prediction had some secret meaning?" demanded Hawker.

"Oh no, sir. There was an indication we think of paragraphs beginning with the letter *b*. Sir Dudley, who is semantics, feels that the little jokes that interspersed the predictions have an eastern European flavour. There was one ingenious adaptation of an old Hungarian joke about a horse. Highly obscene in the original, he said, but ingeniously toned down."

"Well, thank you," said Hawker, heavily. "I suppose you'll report to the military if you crack anything."

"We shan't, I'm afraid," said Mr. Peating cautiously, "but that would be the procedure."

He shook hands all round and departed.

"Spies," groaned Porterman.

"But not necessarily, if you will forgive me, sir," said a bright, up-and-coming Sergeant.

"Nobody in the building except a saucy woman named Tump"— Mr. Porterman brooded—"knew him well. That part of the corridor has no goings and comings except a copy boy named Alfrid, with an *i*. A nosy woman named Miss Bottle has an office opposite. She keeps the private ledger—directors' fees, fixed expenses, that sort of stuff. Not onerous, but paid for being as close-trapped as a mussel. She'll swear that only Tump went into Button's office until the wretched boy entered, dived out abruptly and used her phone to notify Bocker."

"Surely Q.E.D.," said Hawker. "Motive?"

"Hungarian born," said Porterman, "family were always on against Hitler since 1934."

It was strange, thought Harry, that peace-time opposition to Hitler was in these latter days regarded as something sinister in every country except Germany. He felt a trifle uneasy when he thought of recent remarks he had made, more or less publicly, about the Liberal Party. One never knew—premature retirement, loss of pension, big anonymous men saying "twenty years ago the witness subscribed to Oxfam..."

"Concrete motive?" asked Hawker.

"We'll get it," said the heavy Superintendent. "Bed, no doubt."

"Deceased was a stubby, tubby fellow, but powerful," said Harry.

"Her hobbies are fencing and judo, and with regard to the latter she is the head instructor at a club for such pursuits," said Porterman. "Bed or spying, and I'll establish which."

"I'm not exactly happy," said Hawker. "Mr. James saw Miss Tump shortly after the event and reported nothing."

"I got no feeling of agitation," said Harry, "or emotional involvement. When they kill a sleeping partner they twitch."

"A lunatic named Milk was in there at the time, sir," rumbled Sergeant Honeybody.

"Milk," said Porterman, answering idiots, "is sixty-nine, five foot two and of frail physique except his vocal chords."

"So what is your intention?"

"To find out everything Miss Tump—she changed her name by deed poll in 1944, the parents are named Gilonis—has said or done since 1933 when she came here aged five."

The massive Superintendent nodded and left, dutifully followed by his entourage. Harry, Honeybody and one young Sergeant with apple-red cheeks remained.

"The Superintendent nearly had me convinced, Inspector," said Hawker scooping his yoghourt with a spoon which, from its peculiarly tinny appearance, Harry deduced had been filched from the canteen. "Then I remembered that Porterman believes that anti-fascism means communism, a fallacy of which I shall never rid him. It *is* difficult for us poor coppers of course to be dispassionate," he glanced at the Sergeant.

"I'm Labour, sir."

"One might surmise that from age group and background" —the Sergeant flushed—"but if the situation ever occurred you would bash a Labour bod on the sconce. Right?"

"Never thought of it, sir."

"You may one day find I am right! Mr. Porterman, when there was capital punishment, was instrumental in seeing that four High Tories were hanged—they tend to poison for the insurance—although he is of their persuasion. But—do you know Sergeant Shum—Inspector James and Sergeant Honeybody."

Hands were shaken all round.

"Now," said Hawker, "Sergeant Shum is one of the brighter young men. Don't blush; you have a hell of a lot to learn and I have no objection to praising the lowest forms of life. Inspectors I rarely praise; my peers never. Now let me tell you something about espionage. One form is in fact industrial; new processes. However this is a small highly specialised branch. Two, military installation which is now more or less a matter of long-range probings by incredibly complicated instruments. Three, the Order of Battle, plans of which used to be periodically pinched from the War Office, but I have reason to believe they are now inaccessible to the extent where hardened old generals are quite ignorant of what and where their command is"—Hawker had a penchant for exaggeration—"but, and most important, is four, which concerns intention. Two world wars have occurred precisely because Intelligence fouled on this point. What the boys always pray for and rarely get is the defection to them of a major figure in the diplomatique. Your hypothetical ambassador may not know what is happening about underwater installations, but he can tell you how his Government will react to anything. So you know how far you can go. Mr. K. knew he had pushed John Kennedy too far and scuttled back to dry land. That's one example. Today there is a certain amount of deliberate leaking—'look, old boy, we *mean* it'.

"But in this spy work communication is the bastard part. It

has now become impossible for a Fourth Secretary of a foreign power to sit next to a Foreign Office cipher clerk and exchange tapes. Believe you me they've screwed that down, plus telephones, and 'drops'. Try to put a letter down a disused sewer and an official hand will emerge and grab you—we put failed sergeants on that detail." Hawker gave his crocodile grin; one never knew whether it was real or assumed. "So," the Superintendent noshed the last of the yoghourt, "instructions were disseminated by the ingenious Mr. Button. Forensic say he was possibly Bulgarian or that way. God knows how they can tell. And he was older than he made out—shrapnel scars in his back indicate that he fought somewhere—but not on record for us."

"Isn't there usually a minder? Forgive me if I presume, Sergeant Shum," said Harry, "but the Spy Master, the Shop Steward, so to speak, is a real person; that's obviously what Mr. Porterman thinks Miss Tump is."

"The landlady, Mrs. Curl, is the more likely candidate," said Hawker. "The late unlamented Button must have got some supplies in—breakfast, toast and Marmite. The rest was steak and kidney pudding. Iron discipline!"

"Probably you're right," said Harry, "I would suggest I checked around Pepper Lane. The bitch must have dealt with somebody."

"Named after a certain Ralph Pepper who was hanged for simony in 1578," said Hawker, absently. He possessed a fabulous knowledge of London. "What I am getting at is that somebody gave the stuff to Percy Button. You'll find perfect anonymity. Pepper Lane is that kind of place. Old clerks, a few warehouses, a big supermarket half a mile away where you could have three heads without anybody noticing, providing you have the money for the battery chicken. But somewhere there must have been a hand-over. Either to Button or to Mrs. Curl; a handshake and something palmed. Now Sergeant Shum will have his pick of ten constables. The Sergeant, wearing his most threadbare suit —he did three years on the *Isle of Thanet News* before he joined us—will be our old friend the unsuccessful freelance, hanging on to a half of mild in the pubs where the journalists who still drink are found. A policewoman will be detailed to do the coffee shops and health juice emporiums. Sergeant Shum's detail will examine the pubs within a radius of three miles of Pepper Lane—choose topers, Sergeant, there are three hundred licences plus drinking clubs—with pictures. The usual listening first and then shaking down the Manager. Sergeant Honeybody, a man of infinite experience of licensed premises..."

"In the line of dooty, sir," said Honeybody.

"...which the accountant rather disputes, will help you there. And, Mr. James, fiddle around the *Bulletin*! Chance your arm if necessary."

Harry glumly took a bus which passed the *Daily Bulletin* building. It looked shabbier than ever. Sir Peregrine was obviously a man who paid no attention to externals. Opposite were seedy offices over a shop selling medicinal herbs. The Inspector thought that probably somebody with binoculars would be watching the *Bulletin* foyer for Miss Tump. On the third floor there was a dull knocking and he remembered that Superintendent Porterman was fond of having the scene of the crime taken to pieces. His critics alleged that some municipally-owned flats had partially collapsed after a Porterman-conducted search for a stolen hearing aid.

"For Christ's sake," said Miss Tump, cigarette-ash dripping from a drooping *Gauloise* as she used Chinese white to mark up a photograph of a consumptive-looking girl clad in long hair and a bikini, "do you public eyes always makes noises like rutting elephants?"

"I'm afraid it's years since I was zooward," apologised Harry. "Have you made a statement?"

"So I'm suspect number one!" she said calmly.

The Inspector tossed up mentally, then said, "It appears you and the wretched boy were the only ones to see him during the relevant period."

She pierced him with her sharp, intelligent, almond-shaped green eyes. "So he was one of the lesser breeds?"

"Forensic think Bulgarian."

"I always wonder why Dr. Johnson said it was a Bulgarian vice," she said obscurely, to gain time. "They always seemed to me mad about women."

"We used to giggle about that one in the Sixth."

"Just don't trouble my remaining parent. He's seventy-one and has heart attacks. Having ruined himself financially and physically helping a lot of poor devils, he was rewarded ten years ago by having a swastika drawn on the front door, and 'You should go back to Rusher' neatly chalked with the esses reversed."

"Chips like epaulets?" said Harry.

"He hasn't. I have just a few. Sorry they show. Well I did not kill the poor bastard and had no reason to."

"Sorry to have to ask, but did you see the late Mr. Button outside of office hours?"

"My good man, twice a week I attend a women's club where I teach fencing and judo. The rest of the time I spend at home with my aged father. That is my life." There was a little bitterness in her voice.

"Miss Tump never murdered anybody."

The girl—Mabel he remembered—had been mouse-quiet in her corner reading proofs. A good-looking kid, he registered, or would be when the fat had abated.

"Character reference or proof, miss?"

"Both. Tump—sorry Miss Tump..."

"I am well aware you tiny slaves call me Tump," said that lady icily.

"Well, then, Tump would literally not hurt a fly. She got bound over for throwing a man tormenting a cat down some area stairs... she's famous for her, um, humanitarian qualities. I s'pose it was old Bottle over the way. But she couldn't say because she was in the lady's loo from three fifteen until nearly four with the Georgette Heyer she keeps in her handbag."

"Would you swear?"

"Sure. I got tired of the cubicle—I think old Peregrine has uncomfortable seats made bespoke to discourage us—and sat on the chair opposite the mirror as if I were making-up. Finally old Bottle waddled out and I thought I'd better scuttle back because if anybody would put you in it's old Bottle."

"But why, miss, should you wish to spend working time in the loo?" asked the Inspector.

"Because I know Tump, Miss Tump's, mind. She was getting round to sending me out to collect a press release from a flack in Knightsbridge. The journey is too killing and he always tries to pinch my bottom."

"Then why do you not join a judo course?" asked Miss Tump.

"Frankly," said Mabel, "between being pinched on the tail by a P.R.O. and thrown on that practice mat I would opt for the former."

"I was, of course, aware of your habit of locking yourself in the loo to avoid honest work."

"Sorry, Miss Tump, but Kereeest, Knightsbridge in the afternoon! And the man lisps!"

The Inspector sighed. "But why should Miss Bottle immolate herself in a toilet?"

"I thought that meant burning yourself to death with petrol," said Mabel with interest.

"It roughly does," intoned Miss Tump—Harry was reminded of a woman who tried to teach him the six times tables, "from the Latin *immolare*, to prepare a victim."

The Inspector felt the blood creep into his cheeks. "I meant incarcerate."

"More like a policeman," said Miss Tump judicially.

"Look," snarled Harry, with a lurking thought that his Amanda would probably be talking back to him in sixteen or seventeen years, "was she in the habit of locking herself in the bog with a book?"

"She hasn't much to do, really," said Mabel calmly, "just fill in a few entries and make out cheques on the private account. But she has this ruddy great window—anybody who handles money here has to have a big window so that Jolly can have a snoop. So she gets bored and uses the loo."

"You are not trying to protect Miss Tump?"

"I would if necessary, but I'm not. I can produce three people who came into the loo while I was shirking."

The Inspector felt himself involuntarily scowling.

"Have you a daughter, Inspector?" asked Miss Tump.

"A few months old."

"I find that young men with small daughters register a great deal of perturbation after conversing with Mabel."

"You'll make a sweet old charley-dad," cooed Mabel.

"Good day, ladies. Cut down on the carbohydrates, miss." With this Parthian shot he left. He wished the Marquis de Sade had not placed bottom smacking in such dubious twilight.

He checked that John Jolly was, as expected, not in, but in the news room he found Peter Leeming, seamed as ever, conversing with a heavy man with a shortage of breath. Possibly he hadn't moved.

"Sir P. says we must press for total political union with Europe. Said he had been dining at Trinity College the night before and it was all fixed. The Professor thinks that he could get in Hungary and Turkey if given a free hand."

"If you want to lose circulation," said Leeming without emotion, "Mr. Bottomley, tell the clerks and the working men that they'll have the Germans, the Dutch, the French and the Chris' knows who coming here and taking the jobs. Don't you realise that *they* are better? Who would you have your car done over by, an Englishman or a German? Don't be silly. We *know* it."

"We won the war," said Mr. Bottomley—Harry remembered that he was the Editor.

Leeming laughed like a creaky iron gate. "Heard of Russians and Americans? Now, Mr. B., tell Lemski or Butterwisk—they are good at the stuff—to do a job of fancy skating, but not to come out with it straight. God Almighty, how I'd like some good Italian bread and some decent Normandy butter! But, Mr. B., we have to suffer for the good of our shareholders."

The heavy man retreated, like a baffled bull.

"Sit down, Inspector," said Leeming with easy grace, "I would not have inflicted that on you if I hadn't known you fellows know the score. I keep telling the young chaps that we sell paper at so much a pound, like the cigarette boys primarily sell water. The most valuable man we have is the classified ad manager."

"I want to know about Miss Bottle. Reliable?"

"Been here longer than I. Retires next year under a curious edict that the women serve four years less than men and at decreased pension. Efficient—she keeps the private ledger and does any top security figure work. A highly qualified accountant. What you might call a martyr to her job. I do not suppose the company has a more faithful servant."

"'Um," said Harry, "forgive me but she could not be a dedicated Communist? So dedicated as to be over the edge?"

"All vetted. Sir P. hires a firm of private investigators. You are not engaged if you are left wing. Don't mistake that for our policy, for God's sake. We're selling paper. Matter of fact it's the right-wingers who write the best watered-left copy, which is what we feed them on. Plus stuff like this." He turned round a proof with a four-inch headline: 'Opium Dens in Blackpool?'

"Never heard of those," said Harry.

"We sell forty thousand in Blackpool in the off season. Tomorrow we'll get through seventy. Now, if you don't mind..."

Harry thanked him and left. It seemed to him that people were perpetually getting tired of talking to him.

He ate a leisurely lunch at his club, forbearing to telephone Elizabeth in order to punish her, but uneasily conscious that since Amanda had arrived the luncheon phone call was no longer much in his wife's life. After he had finished his cheese, he called his office and was relayed to a sardonic Hawker. "Fenchurch Gaol, maximum security, has a story about espionage. Where are you, I'll send a car?"

"A club, eh?" said Hawker. "I thought you were happily married!" He chuckled evilly and slammed down his handset. The butterflies in the Inspector's stomach rose and fluttered at the thought that perhaps he *had* been spending more time at the club since Amanda's arrival. If only Elizabeth would take a sensible view about napkins!

Fenchurch was maximum security, having originally been erected in some haste to house theoretical prisoners who never arrived from the Crimean War. Mr. Gladstone, who believed in the therapeutic and cleansing influence of fresh air, especially if damp, had caused it to be set upon a steep hillside overlooking a marsh. Charlie Dickens had written an article causing the building to be circular, on the principle that the turnkeys could perpetually promenade around the walls, shoving in bowls of food or taking out what he called 'the unmentionables of life' through small slits, so designed that nobody over four feet three could worm through them. Ruminating, the Inspector, under medium height himself, considered that probably the smaller you were the better.

After six weary hours, the Humber went through the large, clanking gate and Harry, roused from a doze, creaked out to see the Governor.

Governor Blight had been a Gunner of some distinction, and had in fact been vaguely considered for New South Wales, tried in a remote group of islands, where he had fallen into one of the many administrative and political mantraps which beset distinguished ex-Gunners, but was now in safe waters in a gaol, with excellent living quarters and a convict who would still have been one of London's leading chefs but for his predilection for poisoning his wives. The Governor had a rather large notice —he was a forgetful man—over his desk to remind him not to allow his chef access to roach powder.

His remote blue eyes, relic of so many obscure army circumstances which admitted of no solution, surveyed Harry.

"D. Fipping, a poor record, one is afraid, and getting old. The climate, you know..." The Governor slightly twiddled the knob of his central heating. "But they come to Chief Warder Littlejohn with these stories, to curry favour I'm afraid. I have to pass them on. You fellers aren't too hard on us when they go over the wall, and one is grateful. Fipping is 'indeterminate' and has varicose ulcers and, Chief Warder Littlejohn tells me, has no money, so one does not suppose he is any kind of risk."

A young, silent warder was summoned to take the Inspector to see Fipping, D. While there is no great necessity for policemen to visit gaols, a certain amount of traffic is inevitable—Harry had once been an official witness to an execution and it had amazed him how determinedly and tenuously the culprit hung on to life whilst being hanged—but there is a certain stink, as from a very old boarding house with seventeenth-century plumbing. And the place where they keep the old men is never salubrious. Old lags, senile after years under the lock, not badly treated as dogs are not badly treated, encouraged to creep out into what little sun there is, old joints smelling of stale wintergreen.

Fipping D. sat importantly on a stone bench in the small interior yard, while other old men eyed him enviously.

"Fipping, D.," said the young warder dispassionately, "seventy-nine with an indeterminate. Forty years of bird, including violence."

"No, sir," said old Fipping, "'aven't been violent since 1927. The judge said that. You look at the record, sir."

"He came in two years ago, pinching the drawer out of a till in a supermarket," said the warder.

"It had fallen on the floor and I was gathering it up," said Fipping.

"And I suppose you bit the young lady on the calf because you was looking for your false teeth? Q'right, you tell the Inspector."

But Fipping, having his day, was in favour of gossip.

"Is it true, sir, that Lord Montwhatsisname is goin' to be the Guv in place of daft ol' Blight? Royalty, ain't 'e?"

"I know nothing of such things," said the Inspector, truthfully.

"Ah, they say the screws is all to be Hoxford men, educated like. Iggerent lot of effers they got now. Chief Warder Littlejohn 'as to get Mr. Botting 'oo got away with a cool 'alf a million out of fiddlin' in the 'ire purchase to fill out his betting slips. Iggerent!"

It was getting cold, with the mist seeping up the hill. The

other old men were drifting into the curved doors of the gaol.

"Now then, Fipping, D.," came a firm voice. "Chief Warder Littlejohn, Inspector. I had some trouble in F Ward, the sexual maniacs, so was delayed. Give your story straight, Fipping, and you get a nice bit of pickled belly pork on your plate tomorrow. If not I'll have to transfer you to 308."

"Oh, no, sir, the belly pork—and some cucumber p'raps," old Fipping slavered.

"Then speak up like a man," Chief Warder Littlejohn caressed his small moustache, "and I'll see you have a bit of good tomorrow."

"I used to work around Bunting Street, sir," quavered Fipping. "Never no violence for years, the judge said that. Not violence."

"Get to the point," said Chief Warder Littlejohn.

"There was a spy down Bunting Street, sir. I always heard it."

"Why didn't you tell the local policeman?" Harry asked. Bunting Street was contiguous to Pepper Lane, but overlooking London Pool.

"None of us wanted nuthink to do, excuse me, sir, with the perlice. Live and let live."

"Whereabouts?"

"Dunno, sir, you don't ask questions down Bunting Street."

"All right, Warder," said Chief Warder Littlejohn, "return him."

They watched the little old man hobble off.

"What's this about 308?" said Harry.

"Next to the kitchen. Cockroaches. The old bastard's afraid of things that crawl. So if he gets mean I give him a spell. A vicious beast in his day, now gone at the muscles and bowels like they do after ten years, off and on, of bird in this place. Bad enough for us officers. All the screws get the screws." Chief Warder Littlejohn showed bad teeth in faint amusement....

The Inspector got home a bit before midnight. Disconcertingly, his wife was awaiting him.

"Why didn't you phone?" she said, kissing him and removing

—a process to which the Inspector had a concealed but built-in objection—his duffle coat. "I had to get in touch with Hawker. He said, the old beast, that it was your turn to visit ladies' gaols."

Harry mumbled something which his wife did not listen to. Presently he was in front of the gas fire, shoes removed for slippers, eating rump steak accompanied by half a bottle of fairish red wine and wondering what made women tick.

3

WHILE AMANDA IN her high chair was reduced to temporary quietness by the tops of the Inspector's two boiled eggs which she busily mashed with a spoon, and the dog, Mr. Bones, lurked uncomfortably under the table and thought of toast, the Inspector read the *Daily Bulletin*.

"I ordered it yesterday for the duration," Elizabeth had said.

He reached out and administered an approving pat.

"I suppose one has been kind of neglectful since the Monster arrived," his wife said.

"Nonsense," he lied.

He spooned up egg and read 'The Man I Knew: John Jolly's Tribute to Slain Staffer'. Obviously Jolly was embarrassed by the name 'Button', which was scarcely tuned in to obituary. It was skilfully written in the short pungent sentences which were the trademark of the paper. "A quiet man with a passion for animals whose life had been the study of the Occult which he had begun when a trader in the Far East," the Inspector summed up to himself. It looked as though Jolly knew more about Button than he admitted. There was no photograph, only a reproduction of a prediction, 'There will be momentous Royal News', coupled with a later headline announcing the engagement of Princess Margaret. "There is always some Royal news somewhere in the world," the Inspector mumbled to himself.

Miss Wasey Tump and her factotum had kept their mouths buttoned, for Jolly would hardly have expatiated on the virtues of somebody with a phoney background. "Hmph," he shared his toast with Mr. Bones and rose and kissed Amanda who managed to daub his lapel with egg white in the process. Once this would have maddened him—once dressed he loathed to change, but now there was only calm recourse to the bottle of Dabitoff, prudently kept behind the electric clock.

"Can you get home early, dear?" said Elizabeth, "I'll arrange for a sitter and you can take me out. Surprise me, such as with that play with the rave reviews. I'll pay for the sitter."

It was nice to be comfortable, thought Harry, on a bus to the city, slippers by the fireside, nicely dressed steak. But what the devil *was* the bitch after, queried a little inbuilt married man? Last time it was putting Amanda down for this hideously expensive school. He thought of his nervous dyspepsia and stared out of the window.

"Got the wind?"

It was a red-faced fat man next to him.

"Well, yes, I have."

"I know the look," said the fat man. "In the debt-collecting line myself and my missus says sometimes I could drown out London Airport. 'Ere, take two. One of the old patient medicines, Sharb's Belch, Heartburn and Bowel Regulator. Works miracles for me. As used by the legal and military perfeshons, it says on the paper. Good as a book with testymonals, but very fine print."

This would be a good way to poison somebody, thought Harry. Ten to one the Good Samaritan was really strangling the publican.

"Suck 'em," said the fat man. "Slow, and you'll find it eases it and soothes the nerve ends."

Strangely it did, more than the little pinkish tablets that the officer doctor—feet, ulcers, nervous dyspepsia and, but rarely, insanity was his work load—prescribed. There was a kind of warmth in his stomach. The only trouble was that his neighbour embarked upon clinical details, but Harry thanked him as he squeezed past and went to see the oldest Inspector on the City of London force.

Old friends, they greeted each other warmly.

"Thank God that *Bulletin* job was two hundred yards outside our manor," chuckled the City man. "The boss laughed like a stopped-up sink and actually okayed a taxi fare. Though I suppose we'd have called you Brains in."

"Fipping, D., Charlie."

"I thought he was inside?"

"Is. Indeterminate sentence; he'll die inside, poor old bastard."

"Don Fipping predates me, Harry. He could be your granfer, but God forbid. When I joined, the old-timers—and tough, boy, as you'll never be—told me all about Fipping, D." He stuffed tobacco into his pipe. "Years back, telephones a novelty. When Fipping was in his cups, and he was below medium height, he fought like a mad threshing machine. It always took three with a thing they had then like a straitjacket on wheels to take him in. He favoured a cosh loaded with buckshot... let's see, he was one of the Bunting Street lot. Funny place that was years ago, but, then, there were plenty of Bunting Streets. Some survive, but it got badly bashed in the blitz. The people, all close-lipped and intermarried, are God knows where and in what sanitary council estate. Somebody else's headache. I believe in heredity, like the Jukes girls' study. You'll find the Fippings were thieves right back until they came out of the trees."

"Surely environment," protested Harry.

"Me foot," said the Inspector. "They can get so they have big cars, but the stench is there."

"Okay, uncle."

"You'll learn, young 'Arry, and I hope it doesn't cost you *all* those fluoridised teeth what the Welfare State gave you. Now Fipping D. had the skill of being practically able to shinny up a blank concrete wall. The original cat burglar, except he went for warehouses. He done his few years as a boy round the Thames workin' in the bulk stores. He registered the fact that in those days there were the so-called 'dead lofts' at the top. Slower ships in those days and you got stuff in five months before you wanted. Now Fipping could get up the wall and into 'em.

There was usually some hydraulic sling inside and the nightwatchman didn't go up there. Fipping used to force the fire escape door, put the loot into canvas bags he carried rolled round his waist, and lower them with thin rope to a mate below. Many times it wasn't discovered for months, except we got to know it was Fipping, D., the only man who could get up those walls. He could have done Everest!

"But he wasn't too smart on top. The local P.C. would see him slinging money about—his top was six thousand quid's worth of furs in 1923—and he couldn't resist trying to cache a bit of the swag for a rainy day. So we always got him. Then his joints went—the gin and the fen—and he had to go to sneak thieving. Small grocers usually, but then the Conservatives got rid of them and he had to turn to the supermarkets, like trying to pinch my boss's dentures, closed TV circuits they've got."

"I cannot see how your boss's dentures have closed TV circuits."

"They say he has a small microphone embedded in his navel, and that the new Testament which he keeps so conspicuously on his desk—I've seen many a Home Office official look nervous on an official visit—contains a tape recorder. And now I've given myself time to think, what exactly is this about?"

"The late Percy Button was almost certainly a spy; Fipping coincidentally—but you know the grape-vine though they aren't allowed crime news—said he'd heard of a spy in Bunting Street."

"Did he sell you a gold bar as well? Guaranteed?"

"Tough Chief Warder, desire to placate."

"H'm, I've got to get out some goddamned report on vending machines—a two-hundred-pound investment makes you a capitalist for life, I'm thinking of cashing in my Government bonds—and I'd as soon be out of here as in. There's a good pub around Bunting Street where you can get a mixed grill that sends you : pinched from Smithfield, of course, but eat and let live."

Bunting Street was like some old carnivorous beast dug up by an enquiring scientist. Once it must have been lived in; there were footprints of time, but a peculiar, desolate look as of a deserted village in a jungle. It was not very long; half a mile, thought Harry.

It was waiting, as the Inspector supposed it had always been waiting, for new speculators, the Celts, the Romans, the Normans and now the developers who would take over its aged arteries and rework them into money.

"Spies my arse," said the City Inspector, "but half an hour until opening time."

Aroused, Inspector James grabbed the arm of a small man scuttling by.

"Now, Duck," said Harry, "I want two stalls for that sleeper and ten bob over for you."

"The American show?" Duck's nickname stemmed from pre-Welfare State adenoids. He fumbled in the breast pocket of a greasy black-and-white striped sports jacket.

"The English one about a boarding house filled with old whores who eat a Methodist clergyman."

"Very scarce, sir, never knew 'em so scarce," said Duck. He was a useful informer, though principally to Inland Revenue; men tended to boast over cigars in theatre queues.

"I could tell Johnny D. who put him in," said the City Inspector, casually. "Raring to go is his brother, the one that uses the bicycle chain."

"O'right, two in number G. I can't do better. Fifty-seven bob which leaves me the price of half a pint."

Harry took the tickets and counted out the money.

"Ta," Duck paid him the compliment of not counting the shillings.

"Half a moment, dear boy," said the City Inspector, "born and bred here weren't you, you little bastard."

"Visiting my old gran, sir, she's down on the river."

"With the three girls she manages."

"Live and let live, sir, no trouble I'm sure and always willing to assist."

"Where did the spy live?"

"The spy!" Duck double-took as he honked. "Blimey, guv, I was buyin' Tiger Nuts outside the old school wot was bombed when I 'eard of 'im. You're joking a poor man!"

"Where?" said Harry coldly enough to receive a faint smirk of congratulation from his elder colleague.

"It wus jess a joke around the playground, mister. 'There 'e be, the spy, you try to spit in my eye.' Then a bit of a punch-up, like. It was that building"—he pointed to a gaunt apparition. "A Zepp got it in 1917 and they never rebuilt except for somebody printing dirty postcards in the basement."

"Who owns it?" asked Harry.

"I forget 'is name," said Duck. "What they call a developer—like my old gran. Can I go?"

"Get off," said Inspector James, "before I hate you, and if those seats are behind a pillar, I swear..."

"Wonderful seating, guv, they say the leading lady don't wear nothing on under her mini...."

The rest of the proceedings seemed to entail the summoning of two old and depressed constables and somebody, rather brightly lit, who represented a syndicate which proposed to replace the old warehouse with a fabrication known as King George's Gardens, lined with boutiques.

"Nobody in there for years, sir, badly shot up in World War One, insurance claims to the thirties, then nobody wanted premises," the Inspector was told.

The lock of the main door was of a complicated nature, rusted, gnarled and set in when craftsmen knew how to do it.

"Never get in there!" said one of the Depressed Constables.

"The key is unfortunately in Glasgow," said the agent. "Not that one would imagine it works."

Harry tapped. "Teak," he said, "wish I could have it for a table top. The lock would be the weak link, although heavily morticed. Fifty years of London air doesn't do locks any good."

"Have to cut the lock out," said the City Inspector.

"Only if you provide a new door," snapped the agent.

"I can get a warrant."

"And I can apply for an injunction within the hour. Mr.

Snodd, of Furphing and Johns, is not a hundred yards away." There was a flash of gold teeth below a raised upper lip.

"We'll replace it with a steel door," said Harry. With luck he might wangle a magnificent piece of teak.

"It will have to be drilled. No heat, unless you sign obligation for fire risk."

"We use a man a quarter of a mile away," said the City Inspector.

"I know 'im," said the elder of the Depressed Constables, with the air of one who would prefer to be elsewhere.

"Get him out here quick," said Harry. "A drill job and no heat. If he's got a fire extinguisher tell him to bring it."

The Constable moved away at the prescribed four miles per hour, and after a slight wrestle with his conscience the agent produced a packet of cigarettes, glanced at it momentarily, swiftly replaced it and handed round the Cheapest Brand.

"Those coupon smokes is no good," he said, "stands to reason. My wife is saving 'em for a granfer clock. Women!"

"Ta," said Inspector James, "so empty since 1915-ish, eh?"

"About that. It's 'ard for us to envisage. But now this Glasgow syndicate is to erect a soup block of flats, but rilly soup. The river's gettin' that fashionable. I like to think of the titled bleeders gettin' more and more rheumatics and phlegm in the mornings." He gave a laugh of pure enjoyment. "And then the Income-taxers on 'em."

"Local boy, eh?"

"Born, sir, but bettered myself. Notting Hill Gate now."

"Spies here?"

The agent did not flinch. "Used to be a school over there until old Hitler got it. We used to play 'I spy', a funny game. Strange old place it used to be!"

A small truck arrived driven by a brisk technician. "'Oo signs the requisition?"

"Inspector James, C.I.D."

"Ar," the technician inspected the lock, "proper old thing, ain't she? The 'ouse on the corner, Constable, will plug us in.

Run out the flex, please. It's stepped up in stages, those little green boxes."

"This drill, sir," said the technician, "is plastic. It does not actually touch the wood, but generates sufficient molecular..."

"Just so it works," said Harry.

The technician sighed with the air of a man whose wisdom is always being dried up at source. "P'raps one of you gennelmen will sign the pro forma invoice."

Harry rested the docket against the door and scrawled his name. Presently the constable plodded back and the technician plugged his drill in.

As he said, it was a cow of a job and the thickest door he had ever encountered, part of some foundered old sailing ship he shouldn't wonder. Finally an oblong piece of wood fell out, but the bolt remained, and the technician produced small tools and fiddled for fifty minutes before saying that he would now have to tickle the lock, a process entailing long-nosed pliers.

At last, under the influence of oil and pliers, the metal grated back and the door, creaking but game like an ancient roué, swung outwards.

"Ar," said the technician. "I suppose I'll 'ave to take that ole bastid orf 'is 'inges."

"A lock-down metal roller installed," said Harry. "Give me an order form and deliver the old door to New Scotland Yard. To Superintendent Hawker."

The technician was a gloomy man who reckoned that the man who took *that* door down should receive two state-provided trusses in advance, but he followed the four policemen and the dubious agent into the darkness.

Harry produced his torch. "Is there a light?"

"Turned off years ago, sir. In fact I don't think they ever 'ad the electric; gas in them days."

The Inspector probed with his torch among cobwebbed partition walls and rotted wooden shelving. What windows there were—and it had been rather a dark satanic sort of mill— were boarded.

The agent jerked a thumb. "The entrance to the basement

was stopped up. There is a door at the side. It was let during the last war."

"Dirty photographs," snapped Harry.

"Don't know, I'm sure, sir, a journalist the gent did say 'e was and paid three months in advance like. A *proper* gent, my guv told me he were."

"Bah!" said Harry—it was an expletive he was fond of, as it for some reason infuriated his wife.. "Pish!"

"There's a stairway on the side," said the City Inspector. "Over there on the left."

The iron stairs were rusty but stout Victorian, approved by obese and prosperous ironfounders with colonial interests, thought Harry.

"We'll have a look; if I break me neck, just a quiet burial and a chaste notice in *The Times*, with 'dearly loved' very prominent."

There were some tremors in the stairway, a kind of inbuilt alcoholic shake, barely perceptible except through the feet. The technician was whining with terror as they met an iron barrier.

"For God's sake, sir," he mewed, but Harry had kicked it and it grated inwards.

"Shove," said the Inspector. They did and the door moved with the alacrity and pleasantness of a television critic; and the whole stairway conveyed the impression of disintegration, stray noises of mated, elderly metal, past impotence even, shook the very walls.

"God," said the technician, "we're forty feet up."

"Be calm and remember Whimper," said the City Inspector.

"'Oo's whimperin'?" demanded the technician, stung.

"He climbed the Matterhorn and got his lot."

"The dolly wot got shot in the First World War?" said the eldest police constable.

Sex always took their minds off it, thought Harry accelerating.

"She was Mata Hari, an assumed name, and looked like the back of a bus," said the City Inspector, after a pause. They were nearing the top. "The Matterhorn is a Swiss mountain."

54

"She runs the spaghetti and meat sauce near me," said one of the morose constables; "I must say her food isn't bad, but the other... sixteen stone stripped I'd say and my dad was in the butchery...."

Harry stepped off the stairs on to the catwalk. Iron-lined stout cement bricks and a door, protected on the outside by a massive wooden girder anchored into a heavy wrought-iron slot. The two constables heaved and, groaningly, the wooden bar came up and back. They applied shoulders and the tough old door opened inwards.

"Good God," said the City Inspector.

On the floor were two suitcases, a litter of empty cans and a skeleton in frock coat and striped trousers plus the vestigial remains of a striped shirt and a black tie upon what Inspector James recognised as a celluloid collar.

"An apparatus in the corner, Mr. James," said the City Inspector.

It resembled the switchboard of a small office, except that instead of plugs there was a flat key mechanism.

"The Spy," said the technician with awe.

The City Inspector was already on his way down the stairs.

The agent's representative said, "Positively no responsibility of the owners. Please record this denial. No financial liability admitted by agents or owners."

"Steady on," said Harry. "This looks pretty old to me. All we'll want is factual stuff, dates mostly. You both," he looked at the technician, terrified in the presence of death, "better get along. You may be wanted to testify, but one doubts it."

It was Harry's experience that once you got into the sphere of espionage you also got within the orbit of froglike men who favoured ugly brown or tan suitings and raincoats. It was a kind of uniform, he supposed, with froglike looks indicating some kind of ability in the field of unearthing spies.

Two hours later, without lunch—the City Inspector and the constables having discreetly bailed out of the affair—Harry found himself in a room with an immaculately groomed man, a trifle on the tweedy side, with no discernible jaw. Harry remembered that he had favoured Hitler, rather, and was thus stuck in an immovable pocket on the hierarchial billiards table. That was the trouble. Those that had opposed were stuck and those that favoured were equally in chancery.

'Mr. Smith', which was not his name, was rather pleased. "It's something to do with the decay of the bones, Inspector, according to Sir Plunkett, who gave a rapid carbon test. From 1914 onwards, he says. There was a 1917 copy of the old *Morning Post* in the loft, though we should not suggest that journalism aids science." Yellow buck teeth showed in mirth.

"Yes, sir," Harry was deadpan and the old, built-in unease, product of God-knows-what government policies, showed on the long narrow face. Mr. Smith said, very business-like, "The radio transmitter is approximately 1914-1916, the newspaper date approximates to the date the Zepps got Long Acre and the newspaper publishers; the empty tins were sausage, iron rations, and chocolate. He was about forty-five when he died. On supposition he got ashore from a neutral boat down the river, set the thing up with accomplices—three men were shot from that area in 1917, all traitors—and then somebody from the Agents, completely innocent, came in to see the damage, saw that the wooden girder on the loft was not in position, and, without looking, swung it down. Starvation! You may well imagine the final hammering and shouting; and the rats!"

"Christ," said Harry, "I'd rather not be with that one."

"Precisely," said Mr. Smith. "I have had a word with Sir Jabeez Lusting, the Senior Treasury Silk, and he thinks that under a fifteenth-century Act—Conspiracy Against the Throne —we don't have to get in the Coroner. I would impress the constables and all concerned, which is where *you* come in, that a closed mouth is a safe mouth."

"Indeed," said Harry.

"Confidentially," said Mr. Smith, "we propose to exchange him."

"Exchange him!"

"Oh, quite decently. We are getting quotes from the leading undertakers. But, perhaps you remember, we had the man in the Eastern Sector—sewing machine needles was the cover—which they got because he couldn't speak the language, one does not know why the London School of Economics recommended him. We have put out feelers to exchange him for an East German spy."

"I don't follow you, sir," said Harry.

"I do not propose that you should. Admiral Canaris in the 1914-18 always picked East Germans. My Master says no deception is involved—a quick turnover at the Border. We get the man from the London School of Economics—there's a decent job on wage structure awaiting him in Whitehall."

"Strict discretion, sir."

Back in free air the Inspector found a telephone box and reached the City Inspector, sardonically amused, and Superintendent Hawker who mentioned that he was placing Harry's ability to discover fifty-year-old cadavers on his record sheet. It was thus in foul mood that the Inspector entered a small restaurant, tried to bolt back when he saw the dainty little candlesticks on each immaculate small table, but was confronted by a fat, genial Greek in knee breeches and, his moral courage sapped by the morning's events, meekly suffered himself to be seated, ordering the cheapest thing on the menu, a Spanish omelette which no Spaniard—except perhaps the ignorant denizens of the irrigation areas around Cordoba—would have recognised. By some kind of inverted snobbish pressure, at which maîtres are adept, he was persuaded to order half a bottle of frightful claret from the middle of the list; he remembered his father, in the wine trade, telling him that restaurateurs got rich from the middle parts of their wine list. The coffee proved to be Turkish, microscopic and cost two and ninepence.

He overtipped to compensate his ego and as atonement walked to the *Daily Bulletin* office, munching little pellets of Milk of Magnesia, Elizabeth having read somewhere that ordinary bicarb did you no good. These cursed little medical articles she was always conning since the baby arrived, he reflected, irritably, and nearly collided with an assistant porter as he mooched into the *Bulletin*'s foyer.

"Mr. Jolly in?"

"Yus, Inspector, sir." The man was stout and oily and in due time, thought Harry, would make an excellent successor to Bocker. "In the newsroom, sir."

"You'll want the Managing Editor, no doubt," said Peter Leeming, crumpled in the same suit and staring dismally at some slips of paper. "These 'Famous Crimes' get me down. One a day. This fellow Chapman, have you got a new angle?"

"Killed for fun, antimony, and liked shooting rats. Polish butcher originally. He might, just might, have been Jack the Ripper, but it infuriates criminologists if you say so."

"Thanks." Peter Leeming took his thick black pencil and scrawled 'Fun Killer, 24 pt. Times' and 'Was he the Ripper? 16 pt. Gill sans.' "Oh," he said, "to the right. Jolly's in that little cubby-hole."

John Jolly was closeted with Bocker the Head Porter and did not notice the Inspector's approach. Harry waited patiently while Jolly outlined his scheme to provide the machine room with a gas jet, a kettle, a teapot, one teaspoonful of tea per man—to be dispensed by Bocker—and an accompanying Marie biscuit. He seemed to think that the Chief Engineer should be the man to manipulate the gas jet.

"The unions wouldn't stand it," said Bocker, firmly. "Lor', sir, you'd have the whole street out within the hour. My Dad, in the licensing trade it's true, used to say if you got between the British working man and his beer or tea he turned into a raving tiger. Mr. Churchill knew that, sir. During the war he saw there was plenty of tea and beer. I remember..."

"Yes, yes," Jolly's face was scarlet with venom, "but Sir P. is worried about the time spent on swigging tea. They dawdle up those stairs. Why can't they run, a lot of healthy men! He wants something done at once."

Bocker coughed. "If I may say so, sir, there are various sorts of tea."

Jolly's small eyes became even narrower. "Go on."

"There is a certain tea-bag, sir, that is undrinkable. Turned out for export to the U.S.A. by a wholesale grocery with Sir P.

on the Board. He happened to mention to me that the rats—the warehouse is full of them, but usually among the coffee, fond of it as the beasts are... Oh, good morning, sir," Bocker's cod eyes had swivelled round to Harry.

"Get on with it, man," said Jolly.

"A rare funny taste rat's dung gives tea," said Bocker.

"I know nothing of rat's dung, curse it, get to the point!" snarled Jolly.

Bocker was obviously a man who loved an orotund anecdote. "Anyway, sir, the beasties got in the tea meant for the tea-bags, a matter of ten tons, and the American shipper would have none of it. Even the White House wouldn't have had it, so he said. Sir P. is very exercised. He 'ad words with me in the 'all. I suggested he gave it to Homes for Old People—the columnists could splash it and it might help him towards the Peerage. But he said no, it surely had a residual value, and that he knew somebody in the N.A.A.F.I.—some retired general—who was after cheap tea, the other ranks always being after a swig of it as they can't afford beer no more."

"Ah," John Jolly's mind seized and digested. "Not even a printer would walk up two hundred stairs for a cup of foul tea, eh?"

"Not unless he was daft; some of 'em are," said Bocker judicially.

"I'll get Smallpiece, our solicitor, to look at the Union Agreement and then phone Sir P. Meantime alert Mrs. Biggs that a new consignment of tea may arrive, in which case she is to sell existing stocks to... er, some café or other, plenty of them around—at two per cent reduction. Tell her to keep the water below boiling point in future," said Jolly masterfully.

"Not the boiling part, I wouldn't, sir. The Agreement don't say what quality tea, but the boiling water part would cast you, legally speaking."

Bocker's omniscience caused the blood to creep up again from John Jolly's throat, but he said, "Thank you, Bocker, carry on. Ah, Inspector, I did not see you! Pardon me for involving you in, ah, domestic discussion."

In silence the Inspector watched Bocker's stately retreat.

"You can talk freely," said Jolly, "completely sound-proof, Sir P. has everything soundproof. Even the Administrative Lavatory," he gave his false chuckle. "A lot of business has been done there in its time. When he bought...oh, never mind, but I've seen a couple of Cabinet Ministers there discussing things...."

Something odd, recorded the police part of Harry's brain. They tended to burble when a legal porpoise was close behind them.

"Did you happen to know Mr. Button well?" he asked very coldly.

"Good God, no. Oh, you mean the article this morning. I had to make a tribute to deceased. Sir P. was adamant; and there's an ex gratia payment of seventy-six pounds to the widow if located—he didn't qualify for the pension fund—but Sir P. sets aside a sum for these cases, and although Button hadn't strictly been a staff member over the years, Sir P. ruled that he qualified for the whole thirteen years, less income tax, of course."

"This business of him loving animals and travelling in the Far East?"

"Pure invention, my dear fellow, and cleared for Libel by the Solicitor."

"He was a spy from the other side of the Curtain."

Harry thought that the creased, wattled face was chap-fallen.

"Will it come out? I don't know what Sir P. will say," Jolly sat down on the kitchen chair.

Harry shrugged. "If we get the fellow, and it's political, your answer is 'yes'. If the motive is civil, as you might say, I would not imagine it would be brought out. We do not wish to alarm the public," he added cattily, "with the thought that the great organs of opinion are manned by spies."

"I do not know what Sir P. will say," reiterated John Jolly, overwhelmed. He brightened and seized the intercom as if it were his feeding bottle. "Jolly. In the sanctum, pray."

One could almost hear the creakings of Peter Leeming's joints as he entered.

"A fine thing you gone and done," Jolly was capable of the sepulchral, freezing whisper that had been the most valuable weapon of his countryman Lloyd George. "This man Button was a spy."

"He did his work well," said Leeming. "I have my doubts about Miss Tump on astrology. Her trial column was, well, flippant."

"She well knows today is my birthday, the hag," said John Jolly. "Since she haunts the library for *Who's Who*, and I, um, got in the last edition. 'Beware of strong waters', the bitch put in among a lot of other crap."

"Now," said Harry, "this is not relevant."

"Sorry," said Jolly, "get the point and stick to it is my motto and I rarely forget it. It was before my time that this happened—and also, of course, Sir Peregrine's."

"Four owners since," said Leeming, impassively, "the one we had then jumped down the lift shaft the day before the annual general meeting of an insurance company he was chairman of."

"The point," said Jolly, well in control of the situation, "is did he just apply out of the blue, or what?"

"He wrote from Margate," said Leeming, slowly.

"Never trust 'em," said Jolly. "Blackpool is worse."

"The point was," said Leeming, "that we were bringing in this format of topical features—'Your Baby', 'New Slant to Beauty', 'Horses for Today's Courses'—all that. We kept running a classified—six lines—in *World's Press News*—like drawing teeth to requisition the money. I think the application came in answer to that, with an amusing specimen column, something for all the family, as we used to say then. Now it's 'The Swing with it Daily'. Things change so."

"Where would his original letter be filed?"

"Nowhere," snapped Jolly. "We're not in the dark ages at the old *Bully*, my dear sir. Sir P. has a rigid system of jettisoning everything on a yearly basis, except long-term contracts held by our bank. No wasted space in our building; everything productive. And of course, it does make things difficult to prove against us, come litigation."

"Margate's one of these odd towns that expand and contract," said the Inspector. "In winter people know each other. Button lived in a small, cosy flat—an ex-girls' school, long since bankrupt, with a lot of entrances. He must have had a car; none of the local tradesmen knew him. They generally know the residents. Come to that none of the publicans knew him. He paid for the flat by money order : no banking account. How did you pay him?"

"Cheque, naturally. Jesus!" Jolly snapped erect. "The head accountant has mentioned a discrepancy to Sir P. A credit one. Usually it's fiddling, but the discontinued Outside Contributors' Account has a funny lump in it on the credit side. It worries Sir P. You know," said Jolly confidentially, "when they get honest it means they're doing something worse. We had a man once who stole all the metal from the composing room store; he wrote the 'Inspiration from the Bible' para each day."

"What you are saying," Leeming said to Harry, "is that he destroyed our cheques."

"Of course," said Harry, "how the hell do you think we get 'em generally? Through the banks!"

"I suppose we could write it off," said Jolly, "over thirteen years it's a nice sum, and transfer it to shareholders' funds employed. That might placate Sir P. And there's the sum earmarked for the widow or heir. You could hardly give that to a spy. A nice bit saved."

"How was he paid here when he joined the staff?"

"By cheque I s'pose," said Jolly. "We encourage that as long as it's the bank Sir P. is a board member of."

"Sure?"

Jolly was at his best, bellowing down the handset at a member of the payroll staff, who obviously lost his nerve and was gibbering, judging by Jolly's encarmined cheeks.

"Packs of fools over there," grunted the Managing Editor, making a note. "They need a good shake-up. Heads will roll over there tomorrow, I assure you. No, when he first joined he queued up at the pay office window, presented his card with the number on it—we take no responsibility if the card is lost or stolen—and took his pay packet, less tax deduction."

"The banks to an extent co-operate," said Harry wearily, "but Inland Revenue—correctly in my opinion—are cagey on the source of income. But I dare say that if the Beautiful Spy did mark her return in such a manner there would be some discreet word in a club not far from Whitehall, and then would come the men in mackintoshes whom my superior officer hates. However it is obvious that your astrologer was on his last lap. Let's see, say some time in May, you'd have had no astrologer."

"An N.U.J. member," protested Jolly, "and a month's notice on either side!"

"He was N.U.S."

"The railways!" exclaimed Jolly.

"National Union of Spies. There is one in the dog-don't-eat-dog sense. Pro rules and all that. But he would file no return; he couldn't, because of the inevitable 'where did you file your *last* return'? query. But you had been deducting tax and eventually there would have been an unbalanced item, and men in bowler hats with black briefcases. So before then he would have gone for it. Which also brings me to the point that he must have been planning a really good final coup before retirement to a little country estate in you-know-where."

"Could we print that?" asked Leeming.

"Ask your solicitor. It'll frighten him so that he can't judge the geraniums at the Chelsea Flower Show. He will rightly advise you of the penalties handed down under Official Secrets. They put you on weaving little mats these days. No oakum picking, but the food is still rather bad. Well, good-day to you both."

Descending in the lift, he found Miss Wasey Tump seated surrounded by books, with the peculiar emanation given off by those kept for a long time in damp places. The girl Mabel was pouring tea from a kettle reposing on some kind of patent apparatus actuated by a gas bottle.

"This is Archer McClout. Inspector James, of the General

Nuisance and Parking Offences Department." Harry thought she bridled a bit. He noted that there was a bottle of gin among the tea cups.

McClout, from his accent, was Australian, a smallish man with a huge nose around which generally flickered a smile. His voice came from afar, seemingly from the bottom of a disused gravel pit. He poured a slug of gin into the black tea.

"Have a shot, Inspector, warms the blood weakened in semi-tropical climates."

"Have you got lemonade, love?" The Inspector addressed Mabel.

"Two bottles. She," Mabel scowled, "says I'm too young for gin and sex, but you'll have to pay for the Schweppes." She delved into her desk.

The Inspector ceremoniously produced a two-shilling piece and Mabel made change from a grubby-looking petty cash box.

"One day you'll find Mr. Jolly will flounce in and check that box—it's been known. I hope you know what you're doing, getting your own money mixed up with it. Jolly will prosecute over anything more than one and fivepence," said Miss Tump.

While Harry poured gin and lemonade Mabel made intricate calculations in a small notebook. "It owes me three and fourpence," she said triumphantly, "less a meat pie I bought for lunch."

"I have cautioned you against pastry," snapped Miss Tump, "but any surplus would be immediately confiscated."

"There was the case of a sub once," grated Archer McClout, "who won seventeen pounds four and nine in mixed doubles at the betting shop. Of course," he had a laugh seemingly connected with his navel, "he had a few mixed doubles himself to celebrate, so when he got in two hours late it had come down to thirteen pounds ten, which he put in the waste-paper basket under the impression that it was his desk drawer. Sir Peregrine comes round, peering, because he's upset about the amount of copy paper being used. He seizes the dough-ray-me and says it's for shareholders' funds employed—they say we own a chain of knocking shops in India—and the sub can't complain because if he opens his mouth there'll be an explosion as Sir P. is puffing at a sixteen-inch cigar."

"These scabrous and apocryphal anecdotes are the bane of every newspaper," said Miss Tump.

"Don't be biblical on me," ground out McClout.

"Do we really own cathouses in India?" asked Mabel, fascinated.

"Dozens. Place named Grant Road."

"Mabel," said Miss Tump, "take your book into the ladies' for half an hour. If anybody, including Miss Bottle, challenges you, tell them that you have my permission."

"I wanted to help with the astrology. Do you know that..."

"These books which I obtained from Foyle's yesterday, though smelling of age, will suffice. Sir P. has his birthday next month and I shall plan a prediction that will make his ghastly blood run cold. Avaunt!" A portion of cigarette-ash fell into Miss Tump's tea.

It was *Tropic of Capricorn*, Harry noticed, as Mabel sullenly opened her drawer and produced a paperback from under a pair of green galoshes. With a waggle she departed.

"She'll be the death of me," said Miss Tump, ash dropping.

"You've had enough gin," said Archer McClout, clinically, filling his own cup and Harry's glass and withdrawing the bottle.

"Her father," said Miss Tump, "is a minister of advanced persuasion who used to write our Daily Snappy Sermon when we had outside contributors."

"I never read it," said Harry.

"Natch. Our readers are atheists to a man," said Miss Tump. "But we have to have a bit of spiritual uplift—all of 'em do. Which is why he's here," a long finger pointed at Mr. McClout.

"Pardon me for being insulting," said the Inspector, "but the Higher Things of Life hardly look to me to be Mr. McClout's cup of gin and tea."

"I'd be back Sydneyside but for the fact every time I

raise the fare you bastards put the fare up," leered McClout. "I'm a sports sub, but when Sir P. decided to close up outside 'tribs and cut the staff generally, we had time on our hands; that I can't deny. The agency stuff comes in subbed and it's just mechanical work for us, so we do bits of feature stuff to fill in. I drew the Sermon and Lady of the Day on TV. The latter is easy because it comes to me via P.R.O. and I only have to curb his wind, but the religion," McClout shook his head and drained his tea and gin.

"In short," said Miss Tump, "my father, as a hobby, is a biblical scholar. He provides relevant quotes and Archer, in his horrible way, fills in the Inspiration. He's good at it."

"Ah," said McClout, draining the gin bottle. "He nearly got me sacked about the Money Changers. Out I'd have been but for the fact half our desk went to the new Government as P.R.O.s. Sir P. said it had been writen by Stalin and when poor old Leeming produced a Bible he said it was forgery."

"Which brings me to the point," said Harry. "Do you habitually keep your door open a crack? The first two times I was here that was the case."

"It is a matter of record that this is the oldest newspaper office in London," said Miss Tump. "The building inspectors are always clucking away about weak floors—rather like that Arnold Bennett scene with the printing press crashing through..."

"Clayhanger," said Harry.

"I never knew they read." Miss Tump rather ginnily addressed the ceiling.

"Only for obscenity," said Harry. "The last Home Secretary but one had doubts about Bennett, not realising he had been dead for some years."

"Any jokes made here are made by me!" said Miss Tump. "As I was saying the windows of this rat-hole are impossible to raise in any ladylike way and the fug becomes impossible. Sometimes I open the door a few inches, thus letting in a touch of thrice-breathed air."

"And on the afternoon of the murder?"

"I can't remember. In any case I had a tricky problem. Some of the stuff didn't make sense. After I came back from poor old Button's office I was on the phone."

"To whom?"

"A flack named Eros Fay—real name Hawkins. We checked and found that one sheet of the crap had dropped under his desk. So if you think I was peering out of the door you are typically wrong."

"Bye bye and thank you."

When he reached the lift he was surprised to find that McClout was beside him. "Time for a wet and a talk?" asked the journalist.

Harry consulted his watch. "About twenty minutes' worth. You fellows seem pretty freely off the chain."

"Wrong conclusion, but I admit that I know old Bocker pretty well...."

The Head Porter's white hair bobbed in acquiescence as McClout had a confidential word with him. The Inspector led the way to the little pub where—it seemed ages ago—he had drunk with Miss Tump.

"Afternoon," said the landlord, "I found a rare bottle of lovely old pork in the... oh, it's you. And what is your pleasure?"

"If I told you, you'd faint," said McClout, "I got it out of the Marquis de Sade and it involves..."

"Funny man!"

"If you don't want to be amused," said McClout, "half of bitter for me."

"And for me," said Harry.

"No, no," said McClout as the Inspector pulled out a note, "this one I can get through. Jolly never queries buying booze for the police, what with all the stuff on his conscience."

"A lot of you Australians around the newspapers, so I've found," said the Inspector.

"And New Zealanders," leered McClout, "but those you don't notice because they don't speak funny—just bleat away like retired Scottish nannies. Seriously, the next paddock has an irresistible fascination for journalists. At home we have great quantities of English and New Zealand people."

"You intend to stay?"

"Married English, three kids; I must confess that I like London," said McClout, "and so does the wife. Which brings me to the fact that Tump was a bridesmaid, the wife belonging to some wog crowd or other. We go over to her place as often as poss. The wife takes a cake or something and I generally cough up a bottle of gin—the old man likes a shot of it with cake, for God's sake. The *Bully* has no Sunday edition, so on Saturday arvo I go all Australian and do their garden, and I never knew there were so many insects till I came here."

"Surely Queensland," said Harry, afterwards cursing himself for his innate compulsion to debate.

"Sure, fruit bats, tropical creepy things all over and prickly pear, but," McClout's finger jabbed, "also tropical *growth*, at a rate that beats the disadvantages. We live in an apartment, but the Tumps have about an eighth of an acre, and I swear I cannot grow good broccoli! There was an ad. about manure from thoroughbred horses in *The Times* and I tried that—they could have been dray-horses for all the good they did my broccoli."

"I doubt whether excuses about gardening will placate my wife. This is the baby-sitting night out."

"Just so that you know that Tump is a friend," said McClout.

"No need to labour it."

"All right. You may not have observed that the *Bully* office is circular. I don't think you boys have. Naturally, the plan is flat, like Mercator's Projection," observed McClout, smugly. "But fundamentally the thing is built round a large air-well with what was once a fountain at the bottom—vintage 1901—but is now a miscellany of rotted banana skins and worse. So, if you are good enough to bear with me, the circle has two staircases, each equi-distant, for emergency, maintenance, cleaners and however Fat Jolly may decree. The lift is to the right of Tump's office and Button's was to her immediate left. Therefore the murderer could have approached via the left-side stairs. That fat Superintendent of yours, Porterhouse, and his myrmidons," McClout savoured the word as he finished his bitter.

"Porterman," said Harry.

"A steak by any other name."

"You are speaking of my superior officer."

"Well, rilly," the Australian minced. "But a fine-looking man, although gone at the knees. What I'm telling you, sport, and this is Christian upbringing versus ethics as you might say, on the arvo of the murder, at three fifteen approx., I had crep' down the left flight of steps to have a word with my mate in Syndication. The fact is," McClout reddened, "I write things for teenage girls."

"Two gin ands, for God's sake," Harry snapped at the lurking publican. "You *what*?"

"Healthy stuff at thirty bob a thousand words," said McClout, "all about girls marrying the boss's son after the foreman has failed in his horrid wiles; though what with the Managerial Revolution and Nationalisation it's hard to find a boss's son that hasn't emigrated to somewhere and somebody warm. But it sells. My friend advises me as to where the market is—case of Scotch at Christmas. If Sir P. knew it's the sack for both."

"We don't talk," said Harry. "We go through our lives like graves. Yet time ticketh on. Unbosom yourself, McClout. Pretend I'm a healthy teenage girl."

McClout supped his drink, unavailingly trying to oil his gravelled vocal cords. "I'd finished my bit of business with Harry Marks in Syndication—a ten-thousand-worder about a Bradford Mill Girl; we'd had a bit of discussion about whether I could let her sister be ruined, Miss Swish, the editress on that particular mag being on the straitlaced side, and I remember seeing on the clock that it was three fifteen. Mind you it's an old clock, all of 'em are at the *Bully*. I open the door and dodge back because coming from the direction of Percy Button's office is John Jolly himself. He's kind of looking backwards over his shoulder and tip-toeing, so I nick back and Harry and I make like we're doing something legitimate about syndicating the Sermon feature to South Africa. I came out in five minutes' time and there was no sign of anybody, so I scuttled up the stairs and back to the desk."

"Did you report this to the policeman who interviewed you?"

"I was off duty next day when the questioning was being done."

"Surely somebody would have reported your absence?"

"At that hour it's the lull before the storm, the Editor and Leeming holding the editorial conference, perhaps with Jolly intervening like some tattered old God, the cartoonist trying to find somebody to say 'yes', a lot of coming and going, phones ringing, that sort of thing."

"Hmph," said Harry. "No joy in what you've told me. Why the hell should Jolly wish to strangle his astrologer? Name me one reason?"

"This is where I hate myself," said McClout, "like my thirty-bob-a-thousand heroines. Tumpers always has that door open. This afternoon I had closed it because of the gin and Miss Bottle opposite. It's a kind of nervous thing with Tump to glance out when she hears a footstep. From the angle of her desk and the door *I think* she could see anybody approaching from the left, going into Button's office, even though he or she did not actually pass Tump's room. One for the road...."

Harry waited. A lot of police duty consisted of waiting, particularly when 'they' were loquacious.

"Tump will go through hell and high water for anybody she likes," said McClout. "But she likes very few people. F'instance, she likes my wife and the kids, that I'm sure of, but me, after many a long year, I'm not sure about. I think so. If she'd seen me strangling old Button you would not get her to open her trap. But she hates Jolly...."

"So?" said Harry.

"If she had seen Jolly she would have informed."

"And the corollary is that if she had seen somebody she liked she would have kept quiet?"

"Put your corollary round yer collar, sport," said McClout, finishing his glass. "I'm back to the office."

"Austrine, ain't he?" said the landlord, watching McClout's nuggety buttocks as they went out the swing doors.

"Yes, police here. See him much?"

"Newspapers," said the landlord, disgustedly. "Those that drink are free drinkers, but don't give credit!"

The Inspector took a taxi, and at ten past six collected his wife, in a dress he had not seen—although it did strike him that ninety-five per cent of all storage space belonged to her and her daughter. She looked delicious, but an inbuilt wifely circuit impelled her to say, "You've been drinking, dear."

"Do thou likewise!" The Inspector impelled her into the nearest grill room and ordered burgundy and hideously expensive steak.

4

AT TEN THIRTY the Inspector thought it had been all right in its way, a bit of a giggle in fact; the devouring when suitably cooked of a Methodist minister by seven ladies of ill repute, supervised by what Harry vaguely recognised as the Spirit of British Colonialism, had gone over well, moreover his wife was pleased to the extent of proposing a drink and smoked salmon sandwiches.

"Have you ever seen a newspaper office by night?" he asked.

"Should I?"

"Liberal education, but more explicitly an excuse for a taxi home. Perhaps a bite and a glass on the way if the boss feels benign."

"That'll be the day," said Elizabeth, but trotted at his side to the grim façade of the *Bulletin*.

"O God, O Montreal, O ex pot de chambre," groaned Harry, as he saw the fifty policemen in the foyer, with Superintendent Porterman haranguing an impassive and unflinching Head Porter Bocker.

"We're in, we're in," he whispered, as he caught the cold, flaccid grin of Porterman's assistant. "Smile when you say it."

"I gather you were one of the last to see deceased, Mr. James. Good evening." Porterman would plainly have liked to treat Elizabeth as a pick-up, but for the annual ball, where she had scraped a dutiful acquaintance with Mrs. Porterman, a raw-boned lady who knew her duty.

"Death where is thy sting?" Harry was rather surfeited by the Methodist minister.

"You don't *know*?"

"I do not ask imbecile questions, Mr. Porterman!"

There was momentary calculation in Porterman's small black eyes and then he back-pedalled.

"Perhaps you'll stay here, Mrs. James. There's a cubby-hole over there. Pray come with me, Mr. James."

The tiny room was largely filled with mops and buckets and smelled of disinfectant.

"That fellow Bocker gets on my nerves," grumbled the burly Superintendent, squatting—ludicrously, thought Harry—on a projecting shelf. "It's a Miss Wasey Tump—under a tube train and might have been pushed."

"God!" Harry was genuinely shocked.

"She went out of here at six—so this fellow Bocker says. He added that she always had some kind of a snack and spent an hour each Thursday instructing judo at a club off Oxford Street. I telephoned but everybody has gone home. Anyway at approximately nine fifty-five she is on one of the platforms at Oxford Circus. The Transport Board can't find any way of estimating flow of traffic within seven per cent. Like my local pub keeper." Porterman became momentarily human. "Sometimes he's crowded out, other days half empty. No rhyme or reason—no connection with weather or pay days. Anyway tonight was the busy turn for Oxford Street Station. She'd got herself at the front of the wedge of people as the train rushed along; then she screamed and fell—no chance of course. A few feet away there was an oldish fellow who had been watching her profile. He said she looked a dead ringer for a niece of his.

A second before she fell she turned her neck abruptly and he thinks she saw somebody she knew. She started to smile and open her mouth, then down she went. Of course the crowd started to mill around, women screaming and a couple of men in fainting fits... if there was a killer he had time to be almost anywhere within ten miles by the time the witness got to one of the officials.

"Her handbag was wedged under the live rail and in it was her *Bulletin* newspaper accreditation and some letters. A bright constable had the idea of telephoning me."

"Is there a positive identification?"

"Mr. Jolly—I must say he's a live wire," said Porterman admiringly, "sent a reporter... the head.... He's running it as the front-page lead for London and the Home Counties. Now, your report."

Harry spoke for a quarter of an hour. Porterman got to his feet and poked his head out of the door, bellowing. Within six minutes Archer McClout appeared.

"You are McClout?"

"Get stuffed! If you want it's Mister McClout."

"Now, *Mister* McClout, where, pray, have you been since eight p.m.?"

"With six other bastards at a stinking desk rewriting crap. And if ever I saw a demon I'd like to kick in the jingle bells..."

Porterman's large hand stayed him. The Superintendent knew his job, thought Harry, morosely.

"Now, you're tough," said Porterman. "The last time, some years ago, when I played football against your compatriots I was bitten severely."

"I thought the high, falsetto voice meant choir practice!" said McClout, meanly.

"As I said," the Superintendent, "you are tough, but we— and I mean collectively—are tougher. You may recall that under recent legislation, invoked by our Masters, you have no natural right to labour in English vineyards."

"He's correct, you know," said Harry. "You cannot beat the system."

"Have it your way, but Tump was a friend. I heard it around ten forty-five, Jolly roaring around. I phoned the wife to get out quick to the old father. I had previously told the Inspector here that if Tump knew who killed Percy Button it would depend on whether it was a friend or not."

"And who were her friends?"

"I also told the Inspector that it was difficult to tell. Enigmatic, with one em, as we subs learn in our literary way."

"I shall not trouble you further at the moment."

"Balls." McClout did not trouble to close the door after him.

"Difficult to tell!" said Porterman. "A lot of foreigners in this case. I must confess that I was rather shocked to learn that Mr. Jolly was Irish-Welsh."

"Where do you think I come from?" said the Inspector.

Superintendent Porterman, who at Association meetings often proclaimed that on the occasion he had a coloured assistant his resignation would go in directly to the Prime Minister of the Day, shuffled and muttered about spending his honeymoon at a very pleasant Welsh resort, he was sure, and that certainly he had no desire to say that the Welsh, or even the Irish, were negroid. On dry land he said, "I think you might see the Joe Nathan Institute of Judo, tomorrow. Report to me as soon as possible. Pray tell Inspector Goddard to come here. Goodnight to you!"

Having passed on the message to the whey-faced underling, the Inspector found his wife tête-à-tête with Bocker. She might have been seated on his knee, he reflected jealously, had there been a chair handy. Bocker was doing the heavy father act, a gambit which the Inspector had studied, with the years ahead in mind.

"I was telling the little woman, sir," said Bocker, "what a trump was Miss Tump. Pardon the rhyme but years ago I made a few bob on Christmas cards."

"Any ideas?"

"Not an enemy that I knew of, sir," said Bocker, "though she called a spade a spade and that can be a grave-digger's shovel if you do it often enough."

"She always conducted a judo course on Thursday?"

"She got paid, but said it was the exercise to sweat out the grog. Each Thursday at Joe Nathan's School of Fitness. I got through for the Superintendent. Let's see," Bocker produced part of the London telephone directory. "Here, Joe Nathan's School of Fitness."

"It's Jonathan's School of Fitness," snarled Harry.

"Is that so?" said Bocker. "I'm not well educated about names, although I have a pal named Joe Nathan and he doesn't seem the sort to throw people about unless money is involved."

"Come, Elizabeth," said Harry with what he hoped was dignity.

"Take this, sir," said Bocker, producing a pasteboard card from a pocket. "Beautiful Scotch salmon at half prices with the Spanish champers. Mention my name, sir."

"We shall," said Elizabeth, regally, "an immediate taxi."

"At once!" Bocker gestured to an underling and in response to a shrill whistle, which caused an elderly constable to jump higher than he had for years, a taxi miraculously appeared and Elizabeth gave the address recommended by Bocker whilst Harry hunched morosely.

"I must say I cannot stand that man," he growled. "It is rare for me to agree with Porterman. He was rather familiar towards you. Seventy-two, according to the staff list."

"Sometimes these elder citizens exert a strange attraction," cooed Elizabeth.

Harry had learned the hard way. When his wife wished to get his goat his only weapon was silence, a difficult one to use as the crushing retorts ran hard and heavy on the tongue.

"It'll probably be closed," he grunted.

Elizabeth smirked and nuzzled his neck.

Bocker's card gained them entrance to a dubious kind of club managed by a twitchy, elderly man with a drooping moustache which nature or chemistry had turned orange. The salmon was skilfully doctored cod and the champagne Spanish sparkling, but the Inspector's eyes, warily inspecting the two-feet square menu, noted that the prices were not too bad. Presently he thawed out sufficiently to peer out of the dimly lit alcove in which they were seated.

It *was* a kinky kind of place, but the light was too dim to identify any face with accuracy. On a little stage a bearded man softly played a harmonium.

"May I take a seat, Mr. James?" A smallish chubby man in a baggy Harris tweed suit which smelled faintly of beer around the lapels materialised. "We've met at many a press conference." Small chubby fellows smelling of beer were so common at press conferences that Harry could not place a name to him, but fortunately the man introduced himself as he eased his bulging thighs under the fixed table. The Inspector got a glimpse through the dimness of the proprietor peering craftily from behind a pillar.

"We had a tip, Mr. James, that drugs are being peddled here."

"Not my particular alley, I'm afraid."

"I've spent two quid on drink and sandwiches and nobody has tried to sell me any hash. The tip came from Bocker, but God knows what Jolly'll say about the exes."

"Oh, so you're the old *Bully*. Of course."

"I didn't want the job—this crime stuff doesn't work these days. They're all too fly, even the used-car boys. Leeming would have seen my point, but it's his early evening off and that bloody editor rotted his brains with gin when the *Morning Post* was still going strong. But what I wanted to ask you about was poor old Tump! What a woman; she loved her bitter just like I do. And hold it! No running to the ladies' every five minutes like they all do. I telephoned in to the office to ask whether I should continue to sit in this dump in the hope some creep would offer me drugs and got the news. Jolly was loquacious. Of course the bastard hated her. Not that he didn't remember to caution me to switch to coffee or drink at my own expense."

The Inspector sighed, signalled the waitress and ordered a double gin with a pint of bitter as a chaser.

"Thanks, Inspector," said the reporter gratefully, "nothing

like a Dog's Nose, though the present Government make it difficult for a man to get at it outside of Cabinet rank.

"What I wanted to say," his piggy blue eyes were shrewd and sober, "is that you should not get the wrong idea about newspaper offices. They are not repeat not haphazard, particularly a dump like the *Bully* where the cash is doled out in ha'pennies. You're ticketed and docketed and booked in and out. That's from the subs and reporters right down to the boys' room. If any underling was absent from his situation one of the bosses would know why and what for. And Bocker's a remarkable man, old as he is. He knows what time I went out the front entrance and where I am, trust him. And the same with the ten other reporters who are out and about."

"Lavatories," said Elizabeth, obscurely.

"Now, ma'am, I put it to you," his snub nose had a trace of froth on it, "any decent kind of foreman, call him news editor or head machine minder, makes a mental note when a body retreats to the loo. Too much looing and you get your cards. Stands to reason. Your old man would have checked all that."

"Superintendent Porterman has, I believe, produced some kind of graph." The Inspector ordered more champagne and regretfully a further Dog's Nose.

"Now what are you getting at?"

"One of the big shots killed the poor bloody astrologer. A big shot who could move freely around without having to report or book in and out. What about Sir P.? Blackmail, say. Perhaps he'd played fast and loose with Percy Button's daughter. Ten quid a week or a scandal and no peerage, which he's after. Sir P. wouldn't pay—far too mean—so he croaks old Button."

"You may as well know," said Harry, "that Button was some kind of a spy. It'll be common knowledge by morning, the way you fellows talk. His column was a code: 'The British Government will not resist' sort of stuff."

"Gawd," said the reporter, "a Philby!"

"A more amusing writer, one believes."

"Nobody's ever approached me. I would not mind having a go, the way things are going. But they say the climate's that bad and the women are on the big side, parm ma'am, and my tastes are petite. I wouldn't want to take the wife!"

"More to the point," said Harry, "did you ever hear of anybody wishing harm to Button or Tump?"

"Tump, no! She was an Identity, part of the Street. Everybody liked the dear, acidulated old bitch." For one awful moment it seemed as though he must weep into his beer. "Button was aloof, one of those go-straight-home, carefully buttoned-up fellows. God knows how he could have had an enemy as he never had a friend that I know of. Quiet courtesy, did his job well, came from God knows where."

"A foreigner, you think?"

"A foreigner! He spoke the same as you and I do."

"They do! But usually you fellows know each other's background. Button wasn't a member of either the Institute or the Union, by the way."

"Fat lot of good they count with Sir P. He thinks they all should be deported to Australia. But some of the special writers have no background—university and suchlike, army some of them even, and I put Percy down in that class. A decayed something or other. They should tighten the law. You don't find that your surgeon is a failed pawnbroker, do you now?"

"I'd want to think about that," Harry half raised his hand to beckon the waitress, but experienced Elizabeth's stiletto jab on his instep. "Some of them well might be, though the insignia would present a problem. We'd better be off. Waitress, order me a cab if you can!"

"Quite good," said Elizabeth in the taxi, procured by the stout, over-tipped waitress.

"We're over-spending," said the Inspector mournfully. "I keep dreaming of what that child will cost as she gets older. I saw a horrible shop this morning with 'Little Miss Clothes' on the window." But his wife was thinking of other things.

"Bocker did it, of course. Do you remember that old Scottish case about the old gentleman?"

"I wish you would not talk rot," but Elizabeth had gone asleep on his shoulder, and at their destination tottered dreamily into the bathroom and bed, leaving Harry to cope with the mother of the baby-sitter who feared that her daughter, being two hours late—at time-and-a-half she insisted—might have lost her virginity in these dissolute times.

Harry paid them off.

5

SERGEANT HONEYBODY STILL had a heavily alcoholic breath, collected, as he explained, in the line of duty, when Inspector James, in the back of a police car, thoughtfully picked him up next morning.

"It was very trying, but dooty is dooty." Rank had confined the good Sergeant to the front passenger seat so that he had to crane his neck and give the Inspector the full benefit of his labours.

"I played a hunch," said Honeybody. "He wouldn't have gone north, so I worked it out, to Canonbury and low places like that where you stand out like a sore thumb if you're respectable-looking. But say near the Borough High Street; good class of people there, all fiddling and able to dress smart. The Dean Inge Arms it was—one of the new ones under the council flats. Button used to go there, a great mistake because he didn't drink. Lemonade always arouses suspicion, and the landlord is honest; he was a butcher before he got into the pub business. Every Friday night at seven Percy Button came in on the dot, suspicious in itself, and ordered his lemonade. At seven five he went to the toilet; the landlord says a weak bladder, they learn to spot them in the profession. At seven fifteen a small blond man comes in. They are both reading an evening paper, but the blond man switches while the landlord turns to measure his double gin. What he doesn't know is that they have a little mirror one side of the bottle rack on account of you could reach out and steal potato chips. I had a rare job one time with a packet of crisps with chew marks on 'em; we never got to court on that one."

"Sergeant," said the Inspector, "cease to talk. What is the bung's name?"

"One Stafford Blossom, sir, very nice and has some very choice rum."

"On which mysterious note, Sergeant, we shall repair to the Dean Inge later in the morning."

"They say he is a masterly man with a headache and belly pains," said Honeybody, obscurely.

The Sergeant lapsed into a stunned silence. The driver expertly tooled the big car through the heavy traffic and with the omniscience of his kind turned into the dead-end street which housed Jonathan's School of Fitness.

It was one of those grimy but efficient-looking buildings that have survived the planners like an English burglar retired to Portugal and an odour of sanctity. Opposite was another London institution, a faded café with an urn of hot water, buns and bread-and-butter. The Inspector did not investigate, but he knew from experience that there would be a clean but battered wooden counter presided over by a very gloomy man, equipped with a damp cloth and a bowl containing five per cent butter and ninety-five per cent margarine, with a dash of milk as blending.

He consulted his watch. Nine thirty. "You boys nick over for a cuppa and a bun on the old firm." Laboriously and painfully, but gratefully—the Inspector fancied he saw the bulge of a small bottle in one hip pocket—the Sergeant eased his bulk out of the door and joined the driver. The Inspector closed his eyes, but it was not to be.

"No parkin', sir," came the inexorable voice.

"C.I.D. here," Harry wearily found and waggled a warrant card.

"Nothing wrong, sir?" came the voice through the window. "Respectable street this. Two ladies at the end, but most highly 'spec'able: members of the legal perfeshion and no noise. The landlord had the flat soundproofed on account of one highly respected gent likes to tap-dance without no clothes while reciting Acts of Parliament. But a most refreshing street, I'm sure."

"That gymnasium...." The Inspector nodded towards the sign.

"Simon pure, sir; they teach them 'ow to break a man's arm. I wonder if they could be sent to gaol for it; it's 'ardly fair." The constable was young, wistful and a bit on the spotty side.

"Tell your young lady that it depends on the circumstances, but that Eminent Divines—at least some on record—seem to side with her. Judges don't. She should appeal to your better nature."

The constable saluted and trudged away on his weary day of futile walking and the Inspector dozed until, at ten o'clock, the Sergeant, looking flushed but refreshed, returned with the driver.

"Please wait here. The Sergeant and I are going up to the Jonathan place. It should not take more than an hour."

The school was on the third floor as they went up the wide, shallow stairs, typical of the 1890 professional man, but now creaking and uncarpeted. The big oak door of Jonathan's was ajar and exuded a smell of floor polish. A small woman with a pleasant face and cat's eyes parked her mop and came over.

"I wonder," said the Inspector, "if..."

"No need to *wonder*," he heard as he flew through the air over her shoulder. The mat seemed quite resilient, but he was really too old for that sort of thing and the two upper dentures, rather unsatisfactorily fitted, had become dislodged.

Squirming on to his back he saw the small woman dart towards Honeybody who merely thrust forward his huge stomach, increasingly his most potent weapon as drink and the years slowed up his footwork.

"Damn," she said, as she sat down hard on the floor, but nevertheless one wiry hand snaked out and gripped Honeybody's left foot. The Sergeant was, however, immoveable against her tug.

"Assaulting an Inspector means three weeks of the skilly," said Honeybody.

"Oh, my God, have you come about the toilets?"

Harry had gained his feet, making a mental note that he

must spend a few hours a month at the police gym. Keeping his mouth closed as much as possible—because the false teeth were behaving peculiarly—he growled, "Police here. C.I.D."

"Oh, dear." She got to her feet in one swift writhing, a feat which made the Inspector more disgruntled than ever.

"You see we have complained to the landlord and when he put us off my husband approached the council. I'm Mrs. Jonathan, at least that isn't our real name, but we chose it..."

"Silence, woman!" The Inspector nearly lost his teeth and surreptitiously buried them in his handkerchief. The trouble was that without them he had a quite pronounced lisp. And official language seemed to abound with the letter 's'.

"You do both of you look as if you need a course of judo," Mrs. Jonathan said defensively.

"Are all who teach here women?" He nursed his words with care as if they were new-born babes.

"Most of them. It's mostly business girls who learn the judo. I always tell them that if they dressed more modestly... and with my husband it's mostly coaching weight-lifters. Ah, here he is...."

Mr. Jonathan was vast, huge biceps, one tattoed with a python, visible, but with an expression of astonished innocence bordering upon vacuity.

"Good morning, gentlemen," he had a voice like a well-made cheese sauce. "Aha, we'll soon get rid of that." He lightly patted the Sergeant's belly, "and you, sir, a weak spine right from schooldays, eh? Pushed about, no good with the girls. Oh, *we* can tell."

"I don't want to lose it." Honeybody rarely shouted, but when he did it was like somebody falling upon a bass drum.

"Don't want to..."

"They are police, dear."

Away from his huge weights, Mr. Jonathan was frankly a boggler. Somewhere there must be an accountant who kept things going, thought the Inspector, looking around. Probably a nice living.

"Well, you had a teacher named Tump," said Harry.

Slack-jawed Mr. Jonathan repeated the words.

"Miss Tump fell or was pushed under a tube train at Oxford Street Station last night."

"God," said Mrs. Jonathan, "now shut up, Clarence! It's only," her cats eyes supplicated the Inspector, "that he leaves these things to me."

"I suppose your instructresses"—the Inspector was beyond fear of lisping—"habitually fall under tube trains!"

"Shut up, baby," like most men who find it easier to leave it to their wives, Mr. Jonathan could in an emergency exert himself. "First we get chairs. Second you don't carry on. One, two, three, four, like a hundred-and-forty-pounder, slow stages and no jerking. Elbows rigid, thighs slightly parted, feet pigeoned in. Though I must say," he was obviously a man who brooded upon his profession, "that the Russian jerking puzzles us professional coaches, to be fair. I remember at Tokyo..."

"Chairs, please," said Honeybody, obviously with a recrudescence of hangover.

Without apparent effort, Mr. Jonathan lifted four heavyish chairs, two in each enormous hand, and set them down. When they were all seated, his wife said, "I can hardly believe it. Miss Tump had been with us since soon after we started, one of my first pupils, twelve years ago. She used to wear strange hats in those days."

"Now," said Harry, "she learned and then took on teaching?"

"Two nights a week for an hour or so, depending. Beginners. She used to say that if she hadn't got an obligation to do so, she'd weaken and not get a work-out. She kept a lot of the youngsters in order; not that I mind them mucking about as long as they pay monthly in advance, but it annoys the serious students and then there's a drop-off, and soon..."

"How large are your premises?"

"Three rooms up here and Jonathan in the basement because of the weights, not that we think the floor would actually *go*, but when we first came the obese old bag who runs the dancing classes underneath—belly dancing is more her line—wrote to the landlord and..."

"Were you in a position to see Miss Tump instruct?"

"Oh, dear, no. I work in this room. Miss Tump was at the end, with a thicker mat."

"Did she keep anything here?"

"Only a couple of uniforms. We attended to the laundry side of it."

"Had she any particular friends?"

"She wasn't friendly," Mr. Jonathan said. "First day she ever came I was standing watching her on account of I'd never seen a woman so skinny. She said, 'Don't you goggle at me, mindless oaf.' After that it was just nods."

"Of course," said his wife, "her students mostly went to another instructor after three months; the rest dropped out. She was hard to know, but—her name being in the paper so often— she was an asset."

"Could she have strangled a smallish but powerful man?"

"Oh, dear, judo is basically defensive, not like ju-jitsu or karate or unarmed combat."

"Get between them, eh?" said the Inspector.

"What?"

"A famous poet said that to the Conscientious Objections' Tribunal when asked what he would do if a German—I think they made it 'officer' as he came of good family—tried to rape his sister."

"He must be a funny kind of a bloke." Mr. Jonathan's great hands balled and odd-looking lumps of muscle appeared under his tee-shirt.

"If his sister had come to me," said his wife, "he need have had no fear. It would have been the German officer who would have been alarmed...I mean..." she stopped in some confusion.

"To get back to the point, could she have killed a man?"

Surprisingly, Jonathan took over. "If he was just a mug, she could. To learn defence, you have to have some knowledge of aggression."

"When did she leave the club last night?"

"A bit after eight-thirty," said Mrs. Jonathan, "a slack night for once. She poked her head in where I was instructing the advanced course and said goodbye."

"Could anybody have followed her?"

"I have no idea. Miss Tump was a moocher by profession, looking at shop windows to see who had thought up what. Why girls do not spend more time on exercise rather than display..."

It was a day when chairs were nice, thought the Inspector, wearily arising and thanking them for their co-operation.

Harry, back in the police car, consulted his crammed notebook, and prevailed upon the driver to park outside a telephone booth. He looked up the name and found that Eros Fay and Friends, Publicity Consultants, occupied part of a Square which he vaguely associated with bygone ducal families and brothels of superior quality.

This time the parking was quite illegal, so he took Honeybody with him. The Sergeant was increasingly querulous about parking regulations since his wife had taken to delivering the products of her fish-and-chip shop. The once-ducal building was yet unscathed and they had either retained the butler or obtained a rather good film extra who insisted upon a card being placed upon a gilt tray.

"Now, look," said Harry, dangling his warrant card, "I'm forbidden to part with this, like your keys to the cellar, but if I do not see Mr. Eros Fay there will be unpleasantness."

"No offence intended, sir. Perhaps you'll wait in the 'allway."

"His pants look very tightified round the bum," said Honeybody.

"Nineteen-ten until twenty-eight," said Harry. "The masters wore very full pants, so the butler, not to be mistaken in his station, tended to be a bit tightish."

"Only one I saw," said Honeybody, "had taken the plate. Not far from here."

"My dear fellow," as he returned with the butler Mr. Fay was almost swarthy enough to arouse racial feelings and had a twitch between the shoulder blades, "this so stoopid feller to keep the law a-waiting. Do come in. Coffee or something stronger? At this hour we generally have," his boiled eyes shrewdly evaluated, "a smartish drink and a bit of pâté—specially sent in."

Mr. Fay's office had some suits of armour and furniture of uncertain vintage. Harry and the Sergeant perched surprisingly comfortably on the octagonal chairs while Mr. Fay busied himself at the refrigerator.

"Perhaps you would prefer a larger glass, sir," Fay addressed the Sergeant as he held the Dry Sack bottle, "these little titty ones, as we say down west, rarely really wet a whistle."

"It would be a blessing, sir," said Honeybody, looking piteous as he accepted half a water-glassful and declined a biscuit spread with pâté.

"Delicious pâté, Mr. Fay." The Inspector paid tribute and accepted another.

"It's sheerly the quality of the cognac, you know. It goes without saying that the liver and etceteras are okay, but we represent the cognac. I must send—you are married?"

Harry nodded.

"Your good lady our recipe book and a small sample."

"Care of the Yard will do," said the Inspector dourly. "You read of the death in the *Daily Bulletin* of an astrologer?"

"Indeed. How tragic. A wonderful dynamic paper, so ably conducted I always say. Such a respect do we have for Sir Peregrine and Mr. Jolly."

"You want a swift kick in the crutch?" The Inspector drained his glass. Honeybody had recently finished his, being unimpeded by pâté.

"Pardon?" Fay came to a standstill.

"Metaphorically, old cod, since you deal in words. But this is murder. If you want you can have a solicitor with you, but I am asking you to comment upon the fact that Miss Tump told me that she had a very long telephone conversation with you at approximately three fifteen p.m. on the afternoon of the tenth. Now take your time!"

"She's dead," said Fay, dully, "I phoned this morning—the knee breeches campaign—and got on to somebody else. Dead last evening. True?"

"Identification," said Harry. "Tube train. Fall or pushed doubtful."

"I suppose we must have another sherry!" Harry saw Honeybody lick his lips as Fay spoke.

"Nothing," said the Inspector, "just well chosen words."

"She is definitely dead?" said Fay.

"As corpsed as you can get and as only a train can do."

"No," said Fay, "she did not phone me."

"But you were prepared to perjure yourself, is that it?"

"I must say you use words in an ugly way. Let me choose mine carefully." Fay stared at the ceiling for a long moment. "First Wasey Tump had no, repeat no, murderous instincts. To that I will swear. Secondly, when I started out ten years ago—oh, not here and with no staff, 'friends' as I like to think of them—I made a simply crashing error, my dear fellow, of the type that would have ruined me. It was Tump who organised the rescue party, persuading the other girls to give me a second chance and shut up about it.

"Now she was the type of person that needed knowing. She was fiercely independent, but if she had done a favour she expected to be able to ask for one back. There was little I could do to repay a favour of such magnitude. What tips I could, I passed on. She has, had, an old father and I sent him a case of grog at Christmas. So when, on the evening of the murder, she telephoned me, I acquiesced. One moment, please."

He pressed a button and a section of the desk swung open. "Most of our work is done by telephone and we record conversations. There is nothing surreptitious about this; a report of call is sent, where necessary, to the caller." He selected a small capsule of fine wire and dropped it into a slot.

"Seven ten," droned a tinny, mechanical voice.

"Is that you, Eros?" Miss Tump's voice sounded tired.

"Speaking, Wasey, and at your service."

"Is this your private, outside line?"

"My dear woman, it was you who dialled it! Oh, sorry for the brusquery, but it's been a swine of a day and it looks like going on until midnight."

"Anybody with you?"

"Batman just flew in; never knew he had corns, but he winced as he landed."

"No humour, please."

"I am in my deserted, whited sepulchre."

"Some time after three fifteen a man in the office next door to me was strangled. I intend to tell the police that as from three fifteen, on my outside line, I had a long, presumably over half an hour, conversation with you, the reason being that page two of the Flo Nightingale Look crap you sent me had fallen under your desk."

"One minute, dear... you're lucky. From three until three forty-five I was miraculously untelephoned and sans callers, save a brief look-in from my secretary who values her annual two weeks, paid by the firm, to our Bermuda Associates too much to peach. Let's cut this short. Page two under my desk."

"Thanks a lot," said Miss Tump.

"A perjure, I'm sure."

"Mountebank!" Miss Tump hung up.

"There, gentlemen, if gyves are necessary my wrists are ready."

"Bah," said the Inspector.

"If it is only a matter of bahing, I would be grateful not to be tortured by the Crowner. My clients are as sensitive a lot of birds as ever systematically robbed the working class."

"You have not committed any offence," said Harry. "No doubt intent to perjure oneself comes under some Enactment but I am not going to closet myself with a gaggle of musty-smelling old lawyers on the point. When and why did you meet Miss Tump!"

"She fenced, a good second-rater. I was first-class—a matter of record. We got to know each other at tournaments. At that time I was working for an advertising agency, vaguely meditating taking off on my own with eighty pounds in the bank. I must say that Tump gave me a lot of good advice and introductions. So I got myself a room in Holborn, snatched a client, fell flat on my face and got bailed out by Tump."

"I think we might have another sherry," said the Inspector. "Help yourselves, by all means."

Harry meanly watched Honeybody, now in jovial form, flood his water glass. Fay was looking pleased. It was the text-book instruction: 'Get them smug and then hit hard.'

"How many foreign clients *have* you got, Mr. Fay?" The Inspector's voice was harsh.

"Dear me," Fay's eyes were now very intelligent. "Of course, she was middle European. In answer to your rather obvious inference I have no direct European clients. In fact I deal with intermediaries, the chaps who import and export. Personally, I was born in some rather horrible village in Dorset. Spy stuff, eh? You're mad! Wasey was strictly a pox-on-all-your-parties person and G.P.I. to the Germans."

"If you have anything to say, sir," Harry's voice was maddeningly bland, "this might be the time to say it."

"I have to say that this interview is at an end."

"Until we meet again, my dear, and be sure to put it on your tape. Good day to you. And I was being polite about the pâté; only an old creep could have dreamed it up."

"The last bit riled him," said Honeybody sagely as they got into the car. "One of those coves who like mucking about in the kitchen."

The Inspector, who liked mucking about in kitchens and was wondering just how much powdered clove had been in the excellent pâté, preserved a sullen silence as they were driven to the Dean Inge, with its violet strip-lighting, green laminated counter and imitation gold tables and chairs in the lounge.

"Do the talking," said Harry, as they entered.

"I thought your esses were a bit camp." Honeybody was doing his fatherly act.

"These two upper falsies slip and wiggle. Elizabeth says I should go private, but on principle..."

"The lady next door gets false eyelashes, on account of personality defects if she don't have 'em. Persevere, sir."

The Inspector had gone through three generations of English saloon keepers. The original one who generally looked like a retired Regimental Sergeant Major, and often was, then the ruddy-faced, Royal Air Force types, and now those who were apparently retired playwrights of the Old Angry Young Men School. He considered that mild ale out of the barrel had suffered during the progression.

Stafford Blossom, the publican, had a peculiarly whining voice, but enquired tenderly after Honeybody's health. He had a mixture of Fernet Branca and stuff which could fix almost anything.

"A stiff sherry fixed it," said the Sergeant, "and this is my boss."

"Oh, dear," said Mr. Blossom, "I never recommend starting on the sherry, because it makes curing the head pains difficult."

"I don't get head pains," rumbled Honeybody. "Two dry sherries, since we've started, and tell my guv what you told me yesterday."

"A pleasure, sir," Mr. Blossom was dexterous. "Friday nights at seven—since they built this a year ago under Mr. W.'s Plan for Advancing the Country and attracting tourists—I've had the licence—and there he had been, one lemonade and weak in the bladder. Mind you I thought he was jess going 'ome and got caught short. A lot of them do, but they don't know they gotta legal right to use my bog, so they come up and order the cheapest drink. A vicious circle. They say there's one man, gone in his kidneys, who calls in fifteen licensed houses up this road on his way home and a sparkling grapefruit in each. A vicious circle!"

"There was a fair-haired man?" prompted Honeybody.

"Short squat feller, drank one gin. But I always seen 'em swap their papers. Nothink to do with me. Bookmaking, I thought, still a lot of illegal stuff around, or something of that nature. It's a respectable house, sir, no singing allowed."

"I'll have to ask you to come to the Yard and look at some photographs," said Harry.

"Lor', sir, not todye. There's a party of American tourists coming, and two barmen off. One of the 'istorical pubs of London the Tour people say we are. Ol' poets and suchlike. The rill ones they do not understand, old and dirty and wiv bad toilets. Here the ladies can eat their lunch off 'em and the waitresses are dressed all Elizabethan by the brew'ry. And no seasoning in the food but plenty of salad and martinis. Happy as little kings they are."

It was no good antagonising witnesses. The Inspector knew of at least one indubitable murderer—a proof reader in a respectable printing house—who had escaped because the Inspector in charge had offended a key witness.

"Perhaps I'll phone you tomorrow."

"Do that, sir, I've got to get the battery chickens defrosted. Mad on them, they are. I got a genewine Frenchman to design the menoo. Pullet Divine a la Franshish. Seventeen and nine a portion, a bit of deep frozen mushrooms and a soup cube. Happy as little kings."

"Another sherry," said Honeybody, "on the fish, sir."

"We'd better have a bite," said the Inspector, "not the frozen chicken at that price, but perhaps he can do a welsh rarebit and an egg."

Honeybody swigged at his fresh sherry. "They can't do nothing here, sir. Round the corner at the Guinness House."

Round the corner was a bit grimy, but the public bar had clean scrubbed tables and a quite noteworthy oxtail braised with turnips and a good jar of stout. Honeybody, a courier of pubs, mentioned that the gooseberry tart and double cream was quite famous. Harry weakly agreed, and asked the Sergeant to order while he telephoned Superintendent Hawker. The latter achieved the impossibility of *listening* dyspeptically to the Inspector's report.

"Are you eating or drinking?" he said at last.

"Waiting for gooseberry pie and cream."

"Don't talk to me like that," Hawker growled. "That infernal chair. I tried it on 'one' and the way it stirred my lunch up is cruel. In my office at two thirty. I think I know the blond fellow. Went out via London airport at six last night—cypher clerk, second grade, but well up on the you-know-what-list. I'll send a constable out with the candid camera snap taken at the reception for Friends of Democracy."

The pie was good, but the steadily champing jaws of the Sergeant, his inflamed nose and ineffable expression of pleasure ruined it for the Inspector, who refused a suggestion of a little cherry brandy and rather alarmed the publican with the curtness of his demand for a taxi.

Harry and Honeybody found Hawker with Superintendent Porterman. The latter was slyly sneering.

"The landlord of the pub, Blossom, identified the snapshot of the cypher clerk who scarpered," said Hawker without preamble. "Mr. Porterman"—there was a little animosity in the old man's voice, thought Harry—"was good enough to consult the Stealthy Men. He confirmed that communications between the spy-boys are getting damned difficult. Even the wives of consuls tend to be followed into public toilets; and there are obscure listening machines. God in Heaven! The day will come when I retire to Cheltenham gladly."

Porterman brightened, but met the old man's gaze and subsided.

"A few years yet, though," Hawker leered.

"It does seem to be," said Porterman, shifting ground, "that the late Percy Button disseminated instructions, but was getting to the end of his tether. Hence his contact, which sooner or later would have been spotted. There is some big stuff around—what would happen if A did this and B objected. Prolix material. Top guessing on both sides. So Button was instructed to go to bat and hell with the consequences. That is the theory."

"If I may say so, sir," rumbled Honeybody, "one of our side might have done him."

Momentarily the atmosphere was of a bad smell. Hawker, a realist, said, "In which case who do we arrest? I must say that I cannot risk a respectable career and neither"—he looked at Porterman—"could the legal department wish to arrest some fairly senior civil servant acting under orders."

"We would not stoop to assassination, sir," said Porterman.

"Of course not," said Hawker. "In 1943 the two prominent Nazis who happened to have a drink with me in Paris died of acute meningitis. Nice men, I always thought."

Porterman was silent. "I bow to your wisdom, sir."

"You must, of course," Hawker's eyes were very cold as he tapped the table with his fingers. "I did get on to one of my former masters who assured me that Button was not killed by us. I despair of you, sometimes, Porterman, if it has to be done it is in the coffee and medical man waiting with the coronary certificate."

"I would prefer not to know about such things," said Porterman.

"Nevertheless, I telephoned an old friend—one of the small advantages of old age, Mr. Porterman, like eschewing blondes, is knowing old friends—and he said that nobody official had killed the late Mr. Button. So it was *his* side. Not unknown, I understand, if the hounds are getting close to the fox."

"And were they, sir?" said Honeybody who was always a dozen yards in front of any Angel.

Harry was never sure quite what Hawker thought of the stout Sergeant. The snaky eyes flicked round. "As usual," said Hawker, "you put your thumb—a rather fishy one, it is said"—Honeybody looked as embarrassed as it is possible for a man with grog-blossoms to do—"upon the nub of it. There are some rather important conversations coming up. Those snug little confabulations that possibly decide our life or death but which our masters believe we are not adult enough to know about. So counter-espionage have all the stops pulled out.

"Espionage is worked largely on the 'cell' system, with a disposable link, which is what Button was. Once I could have had Button in this office and I assure you that within six days he'd have talked—and not a mark on him, but in wartime it is different. In the piping days of atomic peace it is not done even to question the bloke with the false beard. But the counter-espionage had worked it out that the instructions might be coming through some kind of printed material. You—and in fact I—have no idea of the tremendous amount of money these people can call upon. They thought logically that it would be a potty little magazine, bought for five thousand quid. Then it occurred to them that the limited circulation made exposure more likely, so they were progressively raising their sights. They had not yet reached the national dailies, but they would have, with every damned thing put through computers and grids. We may presume that Button was told to make his final run, then bolt. There has been a continual stream of suspect boats in the Pool; they give them a fair amount of insurance."

"Why did they knock him off?" said Honeybody, dourly.

"The Tump woman," said Porterman, momentarily lowering himself.

"You have some support for that," said Harry, "in view of her endeavour to supply a false alibi." He outlined the circumstances.

"The trouble is," growled Hawker, "that we went over her office with a toothcomb and did the same with her own home—the poor old gent went off to hospital—and there is not one iota of suspicious evidence except foreign language books of an arty nature. This, of course, aroused Mr. Porterman."

"There was, begging your pardon, Mr. Hawker, *Maldoror* in the original French. Quite banned here."

"Nonsense, it ain't, translated here in the thirties. A funny, old bloke thinking he's got moles under the armpits," snapped Hawker, getting mad, thought Harry.

"I'm afraid it beats me," the Inspector said. "Unless the staff of the *Daily Bulletin* are spies."

"Sir P. is on a Conservative Steering Committee," snapped Hawker.

"Kosygin approves of him, which means he's all right," said Porterman. "English commos frighten him out of his wits, but when he was here he proposed Sir P.'s health at the Junior Primrose League lunch for him in Henrietta Street. Security made a special note of it."

"One thing," said Hawker, "the press aren't riding us. I had the P.R.O. have a discreet word etcetera. The bloke from *The Times* nearly wet himself in alarm when the P.R.O. said we were keeping an eye on the third leaders and talked on about Caesar's Wife livin' in Printing House Square as though it was some kind of old Roman knocking shop."

"Which describes it so admirably," said Harry.

"Well you and the Sergeant better get back to the drinking; if you could spare a moment between glasses have a look at this fellow Jolly. What the hell was he doing near Button's office?"

"A most respectable man, Mr. Hawker," said Porterman, "and runs the place with admirable economy." He glanced distastefully at Honeybody, "and woe betide any staffer who goes to the pub too often. Besides we have only the word of a Colonial."

Porterman flinched at Hawker's inimitable slow leer. Harry vaguely remembered a scuttlebutt from his early days to the effect that an enterprising visitor from the Dominions had sold Porterman, then an Inspector, a bolt of fine Chinese silk which turned out to be the cheapest form of synthetic.

"We won't go into that, then," teased Hawker.

"He struck me as a good sort of man to have on your side in an emergency," said Harry.

"Well," said Hawker, "much as I admire your company we must part. The Superintendent and I have two hit-and-runs and a bank robbery, the banks being in their customary philanthropic mood and conveying thirty-five thousand pounds by means of an old messenger with a double hernia and a touch of gout. With the country's money draining away, I shall not authorise car or taxi. Bus perhaps, although a stiff walk would do both of you good."

"What was that old bleeder talking about, Harry?" asked Honeybody who was trudging along the Thames Embankment in obvious perplexity.

"Which one and what?"

"Hawker. About chewing blondes. At his age!"

"Eschewing blondes, which means avoiding them."

"That would be more like it," said the Sergeant, relieved.

The *Bulletin* looked more depressing than ever. The inevitable Head Porter, Bocker, fussed up to them looking rather harassed and wiping his brow. "Fifty boys from a rather low public school, sir, just inside the Headmaster's Conference and with very gaudy ties, clattering round the place and upsetting the Head Compositor who suffers from nerves caused by transposed lines and unintentional obscenities. The trouble is that the readers don't like him and if he leaves out certain letters they shut their eyes. You'd be surprised, sir, how often I have to intervene and how dirty is the public mind."

"Yes, yes, is Mr. Jolly in?"

"The newsroom, sir, giving his spirited address on how the Empire cannot survive without a free press. Nobody's told him it's gone." Bocker raised bland old eyes to the ceiling, which Harry noticed with a start had been plastered in the shape of large, nude women with cornucopias from which streamed grimy words in relief: 'Truth, Progress and Empire' was the burden of the largest figure.

Bocker sensed the direction of the Inspector's glance. "They were the days, sir, when everybody knew their place and a coloured man got off the pavement. Law and order! My Dad, who was in service in his early years, told me that the Chief Constable of the County used to knock at the servants' entrance —the young master being a bit free with the village girls and on the impatient side."

But Harry had stamped off to the lift.

"Bit of an old wag isn't he?" said the Sergeant en route.

"I'd like to see him wag at the end of nine feet of hemp."

"I suppose he couldn't have done it?" enquired Honeybody. "He looks like a man who likes his vittles; a few weeks on bird porridge'd make a new man of him."

"Unfortunately," said the Inspector—his recent experience disinclining him to discuss prisons and their inmates—"he could not have done so, short of nicking out and climbing the outside wall."

"Stranger things have happened, and, excuse me, sir, your lisp is getting worse."

Things went out of your mind, thought Harry, and fumbling in his pocket located the two false teeth.

"Is this better speech, you so-and-so?"

"Perfect, sir, though if I may presume they wobble a bit," said Honeybody.

"The process of getting older," said the Inspector, more to keep in practice than anything, "is the slow decay of the faculties."

"They can cure that nowadays," said Honeybody, aghast, but the lift had stopped.

"We can look back on the great Editors," John Jolly's voice boomed, "Maginn for instance."

"He died of drink," said a gloomy, pimpled boy in the first row.

"Nicholas Byrne," said Jolly, taking the punch but unblemished, rhetorically speaking.

"He was shot long before the *Telegraph* bought his paper," said the pimply youth who was obviously the type who read things up. "A reactionary, he was."

"And in America Mr. Bennett."

Several boys snickered at scabrous memories. The pimply boy had unearthed a book giving extracts.

"The immortal Chas. Dickens," Jolly played his trump card as he uttered the canonised name.

"His mags made dough," said the pimply youth, "but the newspaper he started went bust."

"Now these gentlemen are from Scotland Yard!" Jolly was a man of immense resource, Harry realised.

It was part of the mystique that awe crawled behind the bored youthful eyes.

"I'm here on business," said Harry, "and I can't spare the time to kick juvenile bums. I imagine there are mechanical places where you can better spend your time. So cut off. You," he addressed the pimply youth, "they have molten lead around these institutions. Stick your head in it!"

The boy grinned as he slouched away.

"I'm surprised, I must say," said a snuffy-looking man with the slightly defensive look observable upon people who work in rather dubious schools. "No violence, no military training, no corporal punishment.... I must say that the H.M. will address his Member...."

"No doubt an interesting exchange will ensue," snarled Harry, "meantime your charges are running amuck."

"Boys, boys!" The dominie moved with surprising alacrity.

There was a squeal from the side of Archer McClout who sat immersed among a sea of flimsy paper, most of which he was methodically putting on to a metal spike. His free hand had whipped round and grasped the pimply boy by the nose.

"Now, mate," said McClout, painfully twisting, "do you wish to follow this dreadful occupation?"

"Yes, sir," snuffled the boy and McClout released him.

"Breathing down my neck will only produce a slop round the chops. If you are serious come and see me, Mr. McClout, after you leave that gorgeous school."

"Dad can't afford it, sir, but it's the Welfare State. He says people minus a Tie haven't a chance and get rehabilitated." He scuttled off, watched benevolently by John Jolly.

"The sort of likely, enquiring lad we want. Sir P. believes in encouraging the Young Idea."

"At the union minimum," snarled McClout and the Managing Editor seemed stricken with deafness, but said loudly as he led the way to the small private room, "Fine fellows, these Colonials, but they take a bit of knowing."

Glancing backwards, Harry saw McClout writhe in his seat and turned the knife, "I believe some of 'em were not convicted men."

Jolly's smirk turned to wariness as he closed the door and saw that Sergeant Honeybody had produced a notebook. Actually the Sergeant's shorthand was a breed which nobody but he could read. He had once told the Inspector that he had discovered it in an old girls' magazine during his days as a probationer.

"I'll give it to you straight, Mr. Jolly," said Harry. "You were seen near Percy Button's office close to what must have been the time when, so the Path. bloke says, he was bashed on the back of the neck and strangled with a bit of red twine."

The experiences of years of moral bankruptcy momentarily showed in Jolly's face. All sorts of Official Receivers of the mental variety had wrestled with and finally soothed that shifty mind, thought Harry.

"Let me see," said John Jolly, slowly.

"Would much prefer vocal cordage to optical; otherwise we go to the Yard, and how your loyal confrères on the rival rags would love to take pix! I hinted they might find a story around here," the Inspector added, mendaciously.

"Miss Bottle," said Jolly at last.

"She was in the ladies' loo with a book and doubtless toffees," sighed Harry.

"I know," said John Jolly masterfully. "Two years ago Sir Peregrine installed a closed circuit TV in there and we got a retired hospital matron—all perfectly proper because we stand for the highest Moral Values—to sit all day watching for malingering. You'd be surprised—pinching toilet rolls to take home—makes you despair of the country's future and sterling. But the Union got to hear of it and we had to pull out quick."

"Get to the point, the loo and Miss Bottle," said Harry, "otherwise I'll call for a Squad Car."

"Be careful of me," warned Jolly, "I don't take crap from Inspectors."

"If I, personally, locked you up, Mr. Jolly, it could be interesting."

"No need for us to quarrel, dear boy," said Jolly. "The fact is that Miss Bottle has been with us for a long time—ten proprietors—and the first one, well, he was a lord and had these odd inclinations. So Miss B. got on to this very sweet superannuation scheme, which was abolished by the next proprietor, but we're stuck with Miss Bottle, although the pound is only worth eight and tenpence. But the Agreements all had 'Dereliction of Duty' in 'em. If we can prove that Miss Bottle habitually takes her book and goodies into the loo of an afternoon, she gets about half the pension. So I, well live with it, gentlemen! And many a mickle makes a muckle, as Sir P. says. And Sir P. would be generous—sixty-five per cent in exchange for a total waiver. I came down the back stairs and checked her absence."

"I trust your pension is secure?"

"Share options on the new issues and self-perpetuating seven-year contracts." Jolly glared, "Do not take *me* for a mug!"

"Button was a spy!"

"So everyone has now heard."

"From whom?"

"Well, it was Bocker, to be precise."

Harry, in fury, jabbed his thumb down on the desk top and then brandished his hand in Jolly's face. "This cursed man," and abruptly stopped. Dangling on the end of his thumb was a small bottle labelled 'Cow Rubber Solution'.

He tried to remove it and failed.

"My dear fellow, perhaps I can summon the staff doctor"—Jolly glanced at the clock—"no, he's down the road at the family limitation clinic for Commonwealth Visitors, but perhaps nurse and a hammer."

Somehow the solution, though not his thumb, was seeping out of the bottle. "Goddamn you and your bloody bottle!"

"My dear sir, we must be realistic and I am sure Sir P.," Jolly glanced at his desk top—something retrieved from an ancient seaside boarding house at a sale, surmised a part of Harry's mind—"would not appreciate his furniture being ruined by the constabulary."

"You..." the Inspector stopped as Sergeant Honeybody's immense hand gripped his shoulder.

"I only keep on in the Force because I like my governor," said the Sergeant, very simply, "having a bit of money put away. And I'm a trifle older than you, but knowing the tricks I can smash you up and like it."

"This is surely time for a friendly noggin," said Jolly. "Lubrication without lubricity is the old *Bully* motto." He ogled Harry whilst producing a heavy bunch of keys, unlocking a drawer and producing a bottle of inferior bulk whisky and three small glasses.

"Hospitality of the house, gentlemen, never let it be said that Sir P. stands for Parsimony."

"Pa, who? And I'll have another on him whoever he be, this being on the painful short side," said Honeybody after one gulp.

"Certainly, Sir P. runs Liberty Hall, within limits of course."

John Jolly smiled and poured very slowly, but was defeated by the Sergeant's patience.

During this exchange Harry had left his hand on the desk. Lifting it, he discovered that the rubber solution had rather abruptly solidified, so that a kind of gummy web had attached him to the desk top. As he pulled it stretched while John Jolly smirked.

Eyeing the Managing Editor in a manner which made that worthy recoil, Honeybody groped in his rear-end pocket and produced a large pen-knife and severed the Inspector.

Abruptly putting his right hand into his trouser pocket—he presumed a dry-cleaner would cope—Harry strode ahead of Honeybody to the lift, at the door of which milled the schoolboys. Cursing under his breath he stalked to the stairs. After a few paces down, he felt the two wretched dentures slip and automatically raised his hand to push them back, feeling a fraction of a second too late, the bottle clink against his teeth and the same kind of taste he remembered as a boy when he bit the rubber sponge while being bathed.

He withdrew his hand, but the solution possessed an alarming elasticity. "Ugh," he turned to Honeybody.

"Lor, sir," the Sergeant produced his penknife. "It's that much harder that I'll have to scrape. Do stand steady, sir, and keep the tongue well down—bleeds like hell if it's just nicked." Standing, poised, mouth open Harry noticed one of the younger schoolboys goggling down the stairway.

"We'll have to face it, sir," said Honeybody after a few moments. "It's got stuck to the blade so I can't get it off. I am afraid you'll have to put the knife, take hold of it, sir, plus the bottle and the dentures in your pocket. Do try to use your left hand, sir, because what with the knife it could be embarrassing if not serious."

"I just want to look at Miss Tump's office," said Harry.

The door of the office was ajar and inside it didn't smell too good. The Inspector looked at the old wooden wainscoting and wondered about rats. At Miss Tump's desk was her antithesis, broadly and comfortably built, with a squarish jovial face.

"God, more police," she said, shrewdly, looking at Honeybody. "Your colleagues, led by a most unpleasant Super, have already taken this dump apart. I'm the Cookery Editress."

The girl, Mabel, nodded miserably from her little desk.

"You are her sub?"

"Mr. Jolly offered me three guineas a week, to be disguised as taxi fares, and Mabel seven shillings, ditto, to take over. I know nothing of Women's Topics, except the inevitable and distressing ones about delinquent offspring, but Mabel is destined to do most of the work. Soon Mabel will become able to take over." Her look was very shrewd.

Mabel, whose eyes were red from weeping, hiccuped.

"No clues, girl?" said Harry.

"I made a statement," she talked calmly. "I thought she was the same old Tump. You couldn't tell with her. She once said she had so much misery that it was difficult for her to express emotion facially."

"Excuse me," Harry's feet had begun to ache. He sat down abruptly in the corner chair. Was it his imagination that the atmosphere had grown oppressive?

"My sandwiches," wailed Mabel.

"Your what?" said Honeybody, startled.

"My Limburger cheese sandwiches, he's sitting on 'em."

"By God, so he is," said the Cookery Editress, sniffing like a stout old Pointer.

Harry got up. Whoever had wrapped the sandwiches did not believe in wasting money on paper.

Honeybody, whose sensitivities were so negligible that when anything unpleasant had to be dug up in cellars or fished from the Thames Estuary he was generally seconded to the task, blenched.

"We'll have to scrape him," he said. "An implement is required."

"Take one of the steel rulers," said the Cookery Editress, "and newspaper. Mabel, you will take the result and put it somewhere along the passageway. You learn that with cookery failures!"

"Don't take your right hand out of your pocket, Mr. James, and bend forward, please sir," said Honeybody.

"Why can't he take his right hand out of his pocket?" Mabel was in the semi-hypnotised condition of shock.

"Get back to your work, miss, and no more questions from anybody." The Cookery Editress talked fast. "We are working late tonight and so Mabel provides herself with sandwiches. Lest you think me mean, I may say that our Workers' Model Kitchen consists of a sink, a table and a 1910 gas cooker. We borrow the props, but the food consists of left-overs from a rather good restaurant with which Sir P. has an arrangement. One of the accountants checks it in and Bocker has, after photography, to deliver it to the apartment of Sir P.'s current mistress. There was one bitch from the Common Market that I really fixed. The restaurant had been landed with seven hundred tins of inferior sardines in garlic and tomato sauce for the hors d'oeuvres table, so I ran 'em for a month. After that she got ulcers."

Mabel giggled.

"Did you not get into trouble?" The Inspector sought to divert attention from the scraping.

"My dear man, the importer cleared his vast consignment and placed advertising which made the Advertising Manager—who really runs the place—actually recommend me for another fifteen bob—not passed by the Board."

"Getting back to the two deaths," said Harry.

"Don't raise your head too much, Inspector," cautioned the Sergeant, "it's hard scraping."

"Nobody would have wished to kill Tump," said the Cookery Editress; "a type left over from the 'thirties, political energies drained," she sighed, "as it gets, but just generally nice. Percy Button, though, I dunno. I wondered about him."

"Careful, Honeybody," winced Harry, "careful about those backhand strokes. Was there anything sinister, ma'am?"

"I mistrust moon-faced men, perhaps a traumatic experience when young. But he snuck, definitely creeped, no walking chest-out and good-morning to you. A kind of whey-faced, sneaking progression. Dear, oh, dear," she belched, "I did finish poor Tump's gin—see that I haven't over-written, Mabel."

"It is flowery!"

"Cut on the adverbs. That's always the trick when you step it down. What was I saying? Always where he shouldn't be. We're Special Features and have no business in News. Yet I swear I saw him creeping up the stairs far too often for any good reason. I thought it was money, either lending it or borrowing it. This place is a mass of promissory notes."

"He did creep about," said Mabel, sucking a large pencil.

"Who did he associate with?"

"Nobody," said the Cookery Editress, "a chance word, a note dropped. Bocker says he was a spy. Cunning are such bastards!"

"Have you not finished, Sergeant," said Harry irritably.

"The best I can do, Mr. James." The Sergeant sighed and finished his scraping, "though this grey synthetic... the old blue wool has much to recommend it." He cleaned the steel ruler on the paper.

"Thank you and goodbye," the Inspector straightened with what he thought was dignity. Fortunately the lift was unoccupied. Harry gloomily thought of how difficult it was to be suddenly left-handed.

Bocker was behind his reception desk, disdaining an old, moon-faced reporter who claimed to have a taxi-requisition to an address in Tooting.

"You can't deny it, all signed and regular by Mr. Jolly."

Bocker glanced disdainfully, "No signature, sir. His ballpoint was a quarter of an inch off when you saw him sign. You'll have to watch it. Best thing is to pay it yourself and forget it! No good making trouble, sir."

"Again!" said the old reporter.

"What is it this time?"

"Annual Meeting of the Licensed Victuallers' Association."

"You go home on the bus, sir, I'll arrange for the usual par, rising costs, smoked salmon, the Government, high blood pressure and insolvency. Now, sir," he addressed Harry, who was now rather past discretion. "What can I do you for?"

"You told people that Button was a spy?"

"Gossip along the Street, sir. One believes your P.R.O. gave a quiet briefing. We do not have a police reporter for reasons of economy and so I am relied upon by Mr. J."

The Inspector turned away from the bland face. "We'll get a bus home," he said.

"If I may say so, Mr. James, and with respect, I don't think I would care to sit beside you. And I am not a fussy man! You remember that two constables and the doctor fainted when we found all those stiffs underneath the larder floor in that club in St. James's Street. I had to take the pick-axe with my own hands and even the undertaker said 'e thought the drains might be bad. A taxi, sir, please, it's well known that taxi drivers can't niff anything. On expenses, sir, under 'accidents incurred in the execution of dooty'."

It was probably nerves, thought the Inspector, but it suddenly seemed to him that he was being looked at curiously by passers-by.

"Excuse me, Inspector, but could I have a word with you?" It was the moon-faced reporter.

In the meantime the Sergeant's hand had stayed a taxi. "Make up yer mind," the little old driver, cocooned in what were apparently three ancient overcoats surmounted by an old blanket, snarled. "The perlice don't let you make a bleedin' living. Owner-driver, I am, and wot's Ted doin' for the small man except teaching 'im carols? Carols! He should carol through the traffic all day long."

Why were they so cold? And either ultra laconic or ultra garrulous thought Harry, urging the moon-faced reporter and Honeybody into the synthetic upholstery. With a twinge of advancing years he realised that he had known leather days.

"Where dew you want?" The driver seemed to have the form of blood pressure which affects pilots in very turbulent weather following a hangover. Behind the cab had parked a large white Rolls from which issued a very rancid hooting; the elongated white face of Sir Peregrine peered out of the back window in some kind of alarm, as if the peasantry had uprisen. Calmly, Bocker was emerging from the foyer.

"Straight ahead, quick," said Harry, "south-westish."

"I hope this is all right," sniffed the cabbie through his hatch, "I may say that the Moorgate Monster hired me to take his latest corpus to the baggage room at Paddington Station, but me nostrils told me funny business was afoot and I hailed a constable. Four pages of clippings. He was a little constable, but I did the Monster with the jack."

The reporter was opening the offside window to its full extent. "We have no baggage. I am a reporter on the *Bulletin*."

"No offence, I'm sure," said the cabbie, avoiding a bus, "and Mr. Jolly should be a life peer the way he exposes the nood butlers at these society parties."

"Where do you live?" said Harry to the reporter.

"Maida Vale."

"We go through there. Maida Vale, driver, and close the hatch."

"A pleasure I'm sure. I have me own thoughts." The hatch slammed.

"Thirty years ago, sir," said Honeybody, "he's older but I recognise his mug. The Monster used to publish guide books and kill the contributors when they wanted payment. The driver caught him because out of carelessness—I understand the publishing profession is lazy fair, as Mr. W. says—the Monster had left the corpse in the block room for some weeks in summer."

The reporter was gulping air through the window. "I expect he'll take the short way! Anyway eight years ago I was working on a Kent paper. We were sweet with you local boys and got the hint that the Stealthy Men were down; there was a club with remarkably low prices, too low not to make some thickhead copper, if you'll excuse the term, think hard."

"Excused," said the Inspector, hurriedly because Honeybody loathed the term and had been known to poke quite amiable crooks in the eye because they used it.

"Of course, the Stealthy Men *look* so stealthy that they stand out like sore thumbs. The couple that owned the club took a cultural tour to Finland and never came back—debts all over the place. The butcher said the Government should pay, but he never received an acknowledgment from Mr. Mac except an offer to send some old school books as an ex gratia payment. But it was lovely grub while it was on; beautiful porterhouse with tomato and tarragon and French fries at two and nine." The older reporter, obviously a deprived denizen of Fleet Street, seemed to slaver.

"Percy Button," prompted Harry.

"It's the wife," sighed the reporter, "she's got an economy campaign on. Lentil rissoles! She even says tomato sauce is bad for my liver."

"The same with me, but cheap fish," said Harry, from the corner of his eye watching the Sergeant, who had been known to talk of twelve-mile limits and Britain's briny inheritance, bridle.

"Well, this Button used to go there quite often. I was using my eyes, you know. He knew the couple well—used to wander into the kitchen where the bloke did the cooking—and I swear I never had better sauces or ate so well—but we knew he was the little freelance who wrote the *Bully's* stars. Just window dressing, I thought. They do that—crooks or spies—start a cut-price club, get respectable coves in there as a mask. Well," he reached out and pulled open the glass hatch, "drop me here, driver."

"I don't wonder," said the old cabbie, glancing back with aversion, as he re-engaged the window.

They paused on the way at Honeybody's fish-and-chips emporium where a skinny lady, of uncertain age and with wispy hair, was in charge of the establishment, which, to Harry's knowledge, continually expanded. It was deserted at this hour and staff were pouring out large amounts of oil while a small man expertly dismembered fish. The barrels of chipped potatoes lined the far wall. It was, thank God, thought Harry, thoroughly impregnated by the odour of oil, fish and vinegar.

"Mr. Honeybody," shrilled the *locum tenens*, "your Dodo phoned and she's back tomorrer."

"Ah," said Honeybody stoically.

"And she says not the hake—it being in short supply because the Gumment is sending it to Africa as dried fertiliser—but the rock salmon, so I 'ave six pieces wrapped up 'ere."

Was this woman looking at him or not? The Inspector retreated to the sardonic old cab driver who commented on modern methods of fumigation.

The Sergeant eventually returned with his gladstone bag. "Ten of stout, sir. The old lady looked daggers, but I thoughtfully had 'em delivered; two got pinched, the fish cutter getting at it and you can't stop him. The barometer they gave me after twenty years got broached one time, but tight or not tight he can fillet fish."

"May I drive on, me lord?" said the old driver.

Honeybody growled Harry's address, and at the destination the driver glanced reluctantly at the two-shilling tip, pursed his mouth and drove off.

"I thought you said they couldn't smell?" grunted the Inspector.

"Exceptions prove the rule, but my word..."

"What?"

"Nothing, I'm sure, Mr. James."

Elizabeth answered the door. "You're early," and bent forward to kiss him. "Oh, my God, I left the gas on." She turned to run.

"It's not the stove, it's me!" The Inspector was conscious that he bleated; and hurried to the bathroom.

Presently, padding out to the bedroom with his suit over his dressing-gowned arm, he encountered his wife and the Sergeant in the hallway.

"You'll put those things in the outside clothes-basket," said his wife, "I never heard of anyone who married a man who sat on Limburger cheese."

"Now, my dear," said the Sergeant, "I was once on duty at the Zoo and involved in a strange incident with a camel.... The keepers laughed like the hyenas, but my Dodo was not amused. The dry-cleaning wouldn't take it, and she tried liquid ammonia, but no success though I asked Burton's personally. They said that camels were not guaranteed. Though..."

"Shut up, both of you. I'll cook fish; you guzzle."

Elizabeth had a secret way of dealing with rock salmon involving white wine, chervil and other ingredients which she—metaphorically—kept locked in her bosom. Even Honeybody approved of it and Harry would cheerfully have consumed it twice a week but for the fact that Elizabeth was getting a little social now she had joined a Young Mothers' Club and thought that rock salmon was rather low. However, his satisfaction was marred by his wife's curious glances and he could not face the double Gloucester cheese. The piping hot water had dissolved the attachment between his teeth and the Sergeant's penknife, the former reposing on the mantelpiece, but the bottle, in spite of wrenching and wheedling, was as firmly as ever on his thumb. In fact it seemed more firmly, as if his thumb had swollen. The Inspector, who was a slight hypochondriac, was worrying about gangrene. The doctor? He remembered that the Minister for Health had ruled that children who jammed their heads between railings did not qualify for free treatment and presumably the same applied to bottles and thumbs at any age.

Finally the blow was struck. "Harry James, what is that on your thumb?" demanded his wife.

"A small bottle, love. It contained rubber solution but I think it's all oozed out."

"I do not care if it...what it contained. I shall not waste my intelligence enquiring the circumstances." She reached out and grasped the collected works of Dr. Spock, nowadays never far from her hand.

"Nothing at all," she said at length, but added, loyally, "I suppose babies' thumbs are too small to get jammed in bottles."

"I thought he had dealt with them up to fifty years old," said Harry, meanly.

"Or perhaps babies have more sense than to get their thumbs jammed in bottles!"

"Now, now, me dears!" said the Sergeant. "My Dodo's due back tomorrow so let me have one more evening at peace."

"I know I've read it somewhere." Elizabeth was on her knees leafing through a large red cutting book marked 'Property of the Criminal Investigation Department' which Hawker, intending to be sardonic, had given her at the Christening. Its pages, meant to record dubious classified advertisements, were very useful for retaining the mass of leaflets, hortatory literature from ethical drug companies and innumerable extracts from women's magazines, all of which had descended upon the house since the advent of Amanda.

"Here it is." Elizabeth was one of those largish women who are surprisingly fast movers. She vanished through the door.

"I got a pal in the Post Mortems, Mr. James," said Honeybody uneasily, "who cuts open the bodies so that Sir Plunkett can peer in quick without messing up his hands—he is often in tails before dining with the P.M. He could probably saw it off some 'ow."

But Elizabeth had reappeared with a bucket of cold water, a small jar which contained methylated spirit and some thick twine.

"You soak a piece of twine in the spirit, wrap it round the glass, ignite it, and when it has burned plunge it in the cold water. But quick, Harry James, none of that backsliding and snivelling as when I had to deal with that boil two summers ago."

The Inspector extended his hand and closed his eyes. At the fourth immersion Elizabeth crowed. The bottle had been severed, except for a small ringlet of thick glass which still embraced the Inspector's thumb. Elizabeth applied Elizabeth Arden's finest offerings and wrenched.

"You'll dislocate the bloody thing," Harry howled.

"I'll bash it gently with a hammer."

"No such thing. If I succumb of gangrene my last words will be a Welsh curse."

"Jess a minute," said Honeybody, who had taken various courses in First Aid. "Only one main blood vessel in the arm," he said peering, "so it's not hard to tell." He prodded with a fork and the Inspector yelped. "A free flow, no immediate danger apart from chafing the skin. A little alcohol flooded on —that fellow Jolly didn't look hygienic—and tomorrow we'll see."

The Sergeant attacked the stout and cheese. The Inspector went to bed, huddling pointedly as far from his wife as possible. Elizabeth merely yawned, ate chocolates and read her Book Club offering.

6

It was purely in his Dostoevsky victim-of-circumstance, man-against-society mood that the Inspector, after a frigid breakfast—he knew the sausages were some his wife had picked up by mistake in the supermarket and had kept in the freezer waiting for an opportunity to work them off—had allowed the Sergeant, shortly after eight a.m., to lead him into Post Mortems. He huddled into a chair which prodded him in both kidneys and reflected that Honeybody had wheedled himself into liver and bacon. The place smelled of strong chemicals and seemed, what he could see of it, to be staffed by small, swarthy men who, so Honeybody informed him, were used to working odd hours.

The Sergeant's friend was professionally preoccupied and merely nodded as he took Harry's right hand and after a swift look fumbled and produced a neat file. "It's usually stuck into heads," he said, working swiftly. "There," he dabbed on iodine.

"Forgive the liberty, Bert," said the Sergeant, "and no offence, Inspector, but I brought these along." In his huge palm were the Inspector's dentures.

The technician peered. "About a 3-5-A, as we say. One minute." He padded out and came back with a cardboard box, albeit a neat clinical-looking one. "Open your mouth, please sir."

Harry obeyed. It seemed to him that in the Welfare State one was always getting into positions of undignified clinical examination, not, it was true, ordered by law but the product of public opinion.

"With a little filing, this would be just the job. The lady that fell off the floating radio station! A good, yellowish colour matching your own, Inspector. Let's try...."

Harry's rolling eye met Honeybody.

"Could you stick his own in, Bert?" asked the Sergeant.

"It does seem a pity to waste available, disposable assets," mourned the technician. "Mr. Callaghan addressed our local branch only last month on the subject. However," he brightened, "when we 'put them together' for photographic purposes —a lot of work we get of that kind—there is a sort of glue... for the time being we might try."

"There," said Honeybody, as if he had done his duty, "where there's a will there's a way."

"An interesting experiment," said the technician, "this stuff will stick anything human together. Just lay back, Mr. James."

Harry was conscious of certain dexterous movements.

"There," said the technician, "it dries practically instantaneously does this stuff. You'd be surprised what we can do here, sir, though we don't get any of the credit. It's Sir Plunkett who hogs the limelight and bullies the judge. Yours truly is never called, oh dear no, although when it's the sawing and sticking together it's a different story, with him sitting eating his smoked salmon sandwiches. 'How does the liver look to you?' he said only yesterday, not troubling to raise his eyes from the racing page. The Fulham poisoning. 'Antimony', I said."

Harry explored with his tongue and to his surprise found the two teeth immoveably jammed in position. He effusively thanked Bert, assuring him that he would lose no opportunity to publicise the latter's noble efforts for his country's good.

"One thing about the Welfare State," said Honeybody dourly, as they entered the basement entrance of the lift and went to see Hawker, "is that you get post-mortems free. It's a great comfort to think of when my Dodo's in one of her moods."

"Did you ever have to pay?"

"Oh, dear, yes; a charge against the Estate if there was one. I remembered a cove—Bert's still got an interesting bit in one of his bottles—who had five autopsies and at the end there wasn't enough left to give him a first-class funeral. That's why we never got proper co-operation from the undertakers, they naturally did not like to see the money slip from their 'ands."

The Inspector forced his mind to disregard the possibility of falling into the hands of Bert and Sir Plunkett, and Honeybody, ever sensitive to the moods of his superior, kept silent.

Superintendent Hawker grunted and waited gloomily while Harry reported.

"This man, Jolly," said the old man at last. "I have a friend who is on the Board of a rival newspaper group." He blinked shrewdly across the desk at Harry. "What you're wondering is *why* I have any friends or *when* I see 'em. I'll let you wonder. But he says—and there's kind of tab kept on good editorial managers—that Jolly is far too cowardly to kill. A bully to the staff, but strictly 'yessir' to the moneybags. The kind of talent much in demand today. Very competent, scintillating with ideas, but his wife, a notorious crone, terrifies him and the recourse to the arsenic bottle is not for him."

"Suppose he was Button's Master?"

"If there is any moral anchorage in Jolly, it is respect for his directors, who are right," Hawker exposed his teeth, "rather than left. You never saw a man get out of the Army in 1940 and into writing propaganda quicker than Jolly, though from what he used to pen later you'd have thought he personally defeated Rommel. No vices; drinks, a fairishly heavy man on the ponies, no women—his wife watches him like a hawk—likes peering at strippers; in all Mr. 1975."

"But they might have him netted," said Honeybody. "I remember a little fish, all teeth and gallstones, down Kingston way. Wouldn't harm a fly, but Big Bertie Strout got to know that he had been tickling the peter at his work. It would have meant four years and disgrace—he used to take round the plate regular. Big Bertie worked on him—we could never prove it—so that he 'urled an ounce of vitriol into the face of somebody wot Bertie had an argument with. Eight years it finished up."

"I would like that theory," said the Superintendent, "but for the fact that, far from tickling the peter, Jolly, with share

113

options etcetera, is encouraged at the process. How much do you think a man like him needs to take home? Jack Ketch has to be fee'd. No women. He pays his bookmaker, who is a graduate of one of our more genteel colleges, and, more importantly, he has never been abroad, frightened of it all. Security think he once went to the Isle of Wight under the mistaken impression that it would save him income tax, but after four months of commuting he bolted back to the mainland because he was frightened of the natives. He is no spymaster, Sergeant! Whitehall even succeeded in locating an aged district nurse who attended him as a child—excessive obesity and bed-wetting. Given the years between and the clothing she recognised him."

"I suppose Mr. Porterman clings to the theory that Miss Tump did him?" enquired Harry.

"On instructions from her aged father," said Hawker, tersely, "he said some nasty things about present-day politicans some years ago. Mr. Porterman thinks it was suspicious and 'they' think at Whitehall it was too good to be true. But in any case it is a neatly shut box, which do not open because if you do something jumps out. 'D' notices to the press, special briefings and two Death by Misadventure verdicts by dutiful Coroner's jerries."

"I do not like it," said Harry and heard Honeybody give his short cough of unease.

"Neither do I," said Hawker, "but a year to go and no trouble. Here's a batch of stuff for you, Mr. James, people fiddling over slot machines. I think they want the cigarettes; and the chocolate and mixed vending is a cover."

"How did he manage to get a shoe lace round his neck by misadventure?" asked Honeybody, slowly.

"The surgeon will have an explanation—tying up his shoes. Between us all it transpired to be a bit of the twine they use to bale up the newspapers that got put round his neck. It was a bargain lot, hence the colour."

"All right, I suppose I sign the report for the Crowner," sighed Harry.

Hawker looked at the ceiling in disgust. "I, and Mr. Porterman, our age being taken into account, have pensions to think of. You could always get a job with some Yankee gambling establishment; I must say I have been thinking of it—or serving fish!"

The Inspector disliked his superior in flippant mood, but Honeybody said, seriously, "I must say fish does not carry unpleasantness, sir."

"Do I look as though I served fish?"

Honeybody looked dubious. "It's difficult to know what people look like who serve fish, if you'll excuse me, Mr. Hawker."

"Here's the file," the Superintendent pushed it over. "Small meat pies at a bob each from the slot. The Boss has had complaints from M.P.s who are already looking for a cheap meal. One of the liberals swears it's whale meat and not venison, though how he expects to get venison for a bob passes my comprehension. And there was a member of the Shadow Cabinet who broke his tooth on the shepherd's pie and thinks the Communists or de Gaulle have been at work. I do not want to see either of you today."

"Expenses, sir?" asked Harry.

"Of course."

"Looks like trouble, sir," said Honeybody later, "when they say 'to hell with the exes' it's time to draw your horns in. If I may mention it the fish or second-hand clothing is a good investment."

"I would prefer the pleasure of your silence, except for summoning a taxi. The complaints are from around Charing Cross and extend to Ludgate Circus, from spaghetti to various pies and Scotch salmon in season which is Japanese hake."

"Lord, sir," said Honeybody between expert whistles, "you can never get 'em on the grub. Cars now or a nice case of prostitution, like we had last month... but when you get to meat pies!"

In answer to Honeybody's expertise a taxi materialised, and they went to Charing Cross. Three hours later they had worked up to Ludgate Hill.

"The deadest of ducks, Sergeant," grunted Harry.

And indeed it was, for a smooth gentleman eventually

explained that the managing director had disappeared with £47,000 16s. 7d., representing the capital of the vending company. In addition there were various sums owing; Harry, not too legally, took a brief look at some books; it appeared that the company did in fact owe three thousand pounds and that the venison was indeed whale meat and the steak largely spleen, the latter an old pie-making trick. The smooth man was apparently an obscure but honest accountant. Two interested parties had asked him to investigate the establishment as they had ascertained that the managing director had disappeared. He would offer himself as liquidator.

"When did you get in here?"

"About an hour before you came, sir, long enough to realise the whole sad story. The door was unlocked."

"Any letter files?"

"Masses." The man jerked his forefinger at a cabinet.

Harry looked and half laughed. "Ingenious fellow to call himself M. Tigg."

"I don't follow you."

"The most famous embezzler in fiction."

"All the fiction I get time to read is the bankruptcy reports," said the smooth gentleman.

"My advice to you is to find somebody who can put a padlock on the door for the time being. We can't do too much until after a creditors' meeting unless somebody registers a complaint."

"The interested parties I act for will do so gladly."

Harry produced his card. "Tomorrow at ten, perhaps. You won't see me, but somebody in Fraud. I won't take up more of your time."

It was an old building, smelling of some obscure gas leak and inferior tea. The hydraulic lift looked so sinister that Harry recoiled and sought the stairs, obviously manufactured from stone quarried by generations of Dartmoor labourers. The basement was nauseous, with worn-out old buckets containing decaying paper, and had a locked room with the painted sign 'Janitor'.

Back at the ground floor he stared at the old offices and found an ancient gentleman who somehow subsisted from an obscure religious weekly. Such people were generally excellent observers, but on this occasion there was no joy. It was a formless building generally inhabited by those who, quite legally, sold odd articles by mail. But interrogation produced nothing except some obscure dimensions of Egyptian Pyramids. The Janitor, unknown, came in each morning and did necessary things.

Honeybody trotted beside him into the fresh air.

"A dead end, sir, so I thought."

"The oldest con trick in the world, Sergeant. The man who is not there and never was, as thick as a halloween mask. You will never see anybody who knew the managing director. Everything was done by letter; some kind of shady pastry-cook made the pies, the vending machines were installed by a reputable company, a security organisation collected the loot and paid it in. And the suckers, the old men who want two hundred per cent of a life's savings, poor old sods, are all from the direct mail sucker lists—they usually stem from small ads for lucky charms. A man who will buy a lucky charm will buy Waterloo Bridge if you appeal to his cupidity. You pay out monthly dividends from intake and scarper at the peak—that's the whole art of running a bucket shop. If you stay a week too long, you get *us* in."

"So that smooth bastard gets away with it," said the Sergeant.

"A session of phoning," said Harry, "there's a call box opposite. You keep an eye open in case he bolts, which he won't, I think."

Fifty minutes later the Inspector emerged. The box had been sweaty and he suspected that a mouse had died somewhere in its vitals.

"He seems to be what he says," he told Honeybody. "The six checks I made on the managing director produced nobody who had ever seen him. However, do you know young Stokes in the Lab?"

"Barely, Mr. James, it's Post Mortems that I know best."

"Because of the surgical spirit and lemonade, I know. You want to watch your liver."

"The quack says I must be impervious, sir," said Honeybody, simply.

"Well, this Stokes has been working on typewriting. He says all crooks should buy the electric machines because the touch doesn't register—the pressure on the paper is automated. But by giving the copy what he calls a planogram—a kind of photography registering depth plus various other peculiarities—he says that typewriting on a manual machine is as indicative as fingerprinting and is itching to go before a jury and prove it. The more amateur the typist, the more certain it is, and unless I'm a Dutchman whoever typed the M. Tigg stuff was an expert six finger amateur, untrained. No fingerprints, of course; I spotted a pair of surgical gloves in the waste-paper basket. From now on he has an alibi; legitimate reasons to touch things."

"Experts arguing," said the Sergeant like an old policeman.

"The screw!" said Harry. "That's why I was so light with him once I spotted it. We con him into typing something on the office machine and then do not pressure *him* but his partners. So gradually we open the door."

"Ingenious, master," said Honeybody, "but unlikely."

"For God's sake, yes," said Harry, "but I am off the hook. Hawker will see that another Superintendent gets the job, but no skin off my nose."

"To celebrate that, a drink, sir. I've been thinking of some good keg bitter ale they have near Fleet Street and as nice a bit of fish, and I'm an expert, as ever got past my gullet. Or a nice pork chop if you're that way inclined, sir," observed the Sergeant wistfully.

"Lead on," said Harry, and eventually settled for the chops with onion and mushroom sauce. By the end of the second pint he was ruminating on the sadness of nature in that a man could not immediately have it again. Somebody next to him was eating a wonderful-looking dish of mussels, tomato sauce and white beans.

"A Welsh rarebit," suggested Honeybody. "Light on the stummick and virtually no wind that anybody can tell."

The Inspector, conscious of moral weakness, agreed.

"I always say a drop of sweet Malaga wine goes with it," said Honeybody, "although inclining to lechery they say."

"'Mountain', they used to call it," said Harry, "perhaps it was 'mounting' and Shakespeare made a mistake."

But Honeybody was already beckoning the waitress. "Don't worry, sir, I've never believed it. It's only ever made me snore off."

"Hallo," said the gravelly voice. It was Archer McClout. "Can I join you in your aphrodisiacal discussions?"

"Christ," said Harry, "do you lurk?"

"I have two stiff ones here before facing Mr. Jolly." The Australian seated himself. "And you can buy me the rarebit. Sweet Malaga I do not take, rather agreeing with Mr. Honeybody, and we employ a lot of juvenile feminine labour. When you get to my age... another rarebit, miss, and don't spare the worcestershire."

"The case is finished," said Harry, "finito, off it! Tump did him, somebody, now non resident, did Tump."

"Can't argue with the police. All you want is a closed file."

"What the hell do you think anyone wants?"

McClout grinned. "A point well taken. So I proceed to give you my conscience, confessor."

Harry dug into his steaming welsh rarebit, reflecting on its professional decline. It was not bad, though the quality of the beer in it had slipped, and he refused to talk to McClout until the journalist was munching away.

"Your theology is wrong, McClout. Confession does not work that way. Get advice."

One could never disconcert McClout. He said that he was an Orangeman and low church.

"The fact was," he said, "that I wanted a file-spike, because with all of them flacking away the stuff pours in like drink at a Dublin wake; even the jockeys have flacks pushing out stuff about their wonderful seats. Anyway there's an old wardrobe—

the rumour has it that Sir P. got his first fifty thou running cheap lodging houses—which is used for junk and in it was this file. I glanced at the muck, just in case it was old Peter Leeming's last will and testament, and then I got this. Have a look and don't interrupt my rarebit."

It was a piece of paper typewritten on a very miniature machine. "Spies in Newspaper Offices," it began. The content was vague but suggestive.

"Cripes," said Harry, "bloody dynamite. Whence? And no evasion!"

"You see those little pencil code marks?" grated McClout. "Don't be funny."

"Well, they mean that on the fifteenth of last month this copy went to Peter Leeming who spiked it on the authority of John Jolly Esquire, bless his whisky-sodden corp."

"You have witnesses?" said the Inspector, very coldly.

"If you keep twiddling it like a kid with a yo-yo, you will destroy any fingerprints. One presumes that the C.I.D. have heard of that process, introduced in 1901."

"The trouble with you journalists is that you have scrap-book minds," snarled Harry, blushing, but nevertheless passed the flimsy sheet to Honeybody who expertly produced a kit containing miniature scissors and plastic with which he covered it. The Sergeant, a walking emporium, produced a suitable envelope from the region of his left buttock.

"Sign across the join," said Harry, licking and sealing the flap.

"Delighted, I'm sure," said McClout, seizing one of six biros protruding from his breast pocket. "Now give a working stiff a break. I'm the only man in the game who never got a beat."

"They say there are opportunities on the sunny side of the street near Westminster 'all,'" said Honeybody, apparently gravely considering.

"Do you blokes have to put the TV comics out of business? I mean it! World rights by Archer McClout. Perhaps a book. *Time Mag* with a bit of buttering up the Yanks; it couldn't happen there sort of stuff. Ain't the C.I.A. wonderful?"

"My boss, old Hawker, will scratch backs depending on circs," said the Inspector. "I can only promise you that. But it would be nasty for you if it blew up in your face, eh?"

"I see," gravelled McClout, "the Black List—which they say they haven't got!—for sure. Do what you can, old chaps, old chaps. Me out of it unless it comes good. My advice is lean on John Jolly, a man built like Barney's Bull but frailer."

"Lean I will," said the Inspector, "but we have a back-scratching society, huh?"

"I shall listen at keyholes," said McClout, "except the locks at the old *Bully* collapsed around 1876 and Sir P. would only run to cheap padlocks where things are stored. Good hunting, men!"

They watched him pay his score and depart.

"Have you ever heard Mr. Hawker swear?" asked Honeybody.

"Yes, indeed."

"There was an old Inspector, before your time," said the Sergeant, "who was a bit better, but Mr. Hawker can come very near. I once had to ask my pal in Post Mortems what some of the words meant. I'll phone him, sir, after the four years I did in Lisle Street in the bad old days it's water off a duck's back, so to speak."

"Please do," said Harry. "I think I'll have a drop of port and the Stilton."

He dawdled and it was half an hour before the Sergeant returned, looking awed. "What's the technical term for a man who pinches ladies in crowded tube trains, sir?"

Harry signalled to the waitress and paid before Honeybody could order drink. "I have no idea," he said coldly.

"I think that is what he was describing you as, with due respect, sir. He said a man who could discover clues in ladies' corsets could discover anything."

"And what else?" The Inspector slightly applied the disciplinarian pedal and Honeybody became owl-faced.

"He said go ahead and that personally he will retire to

Cheltenham. If I may venture advice, sir, direct measures are called for. Let's go and twist that fat bleeder's nose."

Harry considered. A man of Honeybody's experience was so often right and he was sensitive about his own reputation of being somewhat devious and soft-handed. Hawker was a man brought up in a bludgeoning age.

"All right," he said.

For once Bocker was not in the foyer. A fattish underling approached and said that unfortunately Mr. Jolly was in attendance on Sir P. and the Board and could not be disturbed.

"Telephone and convey to them that I would willingly provide a police surgeon for the Board and attend Mr. Jolly myself in a cell."

"You cannot mean that, sir," the under-porter was aghast.

"Get Mr. Bocker!"

"He is closeted with the Board, sir," said the underling sibilantly, "being questioned about the missing toilet rolls."

"Impeding a police officer in execution of his duty is six months," snarled Honeybody, at his East End best, "I'll take you in myself."

"One minute, sir," said the underling, sweat starting to ooze from under the drooping layer of brilliantine, "the intercom, sir."

"Put him on, you fool," presently said the confident tones of Bocker. "'Allo, Inspector, I am in the Board Room. Yes, indeed, sir, Mr. Jolly will attend you instanter in the anteroom. Don't mind the head accountant, sir, if he's a nuisance just put him outside."

The plump underling escorted them himself, afterwards making himself scarce, followed by an aged, worried man with a computed look about him, but Bocker was as usual impeccable, pausing to peer into the old gas refrigerator and counting bottles. "You can't trust them, sir, it's all the adding up and the price of Scotch. You wish to see the Managing Editor, very well!" He magisterially gave three knocks on the inner door, and John Jolly, tie flaked with cigar-ash, appeared like a jack-in-the-box. As the door closed the Inspector had the slightest glimpse, a mere whiff as it were, of Sir Peregrine's long, anxious face flanked by several nervous fat ones.

"Leave us, Bocker!" Jolly was leonine and the Head Porter subservient.

"Stay, kindly light!" ordered Harry. "Sergeant, show Mr. Jolly the goods."

From his rump pocket Honeybody produced the sheet of copy paper.

"Read, digest and comment," said the Inspector.

Jolly read with professional haste. "Bocker, summon Leeming, it has his initials. Where did you get this, Mr. James—it's the property of the company. What Sir P. will say, God knows. All waste paper is eventually sold."

Stolidly Harry waited until Peter Leeming, seemingly thinner than ever, came tiredly in, his face seamed with wrinkles of permanent perplexity. "We can't run that story on society whores, Mr. Jolly, I've been on to the Solicitor. He had to take a tranquilliser at the mere thought."

"Bugger them!" howled Jolly. "Take a look at this. Too many mistakes being made. I haven't got three sets of eyes. I haven't got ten arms. And Sir P. perplexed about the competition result."

"I consulted the Editor, Mr. Jolly," said Leeming, "who came to you. 'Spies masquerading as journalists' would not be popular with the Proprietors' Association, the Union, the Institute or the Council. So the order came back to spike it."

"Who wrote it? I'll have his blood, I'll see the swine'll roast, I'll..."

"I wrote it, sir," said Bocker, quietly.

"Then you bloody explain it," snarled Jolly. "Leeming, come with me. You might have some ideas about this competition affair."

The door slammed. Bocker looked at Honeybody and wet his lips. "I am a member of a little club near here, sir. Perhaps we could talk in convivial circumstances."

"It's their nerves, sir," said Bocker as they went down in the lift. "Live on them they do. Of course," he added slowly, "there is the Scotch and the hot-house strawberries."

The club was adjacent and expensive, in that the chairs were gilded and the stripper was not more than twenty-three. Further evidence was that the audience, seven, wore fifty-guinea suits. Bocker led the way to the bar.

"One of my consolations, sir, is that I get free membership to such places and a generous discount, so please accept my hospitality. I must say they make a good champers cocktail."

"Bottled ale for us," said Harry, and the barman, whose hair was immaculately blonded and waved, visibly flinched.

"Double Haig, Tommy," said Bocker, "and keep a civil tongue because these are high police dignitaries."

"I really don't think we stock nothing low, Mr. B., rilly. We 'ave some Imperial Tokay that the old gents say will wake the dead now."

"Beer and quick, faggot," growled Honeybody.

A plump person, of dubious sex, emerged through a curtain. Harry had the opinion that such places abounded with concealed microphones. The person snapped its fingers, said, "The imported Polish lager, two quart bottles, you foolish boy, on the house," and disappeared.

The imported Polish lager would have been all right if there had not been stuff added—the Inspector thought caraway seed but Honeybody opted for juniper berries which he alleged was a Polish weakness.

"Oh, well," said Harry, "they are entitled to their taste. Now start talking, Mr. Bocker."

"On the thirteenth of last month," said Bocker, glibly, "the Features Editor said he hadn't run 'Spies' for a few weeks and could I do the necessary. I have a grand-daughter who is a librarian and a rare fan of Len Deighton. She came up with the idea. I got a lot of them off her, although she's down well in the Will and knows it."

"You invent things!"

"Inventing it!" Bocker sounded aghast. "Sir, it's over fifty-five years of experience, since I was a lad of twelve. I was a runner for the great Northcliffe. I have a framed ten-shilling note at home, sir, which he gave me when I told him my mother had been counting the leaves in the toilet rolls and found over a year that there were sixteen less. He put two men on it and they made a nice domestic story of it. Nothing was too small for his Lordship, or too large. He offered to apprentice me to the journalism, but they're a low class of man, sir, and I took my father's advice and refused. Potman, he was, in the Bodega and he used to see them swilling away without an arse piece to their trousers, if you'll pardon the frankness."

"Do you mean all these exposé stories come from you?"

Bocker looked modest. "Most, sir. They have a quiet word and next day I give them something I've written."

"Fabricated!"

"Sir, sir, nobody believes it! After fifty years I know every story."

"But libel, man!"

"Oh, sir, it's vagueness, you don't use names. I learnt that when I was fourteen. No names, no libel, and you cannot libel public companies as such."

"Full name?" asked Harry, producing his notebook.

"Robert Walpole Bocker. My dad was a rare reader and he said politics had gone down hill since Sir Robert. Lor' you ought to see the ones that come sneakin' into the 'all with their flacks and speech writers, and doesn't Mr. Jolly give them hell?" Bocker blandly quaffed his drink and ordered another.

"Look, you old codpiece," said the Inspector, "do you get paid for this inventive faculty?"

"Very good bonuses, sir, over the years. I put my two boys through the university."

"Oxford, I suppose."

"Dear God, no," said Bocker, "the most dissipated ones on the staff—always borrowing a quid from me until Friday—come from there. Durham, sir, me hoping they'd go into the Church of England—lovely jobs on the accountancy and investment side, so I hear—but they got Doubts and were bred to the

Law. They are both in South Africa, sir, getting a choice living prosecuting the blacks."

"I am a trifle tired of you," said the Inspector, nudging Honeybody whose eyes had strayed towards the stripper.

"Now, sir," remonstrated the Sergeant, "my Dodo is currently approaching Paddington Station with all the speed of British Railways."

"As a matter of fact," said Bocker, at his most fatherly, "I happen to know quite a lot of young ladies. Sir P.—well you might say I am his confidant and adviser; but if there is any service I can do for Law and Order... just ask. And of course reduced rates."

"One thing more," said Harry, as sternly as he could, "you have no evidence that anybody on the paper are or were spies?"

"No, sir, all far too ignorant they are, except reviewers, a respectable body of men—mostly unfrocked Methodist ministers, I understand—but *we* don't have any. Sir P. says our readers don't actually *read*. Mr. McClout just clips off the blurbs on the book jackets and has 'em set in 8 pt. *Times* on the cartoon page. Sometimes he retypes them so he can flog the volumes."

"Come, Sergeant." The Inspector—he hoped majestically, but the stripper sniggered—led the way out.

"What the hell do you make of that?" asked Honeybody. The Inspector groped for the tin of patent pills, the Polish lager, or perhaps Bocker, having given him wind round the heart.

He said, "He's over to the Stealthy Men, but, my God, all those years, and he sounds so plausible."

"Ar," said Honeybody, "remember your little kipper!"

The Inspector did indeed remember Amanda who had developed a strange—Elizabeth, disturbed, said Freudian—habit of biting him on the calf.

"What's she done now?"

"I was watching her the other night, Mr. James, crawling in one door and out the other, into a bedroom, round, through the bathroom and back. You hardly saw her, like that story about the postman. Bocker is part of the furniture."

"You mean he could have done in Percy Button and Miss Tump?"

"Yes, sir."

"I'd better see Mr. Hawker," groaned Harry as they boarded a bus. You'd better knock off and meet the wife."

"Can't I have voluntary overtime?" suggested the Sergeant dolefully.

"I must break the news that Elizabeth has departed with Amanda to Tunbridge Wells for a few days. During my telephone calls I put one through to the flat. Her great-aunt, on a sickbed, expressed by telegram the wish to see her and the child. I told her to go."

"That would be the wealthy old lady?" The Sergeant was conversant with most of the intimate details of the Inspector's domestic affairs. Harry scowled, but Honeybody continued, "If she phones, sir, tell her to keep little Amanda out of the way. Old ladies like 'em in small doses. And if the solicitor should call, no harm in seeing he gets a bottle of sherry in the drawing-room after. My Dodo nearly lost her inheritance—three hundred nicker—but for the fact that she thought fast and got a bottle of gin into the solicitor; by the time he'd recovered the old lady had passed peacefully away, the will unchanged. It was some argy-bargy about a carpet."

For some time the Inspector had become conscious of an odd and unpleasant feeling of constriction in his upper jaw; a kind of drawing together and shrinkage.

He pressed the bell. "See you tomorrow. I'll walk the rest of the way. Give your wife my regards!"

Superintendent Hawker was in the process of resisting his removal to the new building designed to house the Criminal Investigation Department, which as a very old dog he was eminently qualified to do. Delegations from Whitehall placed propositions before him, but as he was the only man to grasp the finer implications of criminal statistics—Harry privately considered himself an equal—the Home Secretary of the day, an able and worthy man, although liable to be meekly jostled in public by senior trades unionists, seemed at an impasse. To resolve this he habitually sent an elderly Civil Servant, reputedly as unpleasant as Hawker, round to wrestle verbally with the aged Superintendent. Therefore Harry was used to hearing shrill noises from Hawker's office, but he was not prepared for the vile language, albeit clothed in impeccable Balliol accents, which issued from within the door.

A gloomy constable was outside, listening.

"It's come to bodily assault, sir, like they said in the course, Sergeant Chumwise in 1880 biting off his superior officer's ear, the right one, if I recollect."

"Stay there, constable." The door was unlocked. The striped trousers which Harry, by virtue of a tomato sauce stain on the left cuff, recognised as belonging to the Home Office delegate, revolved rapidly. "Centrifugal," some ghastly mental schoolteacher prompted in the Inspector's head. On his knees Superintendent Hawker wrestled with a wall plug from which a small, flickering flame emerged. Harry seized the cord and swung his weight backwards. There was a final flash and a curse from Hawker, but the chair's mad gyrations slowly ceased. The man from the Home Office, rather stunted in size, arose, stumbled a few paces and subsided into the Inspector's arms. He seemed in a cuddly mood. "Mr. Hawker said it cured the nervous dyspepsia," he snarled.

Harry got the little old gentleman into a chair.

"I'll murder that girl," said Hawker. "It might have been the Home Secretary himself; he suffers from wind badly and was interested in it—all those elections take it out of a man. I turned it on to 1A and it went mad. Believe me, sir," he addressed the Civil Servant, "it comes under the Inn Keepers' Act. You voluntarily got into it; no liability on my part whatsoever. And the language; I'm not sure that it was not a kind of battery at least."

Harry was peering. "American appliances, sir, generally, are for 110 current. You have 240."

"I'm not interested in these bloody things," snarled Hawker, who the Inspector suspected predated all mechanical objects.

"Did you hammer the plug in, sir?"

"I used my boot."

"You've pretty well burned out the motor. Do you catch that ozone smell?"

"I thought it was him," Hawker's forefinger stabbed at the Civil Servant.

"I must, in fairness, confess that the rheumatic pain in my left knee has abated," grunted the latter, "although it was a massive attack and I have lost my glasses."

"Here they are, intact thanks to the wall-to-wall." Harry returned them.

"Oh, well," said Hawker, shifting ground, "no great harm done in the event. It is a lesson to me not to meddle with these American devices."

"You should not say, Mr. Hawker, that we are wrong about the inter-continental devices. Wipes out whole countries, the staff says. A good dose and you avoid years of slow starvation. So you can start again with scientific planning, like the Americans. I must say that I am personally studying Greater London and Melbourne—lentil rissoles, I believe, will be the answer."

"If I may say," said Hawker whose interior disturbances probably sprang from his love of rich sauces and lobster dishes, "you look as though you lived on lentil rissoles."

"Those and lactic beans," the man from Whitehall said primly.

"About the spy case, sir," said the Inspector firmly.

"I wish to know nothing of such matters," said the man from the Home Office, grabbing his bowler. "I refuse to be implicated. Make a minute of that fact, please. In Whitehall spies do not officially exist, they having been abolished by the committee under paragraph 64, section two. And remember, Mr. Hawker, that my Master has made his ultimate concession. Next his, um, iron hand will appear out of its, um, velvet... good day to you." He scuttled out.

"It looks as though I shall have to get out of here within three months," said Hawker, "he's threatening to have a Parliamentary question put down by that nasty fellow. After all these years and finally screwing complete wall-to-wall out of them for my advice about those prison escapes! I advised 'em to say nothing and people would forget it, same as the Train Robbery. No use running around in lost causes. Ah, well," he brightened, "they promise to give me a computer. I've always wanted to get into the text books like Galton, Spilsbury and that lot. 'Hawker, the man who computerised crime detection.' I'll find a way! The only trouble is it's machinery, like that bloody chair. All machines hate me; I deliberately smashed my brother's tricycle at the age of three and since then *they've* been getting back at me. Well, what's all this? Found another fifty-year-old spy, eh?"

"Robert Walpole Bocker outdates that one, if he is. I thought the Stealthy Men might peer at him. He claims to invent all those sensational stories in the *Bully*, including one about spies in newspaper offices."

"Oh," said Hawker, with a yawn, "it's notorious about Bocker writing the paper. A nasty little man from one of the agencies told me years ago. More power to him. The *Bully* doesn't come round here worrying me. But I'll get him looked into, though a pal says it's mostly the Sundays who have spies; gives 'em more time to get on with the job, if you follow."

It was difficult to tell how serious the old man was in this kind of mood. Harry ventured, "I took a course in programming, Mr. Hawker."

"Ah, yes," the cold eyes flickered, "I'll be going next year; as far as the Director's office in Whitehall. As you may have gathered, for what it is worth, my recommendation will be for you to have my place. I have not recommended you for a Chief Inspectorship, because you are too young and the older men would systematically disembowel you. Next year it might be all right, if you cultivate piles and a slight stoop. Talk about your bad health. It'll reassure them. As far as this *Bulletin* case is concerned, old Mr. Tump passed away this morning—he had been living at the end of a piece of cotton for years and the shock finished him. The Department of Dead Files, almost certainly. This Australian, Archer McClout, is somebody I will have checked. I never liked their attitude to cricket. Instruct you to keep an eye on it, but only that. Get on to your other files; perhaps that fat Sergeant Whatsisname might continue with a bit of journalistic boozing."

It was the Superintendent's whim never to recollect Honeybody's name.

"Yes, Superintendent."

The Inspector departed, looking in at his dentist on the way home and brandishing a cheque book.

"Make it out to 'cash', please," said the latter, who was preparing to go home after a hard day of drilling for Welfare State oil.

Twenty minutes later, two drills—of best German origin, the dentist said—had snapped.

"What the devil is this stuff, Mr. James?"

"All I know," said Harry, indistinctly through the barrier of saliva, "is that they use it to stick corpses together."

By nature and the product of long years of peering into mouths, the dentist was a melancholy man. "I don't know but what it will entail surgery. I could take a tooth on either side and see whether they'd come out that way. It would only mean a bigger plate. If it doesn't succeed it's surgery for sure. I think I could get you in at once privately. They could remove a bit of the jaw fairly easily, and perhaps a minor plastic job afterwards where the face falls in."

"Take the bloody things out," said Harry, and the dentist busied himself.

Finally he said, in melancholy triumph, "There," and brandished a small, revolting dish. He said, "Bite on this cotton wool Mr. James. There should be no infection, but with this substance with which I am unfamiliar one never knows. And we will please keep this on a State footing: that way I can claim for the drills. If you get an enquiry from the committee, I trust you will make the circumstances quite clear."

The Inspector paid and caught a taxi to a club largely frequented by journalists and advertising men, a place where time of day hardly mattered. He saw Peter Leeming, his face as ever bagged in lines of worry, seated with three similar men.

Peter Leeming was eating kidneys in sherry and drinking a

dry white wine. The others man-powered their way through the tough Scotch steak. The Inspector joined them, considered that Leeming had the best of the bargain, and ordered.

"A bad business, Mr. Leeming!"

"Indeed," said Leeming. "It makes me sick at heart. Whoever could kill poor Tump, and I understand that is the suggestion."

The three other men, on different papers, listened. One of them said, "Suppose we say it's within the trade, Peter. For Christ's sake it's bad enough without physical murder. My owner was quaking, so they say, when he came up in the lift this morning. I can tell you, Inspector, that he'll give you a bite you'll remember unless you put a stop to it. So anything you ask Peter will go no further. All right?"

Two heads wagged assent.

"I'm just casting lines," said Harry. "Who could have been near Percy Button's office, somebody who might have killed him?"

"Nobody," said Leeming, "except somebody from outside. A person got past Bocker, walked up the stairs and did him in. I checked as soon as the news reached me. Nothing abnormal. I send the reporters out and they check past Bocker. The head photographer looks after his men, although we mainly rely on the agencies and the staff is small. There was nobody unaccounted for, although the Editor and Mr. Jolly were not within my view, but they'd be above suspicion."

"Jolly would murder his old Mum for roughly one and twopence," said one of the other men. "I worked with him years ago and he had a way of fiddling tramcar fares the like of which you never saw. And throat-cutting and informing! Copyboy to Chief Reporter in three years, largely because of procuring for the Directors, they said."

"Now!" said Leeming, "live and let live. A very talented writer in the grandiose sort of way. The public like him. I don't know a man who can leer about vice better than Mr. Jolly. He can play on prostitution like a 'cello and buggery like an aged bassoon. Wonderful! On drugs he's no good, being of a previous generation, but degenerate sex, oh, dear, we've never seen his like, gentlemen, except a man Beaverbrook had in the twenties."

"And never want to," said one of his listeners, a financial editor. "I'd better get back and clean up for the day."

"I suppose we'd all better," said Leeming, "except it's three a.m. for me."

"You fellows work worse hours than we do," said Harry.

"Not really," said the Financial Editor, "there's time off in compensation. We always say, 'Last night we worked right through', and forget the other four days when we quit early. It impresses people. Well, pleased to have met you, Inspector."

"I wish I could help you," said Leeming miserably as he left.

With the prospect of a cold bed the Inspector ordered Stilton and port. Duty eventually called him and he caught a taxi home. The huge dog was whining in the janitor's subterranean den.

"Gnawed the wife's shoes, sir, irreparable, sir, seventy-nine and sixpence, what she read about in the *Daily Express*."

Harry passed over four pounds, adding five shillings when the man alleged that there had been a piece of New Zealand lamb purchased for the four o'clock meal. Other dogs ate once a day. Mr. Bones, from puppyhood, had never seen things that way. He walked Mr. Bones for the mile that the vet had prescribed. By temperament or nature the dog was costive and it was usually two miles. Whilst other dogs doted on London lamp posts and the peculiarly stunted, soot-ridden trees planted by local authorities, Mr. Bones treated them with contempt. What he loved was statues of eminent Victorians. At one time the Inspector was under the impression that the Metropolis was filled with hideous-looking old effigies, top-hatted and brandishing scrolls. But it was fully a mile to the statue of Thomas Carlyle, which Mr. Bones favoured and to which Elizabeth habitually escorted him. Inevitably three people asked him the way to Queens Gardens, a query which he found difficulty in answering.

"An effing furriner!" said the last enquirer.

Back home he opened two tins of dog-food and went to bed.

7

THE INSPECTOR'S WIFE was blessed with abnormally sharp hearing and with the bedroom door closed could amply cope with nocturnal telephone calls or the demands of Amanda, outside whose little room Mr. Bones possessively sprawled. Not confident of his own abilities—and truth to tell strangely uncomfortable at being alone—the Inspector slept with the door open. The enormous dog, himself plainly disorientated, sought at intervals to get on the bed and when pushed off crept slyly back and jammed a nose like an icy, rather sticky ice-cream cone into the Inspector's face. Not for the first time Harry thought of the deputy-chief-constableship of some small country town and a little cottage situated where Amanda and Mr. Bones could enjoy themselves. A place with cheapish but genteel schools designed for the large families of retired army officers and an old wine merchant with a respectable if badly bred bulk sherry. He thought he did not sleep a wink.

His electric razor did not appear to be working well next morning, there was a nagging pain in his upper jaw and the toast was a disaster. He was opening a tin of baked beans when Hawker telephoned.

"On the tiles, eh?" snarled the Superintendent.

"Wife away, virtuous couch."

"Not at one you weren't. I rang and rang."

"Wrong number, sir!"

"I do not dial wrong numbers," said Hawker, coldly.

Perhaps he *had* slept a bit thought Harry.

"It is now eight," said Hawker, "I wish you to attend the Briefing Room at nine."

"What..." the Inspector started to say, but the old Superintendent had slammed down the handset.

Goodbye baked beans, a cajoling session with a kindly neighbour, a little old lady clad in a wrapper, concerning Mr. Bones. She was full of Christian Charity but did not like dogs. Neither, apparently, did Mr. Bones like Christians of any denomination, an elderly Jewish gentleman down the hallway who thoughtfully carried dog biscuits in his pockets being the only inmate of the flats that he had any time for. By digs and sullen glances Harry instilled some temporary Christian feelings into Mr. Bones and by piteous references to Amanda, who the old neighbour mistakenly thought of as a little darling, he managed to dump the dog and bolt, thinking bitterly of fools who give dogs as wedding presents. At that—and with a taxi at his own cost—he was five minutes late, the Top Brass piously looking as if they never slept and had resident hairdressers, and Hawker looking like a crocodile waiting at an Indian water-hole.

"I'll fill you in, Mr. James." The Chairman was not an unkindly man with people who had a fair batting average (to the others he was). "At twelve thirty a.m. this morning a Mr. Jolly was stabbed through the heart with a metal spike in his private office on the fourth floor of the *Daily Bulletin*. Sir Plunkett"—he nodded to the small, florid-faced man—"was fortunately available and says that death was more or less instantaneous. Is that not so?"

"Oh, dear, yes," said Sir Plunkett, who habitually carried the *Sporting Life* cunningly concealed among the commercial pages of *The Times*. "That way you do not, ahem, even croak. Death is not instantaneous. Traumatic death rarely is, apart from massive collision, but you cannot talk. Perhaps three minutes, mostly internal bleeding, almost immediate loss of consciousness. The brain, gentlemen, must have blood. If it has not," he rolled his little eyes to the ceiling, "merciful nature takes her toll."

"Three deaths on an influential newspaper," said the Chairman. "We can't have this! The P.R.O. has been staving 'em off like maddened wolves. I must remind you gentlemen—sternly but with the proviso that it applies equally to myself—that public opinion in the past has sometimes forced resignations from our ranks."

"As the Superintendent in charge," Porterman had risen and Harry liked him for it, "I will take what kicks may be given—I increasingly think of the peace of retirement and perhaps I am not alone in the public service."

"No, no, no," said a bulbous man whom the Inspector recognised as a senior flack from the Home Office, "that is not the public image we wish to create."

Porterman had been a famous rugby player and the morning light made interesting planes on his smashed face. "You can stuff your public image, sir, like the old dirty rhyme says. I want to apprehend the murderer. If I can, I will."

"The facts," interposed the Chairman, "are that it was Jolly's habit to constantly check back through the monthly file of newspapers. At that hour his work was done for the day, barring emergency. He was, so his employer tells me, a most conscientious man, although one admits from all reports a very unpleasant one. He was readily accessible; anybody could see him, in fact he relished tittle-tattle and the setting of one member of his staff against another."

"When did he go home?" asked Hawker.

"They have a couple of bedrooms," said Porterman dourly, "and a shower—not the kind of men who wash other than their hands—and quite often, nobody is in a position to tell, Jolly slept there. He has two boys in the moneylending business and doing well and a wife with... well, the picture is in the file. What is the quote: 'An inducement to early rising'. One of the Victorians, I think.

"I may state," said Porterman, "that the Stealthy Men—much as I dislike the popular phrase"—he glared at Harry as though he was responsible for office slang—"give John Jolly a clean bill of health. In fact if anything he rather favoured Hitler in his time and it was difficult for a Jew to get a job with him unless he took the Union minimum. A thoroughly respectable fellow."

"I looked through the reports," said an old Inspector of Detectives (not to be confused with a Detective Inspector if only because he earned much more), "and the personality of the Head Porter, Robert Walpole Bocker, reads strangely. Always there, fixes things up, knows too many people."

"I know the chief of the Stealthy Men," said the Chairman, wearily, "fellow with no jaw-line and got there because he had to be put somewhere. But you might say he's half-way intelligent. Attended University College and got third-class honours. Apparently for years the Stealthy Men *got* most of their information from Bocker who drew three thousand a year off the Secret List. It was only last year that they woke up to the fact that he was inventing it all—he slipped up in consulting an out-of-date reference book. But a pillar of his Church, vice-chairman of the local Conservative Association, a widower with two fine sons who took a strong line over Rhodesia!"

"Where exactly are we on our progression up the creek?" snarled Hawker.

The Chairman took it; Hawker was reputed to be the confidant of every senior servant in Whitehall and the man whom Prime Ministers occasionally consulted. But Harry sensed the antagonism of the younger men.

"The answer," said Porterman, "is entirely negative. The building is circular, there are a large number of employees, a newspaper office is a fluid sort of place with a lot of movement. The man who stabbed him took the risk of darting in, using this spike, a routine and anonymous piece of equipment, and making off."

"Who succeeds him?" asked a bright young Inspector.

"The Editor, very much subservient to Jolly, is carrying on. Sir Peregrine, whom we aroused from his bed—we had some difficulty in finding which one it was, but the Head Porter informed us"—Porterman only joked when things had got on his nerves, thought Harry—"said that he had two or three younger men in the race for the promotion. I gather that the Advertising Manager makes the final decision."

"I do not want to labour the point I make in my celebrated lecture," said Hawker, "but the fact is that Jolly must have—even in an involuntary capacity—known something. He could have killed Percy Button; he could not have killed Tump. But there is the sudden blinding thought: the subconscious suddenly fires a shell upwards. Mr. James, how did you read the late Jolly?"

"Ingenious, but sly and cautious, perhaps a bit on the leaning side."

"Mr. Porterman's assessment and my own under-estimated his fondness for gambling," said Hawker. "He was permanently hard up in spite of his income. If he knew the killer he might have weaselled about; what's in it for me, one way or another, kind of stuff. At the last minute, of course, he briefly knew. I may say I am sure about the gambling; I phoned a contact who told me that Jolly was regarded as a good 'pay' but one to whom you had often to give time. A mortgaged house. Sons in a good way of business but not inclined to endorse papa's bills. But the family were on fairly good terms."

"I suppose we shall have to pin our hopes on military intelligence, gentlemen," said the Chairman dolefully, "after all they are the specialists. And the Stealthy Men might as well be asked to sneak around Fleet Street; I do wish they would not *look* like undertakers. Perhaps one might suggest a touch of the bohemian, say a flashy tie or turn-ups."

On that note the meeting broke up, Harry avoiding Hawker carefully, not that it did him much good.

His 'in' basket was well filled and overshadowed by a morose Sergeant Honeybody with a well-defined brown mouse over his left eye. With some trepidation the Inspector remembered that whilst the Sergeant had once been a middle-weight of distinction, though it was true he was now out of condition, his wife, of sparish build, had learned to wait until he was in a drunken slumber and then slosh him. Honeybody had once confessed that it was really no worse than having plastic surgery upon the face in a state of anaesthesia. But unpleasant when you woke up. His own wife, whilst not stout, was a woman of powerful build and will-power.

"My Dodo came back," said Honeybody simply. "That old bitch in charge of the fish sees more'n you'd think. Said I was pissed every night—which is true—and saw a pair of lady's corsets on the line, which is a downright, deliberate lie, but no arguing with my Dodo in her Glasgow mood."

"We married men have to put up with it," grunted the Inspector, shortly. "As I told you my Elizabeth is away and no communications to date. The dog is a damned nuisance; if ever I saw him looking like being sick on the carpet—he picks his time—it was this morning."

"Somebody once gave my Dodo a parrot. It had been on board an Admiral's yacht and you never heard such words in polite society. My Dodo being a daughter of the Manse— money in the family of course—was horrified because..."

"Please, Sergeant, I have a headache. When I drink I do not get headaches; when I don't I do." Privately Harry thought about the corsets. Dodo had hinted, in ladylike confidence to Elizabeth, that a local, female, fish wholesaler had her eye on all the eighteen stone stripped which comprised the Sergeant.

"What with the shiner, Mr. James, and my Dodo's wrath— she's always at her worst when quoting the Scriptures—I left our council flat precipitously as you might say at one a.m. Fortunately I had retired with my boots on which was the crux of her fury, I think. I left her shouting about the state of my shirt, apparently forgetting I always carry a spare collar in me rump pocket."

Harry sat down heavily and looked at the Sergeant with disfavour. The shirt seemed fabricated from blue and white striped flannel—it was a mystery where Honeybody ever got such clothes—and in the region of his breastbone appeared what looked like a bunch of noodles attached by some congealed red sauce.

"Ah," the Sergeant looked down and brushed it off. "A lovely dish that was. Nothing like the Chinese grub to sober a man up. My Dodo was so mad that she hadn't taken my wallet, which is her custom, and there were seven nicker in it. 'Honeybody,' I said, 'give yourself a treat...but first the chow as a tightener and p'raps shark's fin soup which the Chinese say...' anyhow there's a widow lady I know in Wapping, like."

"Sergeant," said Harry, "if your Dodo applies for annulment after all these years expect no sympathy from me. And under the new regime it will do you no good in the Force. As it is there is that entry about the police matron who complained."

"I slipped on the parquet floor," said Honeybody, unflinching, "you remember that the disciplinary board dismissed the matter without even calling her to testify."

"Here," said Harry shortly, "this complaint alleges the theft of five thousand tins of salmon from Shoreditch. Be off with you, the watchman's in hospital!"

"Have you heard of the Golden Snail, Mr. James?" When the Sergeant was excited his basso became a whisper.

The Inspector's eyes narrowed. "Raided it two years ago because we got the drum that about forty thousand nicker's worth of uncut horse was in the fridge. All we found was a quantity of duck and pork meat. Chinese cuisine but run by a Jap, a queer. I never heard of yellow queers before."

"All shapes and colours," said Honeybody who could never avoid a diversion. "I nicked a Red Indian once who'd come over with a wild west show. It was very curious, he..."

"Get to the point or get out."

"I can't remember the early dishes or the shark's fin," said Honeybody, "not being steady, as you might say, and came to when noshing at the noodles in the sauce. This little fellow trots up and says he owns the place. 'All right,' I say, 'and I'm a bogey.' 'I know,' he said, 'you're on the *Bulletin* job—the astrologer what got done over. Can you have a word in private?'" Honeybody gave a gusty sigh.

"I wasn't going to risk any pissed-in-the-execution-of-my-dooty charge, so I said I was merely having my pleasure and I would ask my guv'nor in the mornin'. He finally went off with a flea in his ear. He said there'd be no charge, but I wasn't having that neither. I got the bill somewhere...."

"What time was this?"

"Three-ish, sir, the Golden Snail opening at noon and going on until around five a.m. The widow woman works at a gambling club near there, a very respectable lady whose hubbie was in the undertaking, but she don't get off until four, so..."

"I will meet you at this food emporium at one. Now cut off about this stolen salmon. Ten to one 'Greasy' Spoon is behind it. See if his caffs are featuring salmon cakes, not that we'll prove anything on that little bastard."

Honeybody lumbered off and wearily Harry attacked the work pile. It meant briefing cynical sergeants and, much worse, eager-beaver young plain-clothes detectives. However tired you felt you had to be bright and on your feet, instilling confidence which you so seldom felt yourself. There were, the Inspector often reminded himself with oppression, thousands of crooks on a healthy hundred nicker a week untaxed.

He telephoned Hawker and took a taxi rather than a police car to the Golden Snail. By his infallible radar system Honeybody was emerging from a nearby public house and smelled strongly of gin, but his eyes, though bloodshot, were keen.

The Golden Snail had the slightly aloof atmosphere of a Chinese restaurant, as though two civilisations had impinged but not quite blended. It was an interesting place, the food being, Harry remembered, not the rich viands of Canton but the dryer dishes of Shan Tung and Hopeah.

"If you are known you can get rice wine in the teapot," whispered Honeybody, who was munching calcified water beetles with a grave expression.

"The vilest-tasting substance on earth," said Harry.

"Sir, sir, nothing alcoholic is vile, though I must admit that I had a nasty experience with some metal polish while seconded to the Military Police. And one of my sons, in the Queen's Navy, God bless her, said the stuff they tank up the torpedoes with is fair horrid...."

"Sergeant, those gins you had have revived the strong waters of yester-eve. Shut up and behave."

"You would be the Inspector, I think. We remember each other from that unfortunate misunderstanding about drugs." Unlike many Japanese his 'l's' were impeccable.

"Yes, Harry James. You speak good English, if you will accept it as a compliment. Last time I was here I saw your manager."

"Eton and Balliol; a lot of money to speak English!" Impeccable teeth flashed a smile. "The manager returned to Hong Kong. I now devote more time here. Perhaps you might join me for coffee in my private room."

Honeybody also rose. The Japanese made a small gesture. "I would prefer tête-à-tête," he said very quietly.

"Honeybody, stay here and drink tea. As God's my witness if you get on the spirits I'll have you as a mounted constable on the most vicious nag in the stables."

The owner's office was well carpeted and mildly luxurious. A *Pietà*, all browns and greens, hung on one wall. The Inspector, in other circumstances, would have asked the name of the painter.

"Ah, I timed it well! Do take a pew." The electric coffee percolator was comfortably snorting steam. The Japanese poured dexterously, plus a rather good Spanish Calisay.

All these things the Inspector accepted, dead-pan. The Japanese looked serious. "Let me get it straight that a lot of money has been spent making this office bug proof. Laser beams won't work, tiny mikes and tinier tapes fail. We are private."

"I have eighteen stone of Sergeant outside," said Harry. "He'd tackle a maddened bull."

"My dear fellow, but I suppose you were Red Brick...."

Harry threw his coffee into the man's face.

Imperturbably the Japanese wiped it with his handkerchief. "I suppose I should say, 'Oh, Zen!' but it was hot you know!"

"I do not like you," said Harry, "and I can make my dislikes stick."

"I suppose we could not discuss money?"

"Now look, sonny boy, Eton and Balliol, and no doubt a member of the Diners' Junior Club, I'd trap you like a Japanese Peasant. The ones guaranteed to fall out of trees."

The Japanese was not pleased but continued to smile. "Do you remember how the Russians used to throw the coachman out of the carriage when the wolves got close?"

"Giving me a coachman?"

"Let me refill your coffee cup. There! Troublesome times, Mr. James, a lot of people in delicate circumstances. A bit here, a bit there, but an area of co-operation. The late Mr. Percy Button was Peking-paid."

"So they slaughtered him?"

"Dear, oh dear, no, no knowledge. And—I am an honest broker—not the other side. I assure you of this. That I approached you rather than, um, other branches, is that it might be quicker. My principals do not wish for turbulent waters to fish in. We want general business practice, a bit of change and exchange and perhaps four years' solitary at most. But Button is out of it; there will be a replacement of course. You know that. I do not know his name, it's just a six-monthly cheque for a certain amount. Routine business, one might say, and give and take. Of course, now there are two camps it makes it difficult for a man. But neither killed Button. I would throw you this particular coachman, but he is apparently neither Russian nor Chinese inspired. I also work for the C.I.A. and it isn't one of theirs. It was in short not a political knocking-off."

"Did you know a Miss Tump?"

"Only by report, my dear fellow, a social democrat! Nobody likes those, but they seem singularly peaceful individuals. And she apparently had," the Japanese chuckled, "Christian principles. They just give themselves up, my dear fellow, to the nearest concentration camp. Who killed Miss Tump I know not, but obviously quite outside the political periphery."

"What is the purpose of this exercise?"

"My various masters want the peaceful providence of the rules of the game, without—and you will excuse the compliment, please—rather intelligent members of the Crime Squad making it difficult. Counter-intelligence, as you know, is celebrated for its low I.Q. We have no wish to escalate it, as our American cousins would say."

"You realise I shall report all this?"

"Of course, my dear fellow. But remember if your Government wishes to know things about other countries they often consult me, for a fee of course. Your Foreign Office, if I may say so without offence..." he raised a delicate eyebrow... "I must say I was commissioned to approach a gentleman who for some years was a supervisor on the Baltic States as far as propaganda was concerned, only to find that he had confused them with the Balkans. In any case, old chap, my term nears its end. If you hear of anybody wishing to take over a Chinese restaurant—all recipes supplied—refer them to me. Another Calisay?"

Harry walked to the door, which was not locked, and stalked out, a faint, ironic snigger following him. Honeybody stood massively beside the table. "No tea, but I paid the bill. Cleaned me out, sir, you'll have to stand scot for a pint or two; there's not a call-box within a mile, but the publican along the road is a friend of mine."

As usual in alcoholic matters, Honeybody was right and the Inspector left him poised over a pint of keg bitter as he sought the publican's private telephone.

"Ah," said Hawker, "I heard he's a middleman. Better the devil you know as long as they don't step too much out of line. There are limits and these boys can tell you what's happening when the Diplomatic Corps are reading *Time* and stumbling over the prose. Balliol, eh? All the best spies used to be Cambridge men, but things change. A friend was telling me that there are an increasing number of working-class, comprehensive types which makes it more difficult. It clears it up, though, these fellows don't lie. Portermen will go stark, flaming mad. It leaves money or women as the motive."

"I suppose I'd better carry on with Honeybody!"

"I say the affirmative merely because of possible questions. I suppose your Sergeant is currently drinking ale?"

"In the line of duty, sir, ogling the landlord's wife."

"All right, I'll send poor Sergeant MacGibbon to gather up your 'in' basket—he loves to complain of over-work and his nervous dyspepsia—and so you look around. I am more or less convinced that your Japanese friend was truth-telling."

The landlord's wife was apparently hypnotised by Honeybody's immense bulk and he was telling her of some scabrous experience when as a young detective he had been seconded to London's underground railway system when Harry arrived.

"It was behind a copy of *The Times*, ma'am, in the days when the front page was all advertisements and it was a trust of the aristocracy. That was what the magistrate thought so bad and seven munce without an option and increased to a year at the quarter sessions. I told him, the *Mirror* is one thing being read by the workers—broad-minded the magistrates are—but *The Times* is another. I must say... oh, hallo, Mr. James. My guv'nor, ma'am. A rare nice man."

"Pleased, I'm sure," said the landlady. "Mr. Honeybody looks fitter every time we see him."

Harry morosely bought two pints; the Chinese food was working away at his colon.

"You know the Japanese next door?" he asked idly.

"With the restrong?"

"Slim, small, thick glasses and talks like a toff."

"Well, now, I thought he was an Indian, but you can't tell these days, all of 'em scarpering around. Drinks gin."

The landlady meditated, "'E's usually in about this time. He noshes his nice plain grilled New Zealand chops, not liking Chinese muck, upstairs with that gent over there with the ginger mush."

Harry slyly peered. It was a large man with a vivid shade of ginger fringery who was drinking brown ale.

"You certain?"

"O' course, five days of each week, with French fried."

"Sergeant, get him!"

"No trouble, sir, not on premises." The publican had sidled up. "I run an honest house, sir, there hasn't been a lady of low morals in 'ere over the years. And if by chance always over the age of consent."

"I assure you that your reputation will not be opposed in any way, but can we use your private room?"

"Oh, of course, sir."

Honeybody's bulk propelled the large man towards the entrance of the private room. A few customers looked and the Inspector, frankly memorising, stared.

"Now, sir," said the Inspector, closing the door, "here is my warrant card. I wish you to co-operate in answering certain questions. I have no reason to suspect you of any offence."

"Who's your guv'nor?" the man asked unexpectedly.

Harry was halted dead in his tracks. "My what?"

"I am aware," said the man with clipped precision, "that the Force are now reduced to purblind Inspectors, but hardly, one would have thought, deaf ones."

"Superintendent Hawker." The Inspector shook his head at Honeybody who was rearing up like an aged and bad-tempered stallion with still a lot of go in him.

"Perhaps you would look at the door while I dial my number."

Oh, God, thought the Inspector, in it again! "Walthamstow Rangers," presently said the clipped voice. "Would you please clear me with Superintendent Hawker—yes, apparently he is still there. The usual number here, please."

"For Christ's sake," whined Hawker in about four minutes' time, "what the hell have you been doing now?"

Harry reported.

"I don't want anything to do with it," said Hawker, "your boyfriend is the original secret weapon, fight him yourself."

The handset was slammed down.

"I am sorry about this," said Harry to the large man, who had a nervous smile which flickered on and off like a faulty electric globe.

"I wish," he said, in tones which reminded Harry of his national service, "that you cheps would keep out of our territory. My master will simply be furious, but furious."

"The fellow next door asked to see me," said the Inspector. "He wanted to tell me that the late Percy Button had not been a political assassination. The bung's wife told me you ate with him."

"Ah," the large man fingered his ginger whiskers, "it's difficult to explain to the laity, but there is a certain amount of give and take. We provide the Americans with information concerning Cuba and they brief us about the Egyptians. Frankly, old boy, that little man next door knows all there is to know about Cuba. His daily reports go to the President via hot line. We think he in turn gets the stuff from the Chinese Embassy."

"In duck soup?"

"Frankly, old fellow, we thought dim sims, those suety little dumpling things they make. We had a chef experiment and you could wrap thin rice paper round the filling."

"I think we should see him." Harry looked at his watch. "In any case isn't he bloody late?"

"You may have a point there, old boy," the ginger-haired man was a little on the back foot. "I'll ring him up." He dialled and it took some time.

"He seems to have taken off," he said eventually.

"He *what*?"

"I had a word with the cook—a man in our employ. Soon after you had gone the proprietor had a phone call and walked out. The cook couldn't ring because he was doing something urgent to a duck, one of those imported dehydrated ones. But his files are cleaned out and he took a suitcase. How the hell we can get the stuff for Washington God alone knows...."

"There's Bocker, on the *Bulletin*," said Harry, sourly.

"He got the Roosevelts mixed up, Teddy and Franklin D., hence the Bay of Pigs. An old man with a failing memory, stands to reason. He thought Cuba was still Spanish territory. They say the younger Kennedys were very put out. On the other hand there's a fellow on the *Express* who they say knows everything. I can't recollect his name, but"—he brightened—"it will be in the new computer. I must leave forthwith, old chap. Chin-chin!"

"One of the Stealthy Men," said Honeybody, disgustedly, as the door closed.

"I'll weaken and buy a pair of pints and two small gins," said Harry.

"Everything tickety-boo, sir?" asked the publican.

"I guess so," said the Inspector, ordering.

"On the house, I'm sure, sir."

Harry accepted. It was one of the consolations of police work that you got the odd free drink. When he had been a constable on beat work there had been a butcher who always pressed two lamb chops upon him. He had kept very dark about it when they discovered the butcher's mother-in-law in an obscure corner of the cool room.

Finally they trudged off, with the flat, nothing accomplished feeling which is seventy per cent of police work. They turned the corner.

"Coo!" said Honeybody.

Hawker's sallow face peered out of the police car. The Japanese, a suitcase near his left leg, was gripped by Sergeant Shum. The police driver fended off the large man with the ginger moustache. About sixty ratepayers, of the general class that wished to make some valid excuse not to return to work on time, had gathered in chorus.

"This is classified," said the man with the ginger moustache. "You cannot touch him."

"Models of democracy who own West Australia," snarled Hawker, "the Count from Changi."

"Mind your own effing business," said the man with the ginger moustache, lapsing into crudity and moving towards Sergeant Shum. But there was a shot and the Japanese collapsed like a fallen clown. Shum stared momentarily at the dead man at his feet whilst a small man seized the suitcase and scuttled through the inevitably craven crowd. Harry gaped, but Honeybody's ancient prowess of prop forward registered and he fell to the ground pinioning the small man below his huge belly. A small pistol clattered to the ground. The Inspector collected himself and rabbit-punched hard with a balled right hand. The British public rapidly began to disperse.

"Dead as a mackerel, right through the temple," said the gingery man. "We're not responsible."

"Honeybody," said Hawker, "you will summon an ambulance, etcetera and will wait here. Sergeant Shum, place the suitcase in the back, and sit on this little swine. Inspector, collect the lethal weapon!"

"I'd better come along." Oblivious of Hawker's glares the gingery man clambered in beside the driver, his elbow jammed in Harry's rib-cage.

The killer had recovered by the time he was carried, dazed from the blow, into Hawker's room. Watched by Hawker, Harry, Sergeant Shum and the gingery man, an elderly doctor examined him.

"My," he said, "who hit him?"

"Me," said Harry.

"Ex baseball?"

"Pitcher, years ago," grunted the Inspector.

"No sign of concussion," said the doctor, pulling up an eyelid. "If he complains feed him a couple of aspirin. If that doesn't put him right get me quickly." He bustled out.

Sergeant Shum plunged his hand in the killer's breast pocket and produced a wallet and a passport.

"Joe Estan," said Hawker, examining them and speaking in his immaculate Spanish, "Cuban by birth but domiciled in Florida and holder of a temporary American document. In the *Estados Unidos* since 1966, described as a merchant. Thirty-two years old."

"Speak American," said Estan.

"Beyond me," said the Superintendent in English, "but our laws are roughly the same. I have to warn you of your rights; you are not obliged to talk and you can call an attorney. Understand?"

"Yeah."

"I and two other officers saw you shoot this little Japanese, seize his bag and bolt. Do you wish to make an explanation?"

"I wus walkin' on the sidewalk, mindin' my own affairs when I saw you and the heavy-weight with the red hair arguing with this yellow fellow. I looked down, as God is my Judge, and there was this revolver. I picked it up and it went off. I saw this guy—a Jap, so you say—drop and I guess I panicked."

"And took the suitcase as a souvenir of dear old England?"

"You never seen what I seen, copper," said Estan, "people lined up and shot. I forgot where I was. I acted instinctively. I guess I thought the case might be a weapon, or maybe some kind of armour if you tried to shoot me. Panic! I never saw the guy in this life."

"Why are you here?"

"My brother and me got a small cannery—spicy Cuban foods. Nothing big, but enough. We decided to splash the dollars for me to come here to judge export chances. In the last week I've been busy, I can give you names."

"Take him away, Sergeant Shum, book him for carrying a deadly weapon and show him the list of solicitors."

Harry noticed that the gingery man was hovering over the suitcase like a hen with her first clutch.

"And what exactly do you suppose is in that case?" snarled Hawker.

"I outrank you on that matter. Financial statements, one would guess."

"And why was he gunned down, oh helper of imperial policies?"

"No need to be offensive, Superintendent. I was getting close to the Japanese. Unless you get them to defect they never reveal everything; and so it means complete defection and a guaranteed income from a selected portfolio of shares chosen by one of the Scottish officials at the Ministry. We have quite a little colony of them in nice little bungalows at Sonning-on-Thames—remarkable how they all take to golf and bridge—and we have a small welfare staff there; keep them interested is the motto, *Punch*, the *Spectator* and the *Financial Times* all provided free. I did suggest cricket tuition for the younger ones, although it was vetoed. 'No good revealing the secret of our greatness', the P.M. said."

"Shut up," said Hawker, "or I'll make you wish you had never been conceived by mistake." His cold eyes raked the room. "Was he coming over?"

"I think so," the gingery man sobered down. "A house, three thousand a year and guaranteed protection. Actually that represents about four years of actual work. After that their usefulness is over. We have to keep an eye on them as part of the contract, but if it means a kill it's done before they defect. Afterwards... no good spending good money after bad. Our man, the cook, who is an Armenian—they make the best Chinese cooks—said he was living on his nerves. I would guess he packed a case after somebody had threatened him or warned him and went for his life. He was a hundred yards in front of me as I came out of the pub."

"What happened, Inspector," said Hawker, "is that I started worrying and sent Sergeant Shum out to have a lash at the cold duck and parked myself round the corner in the squad car. When I telephoned you were connected with the car. As the Japanese scarpered Shum put down ten bob and was on his heels. He started to run and the police driver collared him. Then, Mr. um, came up and went into his unhand him act and the Cuban bumped him well and truly."

"Can he get away with it?"

"Damned if I know," said Hawker. "I cannot swear to seeing him take the gun from his pocket. We'll have to see whether we can fluke a witness who will. Depends on whether his fingerprints reveal anything."

"The killers they send are generally clean as far as Interpol are concerned," said the gingery man. He picked up the suitcase. "I'd better trot along with this, old cheps. Toodle-loo."

Hawker watched him go, scowlingly, but without protest.

"As soon as that fat sergeant of yours phones in, get in touch with me," said Hawker, dismissively.

"Thank God that wire recording has cut down the paper," Harry ruminated as he listened to the daily input and made notes. Presently Honeybody telephoned and Harry doodled in shorthand. "The Jap's on the way to Post Mortem, sir, Bert being pleased as he's never had the privilege of investigating an oriental."

"Any witnesses?"

"Six, sir, all making depositions at the local station, where I am. Nobody saw him draw the gun; they were all leering at the police car. One witness thinks he saw it, but he is half seas over—you can smell the rum a street away. But I can swear he was *carrying* the gun when I collared him."

"A bit flimsy, but heyho. Get back to the tinned salmon!"

He briefly telephoned Hawker and concluded by saying, "Elizabeth is away, I'll have to get the ruddy dog kennelled and I am owed approximately six hundred hours. Right if I scarper?"

"I once worked it out that they owe me twenty-five months." grunted Hawker, "but get along. Quick before the Commander puts something else on our plate."

The old lady took a poor view of Mr. Bones who had indeed sicked on her carpet and gnawed a hideous late Victorian commode which had sentimental memories as it had been used for thirty years by Auntie Maud, "and if any woman was a saint it was her, Mr. James."

The Inspector assured her that a French polisher would be sent round. Mr. Bones slobbered over his hand. The old lady looked coy. Mr. Bones had wished to Go. By means of a tin of salmon she had lured him on to the toilet bowl, but though consuming the salmon he had refused to co-operate and indeed had become jammed in it. She had summoned the caretaker and in the ensuing struggle to extricate the dog the seat had smashed. The Inspector said he would replace it. Furthermore the caretaker had refused to walk Mr. Bones under seven shillings and sixpence. Harry paid for the salmon, added seven and sixpence and took Mr. Bones into his own kitchen. "And you were such a pretty little puppy," he mourned spooning out dog meat.

The telephone rang.

It was his wife ringing from Paddington Station. The wealthy relative, in the manner of wealthy relatives, had described her doctor as a compound of seven idiots, arisen and eaten a meal of lamb chops and baked potatoes which Elizabeth vowed would have stopped Mr. Bones, and declared that her malady —diagnosed by her doctor as dyspepsia—had been dispelled by the blessed sight of Amanda. Further she had declared her intention of spending a few days in Elizabeth's guest room.

"And I suppose I shall have to pay for the taxi," his wife said mournfully; apart from her vittles the rich relative did not believe in spending money. Nevertheless things went well. Amanda, tucked into her cot, was charming and as a treat Mr. Bones was allowed to watch her eat her Heinz. The big dog was on his best behaviour, placing his huge hound's head on the rich relative's knees.

"I do believe there's Newfoundland in him," she said. "Pity he's not pure-bred; the puppies fetch an astonishing price."

Occasionally critical of his wife's cooking, Harry was later in the evening proud of her. Mulligatawny, an enormous steak with mushrooms for the wealthy relative, which she chomped her way through while complaining of the agonies of wind, subtly blamed on the National Health which she patronised. For himself chops and for Elizabeth, who was glowing with health, a mere omelette, Dr. Hollybotham having suggested the loss of four pounds.

Breathing a trifle stertorously, the rich relative consumed half a pound of cheese with Bath Olivers and announced that she would retire early. Elizabeth dutifully escorted her to the guest room and Harry harnessed Mr. Bones and led him to his favourite statue. When he returned Elizabeth was in bed. He thought he might as well retire himself; he had reached the age when you took sleep when you had the opportunity.

"Harry James what have you done with your teeth?"

"Honeybody had them stuck in at Post Mortems—the stuff they use to reconstitute stiffs."

Elizabeth stared incredulously and then giggled. "Do other women have husbands like you?"

"The dentist had to take out two more! I get a temporary plate next week."

"But I'll give that Honeybody the rounds of the kitchen!"

"Don't worry, his Dodo's back and he already has a shiner; something about ladies' corsets."

"I'll phone her and say it was a lie." She stroked his cheek and alarm bells rang in the Inspector's sub-conscious.

"Harry," Elizabeth cooed. "Dr. Hollybotham says we are expecting another little one."

"Where will it all end?" bleated the Inspector.

"With a boy, I trust," said Elizabeth, "a brother for Amanda; we'll have to think of names."

"Oh, God!" Memories of those frightful evenings with pull-out supplements from women's magazines flooded back to the Inspector.

"I have always thought Harry is a bit low and book-makerish."

"I wish to Heaven I made a book."

"The punters would skin you alive. I thought that Cedric might be coming back."

"No son of mine shall be named..." The Inspector stopped, remembering his wife's adept technique of raising irrelevant issues. "Do you realise what we are up for as regards Amanda's school fees?" he enquired quietly.

"We'll have to halve it. I mean half such a good school would be a pretty good school. If we go on, of course, there's always the grammars."

"The Government is abolishing the grammars."

"Then we'll all be in the same boat."

"It'll probably be another girl," said Harry gloomily.

"And what's wrong with that?" Elizabeth's tone was ominous, but what with his missing teeth the Inspector did not heed the warning signal. "What do you mean by 'go on'?" he bawled.

"Have more."

"A lot of simpering misses who can't earn their keep and whose morals you have to watch all the time. I..."

"You cannot talk, Mr. James! Besides I was reading the other day what the top model girls get."

"Amanda already looks like the back of a bus."

"No such thing. The doctor said she is sweetly pretty."

"By the time she grows up tastes will have changed; the models will be bald old ladies. Society is growing progressively older."

"They can marry rich men."

"The Government are abolishing rich men, except M.P.s."

"Then we'll go to Australia. You told me that they had a Police Chief who died a Field Marshal."

The Inspector pretended to read a book. This was the reason for the fireside slippers, the bottle of special wine, sweetbreads done his favourite way (which Elizabeth hated herself)! Perfidy!

"And of course Aunty will leave the kids her All."

"I wish you wouldn't keep making me sound like a thoroughbred stallion," snarled Harry.

"I never envisaged *thoroughbred*!"

"In any case your Aunty, overweight and oppressed by wind though she may be, will live to be one hundred and three and probably acquire new favourites as these people do. She thinks policemen are low, she herself having made the cash in wholesaling second-hand clothing."

"Nothing of the sort! She had seven refined shops in Peckham including leases in fee simple. Let's not quarrel, Harry. What is needed is for you to become the youngest Superintendent."

"For God's sake, Liz, that's fourteen years off. And with luck at that! I just have to make one major balls-up and I'm an Inspector for life or maybe in some minor Commonwealth job with more money and a trip home every three years. How would you like being a little memsahib?"

"Harry, I know a flack from my working days. A hundred quid to him and he rushes round like an impassioned cat telling the reporters, 'James is the genius who solved the *Bully* murders'. Then I organise the League of Modest Maidens to keep telegramming the M.P.s."

"How you can still belong to that organisation when you intend to breed like an envenomed canary I shall never know."

"It's only callisthenics."

"Elizabeth," the Inspector swung himself out of bed. "I have to have two of those anti-belch pills the man told me about on the bus. Then I intend turning my bedside light off, if you do not mind."

"I know something. Secret! Secret, but would have told you but for you being swinish about poor little Cedric!"

The Inspector chewed his pills slowly. On a few occasions Elizabeth, who rummaged unashamedly through his briefcase, had spotted solutions.

He went back to bed. "Come, father's woolly lamb and earth mother, what gives?"

"You know I like to talk to people!"

Harry knew. Labourers on roads, old European peasants, there was no end to Elizabeth's curiosity.

"Come on," he said, "quit the histrionics."

His wife giggled, "It's probably because after the Tushington Parva business I am sensitive."

The Inspector groaned. Dead right or dead wrong was Elizabeth. In the Tushington Parva business only Honeybody's experience had prevented him from arresting a retired bishop for indecent exposure, an offence which transpired to be the work of a village idiot. "Sir, sir," Honeybody had said over his fourth stout, "bishops don't commit that offence because the work makes them so cautious. Sometimes a bit of fiddling on the accounts which is hushed up, but bishops frightening the ladies, oh, dear, no!" It had been Elizabeth's impeccable logic which had prompted him to apply for the warrant, which, thank God and Honeybody, he had never served.

"So," said Elizabeth, "I shall proceed tomorrow to the *Bully* in the guise of an earnest seeker after truth concerning newspapers, con introduction from you."

The Inspector turned the light off. "I would think Peter Leeming, assistant editor and workhorse, Archer McClout, a tough Aussie, and, curiously, the young Mabel, Miss Tump's former girl. Intelligent and snoopy. I'll write you a chit before breakfast. God knows if it's regular."

"Do cease talking like Aunty about her stomach," said Elizabeth and snapped off her bedlight.

8

In his microscopic 'study' Harry thought next morning how to carry out his obligation. Barking his shin against the desk he wrote: "Dear Leeming, if it's not a nuisance my wife has a yen to see how newspapers work. I suggested she first saw you and then persecuted Archer McClout and perhaps Mabel" —he groaned and thumbed through his notebook—"Snowberry. If it is not convenient get the inimitable Bocker to throw her out. Yours, H. James, Inspector. P.S. Very sorry about John Jolly, terrible thing."

He passed the quarto sheet across the table to a rather silent Elizabeth. You know when you've gone too far, my girl, he thought inwardly whilst tittering pleasantly to the wealthy relative who was in the throes of a three-egg omelette anointed by chicken liver in white sauce. He ate his sweetbreads in silence.

Presently Elizabeth informed him that she had heard of a Jamaican lady with the knack of soothing small girls and equally quelling large dogs and upon arising had phoned her. She would appear at noon. Aunty outlined her plans for visiting friends, including, she said with an arch glance at Amanda, her solicitor. Amanda burped a long piece of goo which Elizabeth skilfully wiped before it was completely visible.

"At least we shan't have drying nappies stinking out the place while she's here," Harry said sotto voce. Aunty was a little deaf, but Elizabeth annihilated him with one glance.

He wiped his mouth, tickled Amanda, kissed Elizabeth and smirked at Aunty whilst patting one of her meaty shoulder-blades. Putting on his duffle-coat he took the various buses which led to his office. Honeybody stood warming his buttocks against the gas radiator.

"A quiet night, sir," he said. "I worked until ten thirty and then pleased my Dodo by giving a hand with the late fish."

"Elizabeth is back. With her Aunty. She will phone Dodo and perjure herself in re corsets."

"A wonderful woman, sir. About the salmon. They were sent off by Shorty Bill and his boys who all have cast-iron alibis."

Harry remembered Shorty Bill, a peaceful and amiable cockney who resembled a walking coffee table.

"And Greasy Spoon fenced them for tenpence the tin. They'll be fish rissoles in his caffs for the Friday trade."

By then other sergeants had come in and Harry dispensed work files: two apparent hit-and-runs; four petty house-breakings, but in his charge because they seemed to represent the beginning of a gang; malicious damage to railway property. The latter he handed to Honeybody who had an affinity with railway stations and did his best drinking in the refreshment room in front of the glass domes filled with dried sandwiches.

He spent the entire morning with representatives of various insurance companies who suspected arson. At one he telephoned the flat. A pleasant woman's voice answered. His wife had gone out, Amanda had had lunch and Mr. Bones was just a sweetie.

"My God," thought Harry as he thanked her and replaced the handset, "Mr. Bones a sweetie. She should train tigers!"

He lunched alone in the canteen on sausages with mashed potatoes with plenty of onion in it and one of those slices which pastrycooks fabricate from their stale leftovers. He rather enjoyed the revival of schooldays memories, but when he got back to his office it did lie heavily in his stomach. The reports started to come in. Honeybody had had a stroke of luck in apprehending the defacer of railway stations, an elderly halfwit with some grievance and a willingness to talk approaching the garrulous. He told him to take a preliminary look at the buildings allegedly purposely ignited. At four thirty the red light on his intercom glowed.

"Sir," it was the Assistant Commander.

"Are you engaged?" asked the slow, heavy voice.

"Only gathering up reports."

"Then perhaps you will come to my office."

Flanking the A.C. were Hawker, looking grey, and Sir Plunkett, more red-faced than ever.

"Mr. James," said the A.C., "your wife was injured in the

Bulletin approximately two hours ago. She is in Charing Cross Hospital."

A haze of red rage came in front of Harry's eyes, then he felt sick.

"Drink this." The A.C. held out a small glass of brandy. He always had everything arranged, thought the Inspector humbly.

"Now, Mr. James," said Sir Plunkett, "listen carefully. It was a blow on the cranium from a piece of lead piping. It seems that the assailant was interrupted after striking one blow. There is a hair-line fracture, but it is not depressed. She will probably recover consciousness around eight tonight. There is no injury to the cortex, but she will probably experience headaches for some months. Who is her doctor?"

"A Miss Nelly Hollybotham."

"Ah, yes, an excellent young consultant, but tell me is your wife expecting?"

"Yes, sir, just about, I think."

"You need expect no difficulty on that score, but we'll have to keep her in for rather longer, say a month. If you'll excuse me, I will go and telephone the hospital." He bustled out.

"I may say, Mr. James, that she will be a private patient at our expense," said the A.C.

"Thanks," said Harry, his brain racing. "Where, why and how, Mr. Hawker?"

"What was she doing there?" asked the old Superintendent worriedly.

"She thought she had a clue. You know how determined she is, so I gave her a chit to the Assistant Editor, Leeming."

"Just to abate your curiosity, your wife was found outside the office of the late Percy Button, now empty. Miss Bottle, opposite, was as usual having her afternoon read in the ladies. Elizabeth had finished having a conversation with Miss Mabel Snowberry, said goodbye and closed the door. We believe the assailant came out of Button's office and struck her from behind. She was lucky because six young boys from the boys' room suddenly came clattering, yelling and skylarking down the stairs on the right. Whoever it was had to make a split-second decision: whether to strike again or bolt for it. He chose the latter and made for the stairs on the left. As soon as he got round the curve in the corridor he was out of sight. The boys saw nothing, but in any case they paused to exchange some vulgar badinage with Miss Snowberry who was on her own. Specifically they asked her what she wore under her mini-skirt and got a scathing reply. That's all. Peter had taken time off to give your charming wife twenty minutes of dissertation on how the paper worked, Archer McClout ditto, and then she spent ten minutes with Mabel. Finito."

"Now, Mr. James, you had better get off home. Take as long as you like off," said the A.C. kindly.

"I want to be the one who gets this bastard," said the Inspector.

"You must get this into perspective, Inspector," said the A.C. "You know as well as I do that we cannot allow personal involvement, even if it is only because," he gave his wintry smile, "it gives a defence lawyer such an advantage regarding prejudice. Better get off home. Any assistance you may require shall be given. Just ring. One more thing: we are giving out that your wife will not recover and please go along with us, repellent though it be. We could announce that she is not gravely injured, and the killer—assuming that he is the murderer of the other three—might bolt, in which case we'd have a killer at large."

"One thing," said Harry, "was there anything further of significance in the box we found in Button's lodging?"

"Yes, indeed, four perfectly forged passports in various names and a book detailing about fifteen hundred pounds, seemingly out-payments to some unspecified person," said Hawker, "but as the boss says, it's home for you."

Somehow he found himself outside the apartment building and paying a cab driver.

"You all right, guv?" the man looked at him strangely.

"Thanks, but it's okay."

Aunty had returned and was seated comfortably in the

kitchen sharing a comfortably large portion of poached smoked haddock, dripping with butter and comfortably anointed with two poached eggs with a pleasant-faced elderly Jamaican lady. Aunty was dissertating upon the joys and comforts of an English high tea. Harry blearily noticed that the next course was scheduled to be scones, cornish cream and strawberry jam.

"Elizabeth is in hospital—Charing Cross. She was struck over the head."

"How?" When the high chips were down Aunty didn't dither.

"She thought she had a clue and was prowling round the *Bulletin* building when somebody came up behind her."

"Tch," said Aunty, "journalism and police-work. I can't imagine how you came to..." She bit off the sentence.

"It sounded all right at the time," said Harry weakly.

"That girl needs a high hand. However, you may leave everything to me. You go and lie down for half an hour. I shall bring you a good mug of strong, highly sweetened tea, then a nice warm wash and a cab, which I shall order, to the hospital. Get along."

As he shuffled out he remembered that Aunty had been something high in Civil Defence in her comparative youth, but he wished, yes he did wish, that people would quit ordering him about. But the tea seemed to restore his energy and he patted Mr. Bones who was emitting distressed soft gruntings.

"All right," said Aunty at last, "have your wash. The taxi is outside."

As he left he thanked her, awkwardly, feeling once again how easy and how uncertain it is to write people off under cliché headings.

At the hospital he found they had done him proud; private room plus an anteroom with comfortable chairs, in one of which sat peacefully Sergeant Honeybody.

"Sit down, do, Harry," said the Sergeant, "she's all right, saw the quack myself. Hawker hauled me out of one of those blown warehouses and I came along. Remember I'm just your errand boy." Elaborately the Sergeant pretended to nap.

The Inspector peered through the door. Something very still slept in a dimly lit bed and a fierce, small but intimidating nursely face glared at him from beside it. He retreated and sat opposite Honeybody and soon—to his vague surprise—he found himself entering the uneasy limbo between consciousness and sleep.

He awoke when someone gently shook his shoulder. The Inspector awakened to face a very clean-looking man who announced that he was the consultant.

"Your wife has recovered consciousness, Inspector. Everything normal. I have no doubt you have met similar cases in the past; no questioning whatsoever, no cross-word puzzles, in fact cabbage existence for a couple of days."

"Can I go to her?"

"Her gynaecologist, Miss Hollybotham, is due in five minutes. After that—and I assure you no cause for alarm, nature protecting the unborn as she does."

"Oh, God," said the Inspector.

"It does seem, Inspector, that Miss Hollybotham does not approve of our sex, though it has always seemed to me that if our sex were wiped off the earth the good young woman would have to master some new speciality. However, I am assured your wife is 'on private' and no known force will be able to stop her attendance. If I were you I'd go and spend three-quarters of an hour round a sherry and a couple of sandwiches. By which time your wife will be feeling a bit human."

Abruptly Sergeant Honeybody jerked into life, sketching a salute to the consultant. "This way, sir, a place down an alley not far away with smoked salmon."

"The Superintendent said on exes, Mr. James," gloated Honeybody as they found the pub. "Russian stout and caviar on toast, followed by the smoked salmon, eh?"

Weakly Harry agreed and surprisingly found he was hungry.

"What was happening when you were briefed by Hawker?" he said.

"The old gentleman seemed to indicate the slate is as blank as ever."

After a second stout they went back. In the corridor Dr. Hollybotham passed, exchanging her usual wintry nod for Harry's formal bow.

"In my day, sir," said the Sergeant in a reverberating baritone, "they were fat ladies glad to earn a quid for a delivery, plus skivvying for a couple of days. 'Aven't changed much basically except in figure."

The Inspector shuddered at his subordinate's temerity, feeling lancet eyes between his shoulder blades. "Really, old man," he said....

"Ah, sir, they have to be kept in their place and no mistake about it," said the Sergeant as he sat down in his arm-chair, a suspicious protuberance in the inside of his serge jacket pocket convincing Harry, half wistfully, that a bottle of spirits reposed there.

"You may go in now, sir," said the consultant, emerging, "Miss Hollybotham is quite pleased, omitting as I am sure you will wish any fundamental details. Definitely pleased. And so am I; but no questions, sir, whatsoever. One thing I should have said. Your Mr. Porterman cautioned us to give a certain kind of prognosis if we were approached—'patient unconscious and condition grave'—and in the interests of justice this was acquiesced to and will be. But two hours after her admission a person rang up and enquired after her. My assistant, who had been instructed, gave the formula and enquired the name, which proved to be a Mr. Thompson."

"What was the voice like?" asked Harry.

"We aren't used to that kind of detection. He said it was flat standard London delivered in the usual highish baritone, caller probably nervous."

"Thank you, sir," said Harry, giving an admonitory stare towards Honeybody before passing in to see his wife. She had acquired an unusual look of frailty. He took the seat by her bed.

"They have shaved my head," his wife complained, "bald as a bad bat is this poor lady."

"Wigs, stricken one," said Harry, "with matching ones for

163

that Amanda, who is well and with Aunty and Mr. Bones."

"I've always wanted to switch colours quickly," said Elizabeth, "I read you can get them in green. And with the new knee-breeches look, zowie! P'raps you can get one of those menwigs that disguise their baldness."

"Silence and rest! The quack says no real harm done. Brains no more addled than usual."

"And Doctor, um, Doctor, um Hollybotham," said Elizabeth, dreamily, "says little Cedric is as right as rain."

"I'll be outside all night," said the Inspector, "yell and I'll fly on the wings of the fairies."

"You *are* an ass. Certain the fearful child is in good hands?"

"Aunty and the Jamaican lady fully coping."

"How did I get here, Harry?"

"Don't you *know*, love?"

"Last I remember is phoning you from Paddo Station. Would that be last night?"

"Yes."

"Can't remember a thing since. Was it a car crash? Tell me!"

"A wallop over the head."

"Why should anybody wallop me?"

"If you don't know, love, I suppose..."

"Now Mr. James," the sharp-faced little nurse had either been lurking in what Harry supposed to be the lavatory or hiding under the bed, "we'll make Mrs. James comfy and turn off the light, if you don't mind."

The Inspector kissed his wife, "Just call, love," and scuttled out.

"Ah, here you are," said Honeybody, "I wheedled two glasses out of that sweet little nurse." The Inspector noted that he had removed his boots and that a bottle of Scotch stood on the tiny table. "Somewhere," Honeybody groped inside his flapping serge jacket, "there is a packet of hammers for emergency. Ar, here, sir, in case we get peckish! The men's is about ten yards along on the right, but be careful of the hot water which is *very*. Have a nip, sir."

The Inspector accepted and an hour later ate two crushed ham sandwiches. The table light was very low and Honeybody, by some professional skill, abated his usual snarling snore into a low drawl, barely discernible.

At about five, when the hospital was arousing into muted life, a new day of work ahead, Harry went to the washroom. In an alcoved window beside it, rather red-eyed from tiredness, sat Sergeant Shum who got up as he saw Harry.

"What are you doing here?" asked the Inspector blankly.

"Mrs. James is under maximum security, sir. We've got chaps all around the building and women police where we can't go. I'm so sorry about it, sir. Mr. Hawker—well, I've never seen a man more cold and angry—swore at us for half an hour, but honest, sir, how were we to know?"

"Sergeant, it was my fault and my doing," said Harry, rubbing an unshaven chin, "I had no idea there was a tiger at large."

"Mr. Hawker reckons homicidal, sir. He says he recognises the pattern."

Harry felt a chill. "When are you relieved?"

"At six, sir. It's strange to be carrying a gun, the first time I ever have. Sergeant Atley, very vicious at unarmed combat he was in the course, relieves me. You need have no worry, sir, and Sergeant Honeybody will be lurking around, just in case. He's very fond of your good lady, sir, and although slowed up he'll bash with the best."

Harry managed to sequester somebody's abandoned towel—he hoped they were not being treated for any dermal condition, and leisurely showered before finding a plug for the tiny electric razor which he carried among other professional debris.

It was an hour before he returned, during which time Sergeant Shum had been replaced by Sergeant Atley who had hair of a rare carrot colour and an obvious ambition to break somebody's leg.

Elizabeth was drowsy but conscious. "Am I dreaming, Harry?"

"You are in good hands, in hospital, Amanda and Mr. Bones

are being cosseted by their Aunty." The Inspector encountered his Waterloo and said, "Miss Hollybotham says little Cedric is okay."

"I thought I might have imagined it all. I can't remember much of yesterday; was it only yesterday?"

"Somebody knocked you on the head around two yesterday. It'll mean a month of luxury in this room, the cost footed by Work."

"I could have sworn I heard Honeybody."

"Dozing in the anteroom."

"Could I see him, just to make sure it's not a dream... nobody could dream about Honeybody."

The Sergeant proved to be awake and changing his detachable collar. "Can't get the good old celluloid ones," he said in a sibilant whisper, "it was a bad day for me when they went out. You just licked 'em, ran your hankie round and you looked like a new pin."

"Elizabeth would like to view you."

"A pleasure, sir." Lumbering, but with extraordinary lightness, the Sergeant went away, leaving Harry with momentary schemes of producing detachable, plastic wipeable collars for people like the Sergeant; large dowries for the girls which Elizabeth seemed intent on producing. He did not feel sold concerning the validity of little Cedric. On second thoughts he felt doubtful about the number of Honeybodys around. Still it might be worth looking into; a kind of sotto voce occupation for Elizabeth might be the answer and she was no fool businesswise. He heard her laugh and wondered whether she should be with a fracture, however hair-lined. Honeybody had some strange secret which enabled him to have women, beldames and all, cackling around him. Eventually Honeybody padded back. "As good as new, sir," he said, floating the tidings on an accumulation of Scotch. "She'll be bouncing away twice as natural in no time."

Two nurses scuttled in, regarding the Inspector with momentary, impersonal disapproval. He sat down and closed his eyes until Honeybody's husky voice informed him that he had somehow wheedled two plates of grilled pigs' kidney and egg out of the kitchen.

"The dietician ordered it for somebody, but the consultant said he wouldn't allow it so the kitchen was stuck with it and glad to work it off." The Sergeant produced knives and forks from his back pocket. "My Dodo will be in during the morning with a Thermos and some tins of best salmon, so I'll do all right. I met a cleaner who says he'll see that there's always a crate of ale in that little closet."

The Inspector ate without appetite. As he was finishing the nurses emerged and he was conscious that one pair of beady eyes had registered the three-quarter-empty Scotch bottle in the corner.

"Better keep the empties under control," he muttered, "these places are sensitive."

"I have that fixed," said Honeybody, "out of sight and out of mind."

The breakfast was quite good, the places having changed rather for the good since the Inspector's boyhood memories of a fractured arm and immeasurable shepherd's pie.

Elizabeth looked surprisingly well, but her mind dwelt upon wigs, a subject which the Inspector found tedious, particularly as he suspected that it would turn out to be an expensive one. Presently he kissed her and told her that he would be back in the afternoon.

"You need have no fear, guv," said Honeybody, "except to briefly relieve myself I shall be here at all hours."

The Inspector repressed a slight snarl as he went and got his bus. It occurred to him that it might well be a snarling day on which to carry plenty of the anti-belch pills.

Aunty was in her element discussing some rich dish with the Jamaican lady, who had arranged with her family that she could stay. Mr. Bones was strangely solemn, plainly having met his match somewhere along the line. Amanda hardly greeted him, sitting, great-eyed, in her high chair apparently listening to information in re yams. He hoped to God it did not infect Elizabeth who had started off with Chinese, veered into Indonesian, wrestled briefly an unsuccessful round with N. Vietnam on political principle, branched briefly into Indian and, at the time of her admission to hospital, except on the economy days of cheap fish, seemed careering in a culinary way in the general direction of Bulgaria. He felt he could hardly bear Jamaican food on top of the responsibilities which constantly took refuge and fluttered in his colon.

The ladies ceased their dialogue while he told them about Elizabeth. He hesitated—sometimes to force a card was the worst tactic—and added: "I must take you into our strict confidence. Our bulletins will say she is very ill; we wish to lure the killer into a false sense of security; so please not to worry. She is relatively, and by chance, unhurt."

"I hope you kick his teeth in, Mr. James," said the Jamaican lady—Mrs. Smith, Harry remembered.

"I hope so, too," he reached out and patted Aunty, registering the thought that he really must stop treating this nice old lady like a horse.

"If you can cope, my dear," she said to Mrs. Smith, "I should go and see my niece. If you'll write down the ingredients while I change, I'll get them coming back and we'll have a nice lunch. I think you'd enjoy it, Harry, very rich and filling."

At his particular moment in space the thought of rich West Indian goodies merely drove the Inspector into the bathroom and to the anti-belch tablets. He supposed you could take too many aspirin and so raided Elizabeth's more sophisticated codeine. He said goodbye to Aunty and tried to read *Time*. Mrs. Smith seemed to be coping; there were no growls or whines or little-girl snivellings.

"Excuse me, Mr. James," said the calm voice of Mrs. Smith, "but I can cope with the dog, the girl and the household chores, but not with a grown man wandering into my water bucket."

The Inspector found that in fact he had not been reading, but merely staring absently at the magazine while walking slowly from room to room. He had somehow got into the kitchen which Mrs. Smith was mopping and his left foot was about to descend into her bucket. He stood for a moment balanced on one leg.

"Go for a walk," Mrs. Smith looked at the kitchen clock. "Nearly eleven. Walk a few miles and have a drink and a sandwich."

The Inspector thought it was sound in principle and presently found himself walking briskly but aimlessly along streets the full horror of which never pressed upon him when he was pleasure or business bent. Now the basic monstrosity of the Great Wen impaled him and Mrs. Smith's advice no longer aided him. He welcomed a large and amiable burglar whom he had last seen four years ago at the Old Bailey. They walked half a mile together.

"Awful sorry about the missus," said the craggy man, awkwardly, "some of the boys would like to have a word with 'oo done it."

"Thanks D'arcy," said Harry, "I'm walking it off. How is it with you?"

"Came out last munth. I got a bit laid by in one of them investment trusts, so the old lady didn't do so bad apart from fiddling national assistance. But it's difficult times, Mr. James. You fellows and the closed circuit TV make it hard for a tradesman to make a bob or two. Well, sir, I go down there."

Part of the Inspector's mind registered that 'down there' led to the business office, though not the storeroom of a man who fenced bolts of cloth. D'arcy must have had a 'tickle' recently, or was acting as an intermediary on percentage. He would have to pass the word on, rather a pity as he liked the big burglar, although come to that he and his colleagues possessed this curious ambivalence towards their 'customers'. He had been walking for an hour and felt tired.

"Want a lift, Mr. James?" The green Mercedes Benz eased to the curb. The latest model, thought Harry enviously.

It was a Mr. Spoon who had made a fortune from cheap restaurants because all his raw ingredients were stolen.

"Hallo, Mr. Spoon, how bist?"

"Fairly." Mr. Spoon was a Wiltshire man. "Citywards. Must say shocked at the news; no need to rub it in, but if you know him and want him done, like, just the name and address over the blower and I'll fix the rest so that he won't never sit down comfortable again."

"I'll take the ride." Harry got into the front passenger's seat, and Mr. Spoon assiduously adjusted the elaborate safety belt.

"Didn't expect to see you," said Harry.

Spoon hesitated. "'S'matter of fact I'm thinkin' of branching out. Three smart city restaurants, just luncheon trade, for the fat bleeders with high blood pressure and the visiting firemen. Salmon, fresh and smoked, turbot, pheasant in and out of season, straws, and something smart with champagne and truffles. There's a Belgian cook who owes me money and can't bolt. I might as well 'ave it out of 'im in work, supervising. A friend of mine knows how you own Italians and the Maltese to do the work. Get 'em into your clutches and then grind 'em white, the bastards. Britons never never shall be slaves!"

Mr. Spoon was an amiable and cunning rogue.

He drove along in silence. "The trouble, Mr. James, is that I've had the wife going round Scotland and sitting herself in pubs; that's all right."

"Poaching gangs?"

"Yeah. Real scientific today. They stun the fish by electric batteries, there's a little infra-red light that makes the pheasant drop into a sack, and there's a bloke up there that takes venison regular. I got a bloke who pinches turbot and as far as the straws are concerned a lot of the blokes in the Market wear big floppy pants and have a way of attaching the punnets to their backsides. What I'm exercised about is the smoked salmon. I even went over and hung about Ireland—I bought a racehorse, and I'll tell you when he's 'going'—but while I was offered all kinds of things, including the contents of an Anglican church, which I refused as I am a religious man, not a bit of smoked salmon came in sight. And you've got to have it on the 'me and you' otherwise you don't get stockbrokers or the advertising. I suppose..."

"If there is a thief specialising in smoked fish on file I'll let you know," said Harry amused.

"Thanks," said Mr. Spoon, very serious, "and there would be a little quid for the pro in the shape of information. I think I could tell you who's knocking over these sub-post-offices."

They were approaching Fleet Street. "I'll nick out at the next lights," said Harry, who could put up with the wealthy little fence for only short periods.

Apart from three good pubs and as many restaurants the Inspector had never liked 'The Street' as a place and the crime was generally not very interesting. However his watch indicated a drink and he turned into the Falstaff and ordered bitter ale.

"Jesus," said a gravelly voice, "you dogging me?"

Archer McClout's nose was beaded with stout bubbles.

"On it early, ancha, sport?"

"Get... oh, I'm sorry, it went clean out of my mind. How is she?"

Harry shook his head gravely. "Not so good."

"I was even polite about it to that man Porterman."

"What did she ask you?"

McClout caressed his snout, the stout apparently acting as some kind of polish.

"Usually they gush 'Oh, how interesting it must be' but your missus was down to earth; time schedules, mechanical stuff. Refreshing. Of course, old Leeming gave her the old stale one-two about the country's destiny depending on our honesty! Twenty-five years of it and nobody has ever offered to bribe me! I'm here eagerly awaiting seduction."

"How are things?"

"Oh, Leeming and the Advertising Manager are running it. They'll have to replace Jolly and two youngish swine are at it tooth and nail. Though Sir P. can be unexpected; the scuttlebutt is that he's negotiating for some obedient Rhodesian, but I dunno. He's worried about the competition result. The six-thousand-a-year-for-life thing. It went to a great aunt of his, aged ninety-six and frail. One of the rivals ran a story about it which upset Sir P."

"But surely she won it!"

"These permutation things," said McClout, wearily, "go to the least likely entry. Sir P. doesn't want to have ten thousand winners! So it goes to the stupidest coupon. And his elderly relative presumably submitted it. I stress 'presumably', but it does not look well. Jolly advised an ex gratia payment of five hundred pounds for handicapped children to take people's minds off it, but now he's gone. The Editor never made a decision yet and Leeming's too straight to get mixed up with it."

"Sometimes I think my job might be better than it looks," grunted Harry, "at least I don't get that sort of thing."

"Bocker told Sir P. to save the five hundred pounds as everything would be forgotten next week. He's nearly always right, the old swine. God, what a life!"

"Have one with me," said Harry, and added with a policeman's professional curiosity, "You're in early, no?"

"The effing circulation," said McClout, "has jumped thirty thousand a day since Percy Button bought it. They can't see the bodies so they buy the old *Bully* vicariously. The Advertising Manager is off his head with delight because the agencies are queueing on his doorstep with the cigarette ads. Ever notice how people smoke heavily at funerals? I should say afterwards, a packet of twenty and a double Scotch. Oh, sorry!"

"Don't worry about me."

The Australian's eyes were very shrewd as they raked the Inspector and the gravel-pit voice went down an octave as he said, "Not so bad as you gave out?"

Harry could only look at him woodenly.

"I shan't talk," said McClout. "Am just glad; nice lady! Anyway old Sir. P. wants to keep the interest up, so the Advertising Manager suggested a six-day series: 'John Jolly, Champion of the English'. Sir P. offered me a certain sum to churn it out. Trouble is that if you ask about him in the Street, they say, 'What, that bastard!' He got here in 1937 on a magazine, wheedled himself out of the Army in 1940 and then into an assignment in Eire when the bombing started. After that on half a dozen papers, steadily putting his foot on the face of his most recent friend. I saw the widow, tough old tabby, raring for the box to be nailed down so that she can go and live in the sun."

"I heard he lived up to his income," said Harry.

"Ah, but she saw he carried huge—at least to my ears—insurance with double indemnity and there is his agreement with Sir P., a juicy one which included death. She's itching to get her hands on the cheque, but Sir P. never pays under three months and then always forgets to sign the first cheque, to date the second or to post the third. Eight months credit except with the paper makers who are tougher than he is. Ah me!"

Fascinated, Harry asked, "But how are you going to write him up?"

"When he was making his name on features he had a technique. He waited until some dirty case was finished and an appeal dismissed, then he'd rewrite it: 'Lewdness in English Lanes, John Jolly Champions English Maidens'. That sort of stuff; nude butlers made him for life, you might say. Funny how you English get a kick out of nude servitors. Anyway in my articles I simply rehash his own: 'John Jolly Puts Down Nude Butlers': 'John Jolly Defends English Maidens'. Wonderful grub and dead easy once you've thought of it. Thirty quid a time I screwed out of them and the Advertising Manager delighted and suggesting that we photograph a naked butler, of course heavy shadow around the midriff. I thought of asking Superintendent Porterman who has got the right curve to his corp."

"If you ever tangled with Mr. Porterman you'd find he was tough enough," said Harry, coldly.

"The Advertising Manager said we should engage the best-known photographer in the country to take the shot at whatever cost. Who should I get?"

"I gather there are agencies," said Harry dourly.

"I might have something for you," said McClout, "concerning the string round old Percy Button's neck, what you thought was a bootlace but which was found to be a bit of the string they tie newspapers up with."

"They!" said Harry. "You must mean a machine."

"They do it that way in the Common Market," said McClout, "but we stick to good old English manual handling; we can't half tie knots!"

"I do not want to know anything about the Common Market!"

"When you can't get cheap Commonwealth meat you might wish you had a chance of noshing that New Zealand lamb or Australian beef. Although you can have Belgian veal or horse at twice the price."

"I know nothing of European politics," said Harry.

"Very invigorating, I'm told," said McClout, "but you can always live off American canned goods if put to the point. Go West, Old Man!"

"Now," said the Inspector, "give over, son!"

McClout massaged stout into his nose, which was assuming a bronzish tinge. "We keep a month's supply of the *Bully* on file in the news room. Jolly and the Editor have separate ones. But sometimes you need to take a clipping from a back number. Well, yesterday I needed a clipping and so I went to the old cupboard where the back issues—all editions—are automatically kept by one of the boys. You take the edition you want, cut the bit of paper out, rebind the copies with string and replace. It was the Metropolitan edition of the day Button was killed that I was after and the string was missing."

"Somebody forgot," said Harry.

"Our business looks confused," said McClout, "but there is a hell of method in our madness. The first thing you learn is not to make it hard for the other bloke. There would not be a man in the news room who would leave the papers just flopping messily around."

"What was the cutting you were after?" asked the Inspector abruptly.

McClout's eyes narrowed, but then he laughed. "I'm with you, Watson, and you can check until your eyeballs pop out. Every week we print the month's football fixtures, even down to obscure leagues operating in the sticks. Sir P. is fond of proclaiming that the British working man is kept content by soccer. That I frankly doubt, but I cut out the past week, stick down the clipping and add next week's."

"Is that customary?"

"Now look, sport, you do your job and let me do mine. The more anything is recopied the more the possibility of error, particularly with a lot of stuff in seven point. It's standing type; the compositors jettison what I have marked and add the new stuff."

"Who could have got to that cupboard?"

"Anybody, but it is seldom used although you would take no notice of somebody rummaging in it. In fact having it is more or less a custom for all the use it gets; it's a 'part of the furniture' sort of thing." He drained his glass. "I've done me dooty and now off to 'How John Jolly Exposed Nameless Vices'. Chin-chin, nice I'm sure."

The Inspector sat listlessly and ordered a ham sandwich, more or less for something to do.

"Can I buy you a drink?"

It was Porterman, his seventeen stone engulfing the bar stool as he eased on to it. The big Superintendent always found it hard to unbend and when he did his voice had a sepulchral quality.

"Half of bitter, thank you," said Harry.

"I, um, am awfully sorry. How is she?"

"She'll be right."

"Mrs. Porterman sends her very best wishes. I must say," said Porterman, after ordering, "I was surprised to see you here. I thought you were rather to keep away."

"Just mooching. I came in here and found Archer McClout."

"I saw him going out," said Porterman. "It is difficult for me to conquer my repugnance for colonials."

Harry kept silent. Finally, Porterman weakened. "What did he have to say?"

Harry told him.

"There's masses of that string around," grunted Porterman, "Sir P. having bought several tons of it at a fire sale."

"But mostly in the machine room," said Harry. "They bundle them up and send them down a chute into the loading dock. The provincial editions go to the railway stations, thence to wholesalers and finally to Mr. Smith, the friendly newsagent, and the person who pops it on to your doorstep. From what I know of Sir P. and the late John Jolly nobody is likely to snaffle half an inch of that string unless for lawful purposes. Whoever did it was editorial, or at a long shot on the business side."

"A newspaper office is unfortunately the ideal place in which to commit murder," sighed Porterman. "Hawker tells me that those on record have never been detected.* Intelligent, egotistical men bustling around, deep in thought. Blasé; if they saw a corpse under the table it would not register as it would to an ordinary person. I must say the business manager has been helpful—a sound man who came up via the door-to-door touting—to the extent that we've infiltrated six constables with laser beam listening aids into the place as cleaners. He had to consult Sir P. who refused outright until he realised that their wages were not his responsibility. I must say, Mr. James, that, ur, um, your wife"—Porterman always seemed to consider himself as the only man with the benefit of clergy—"was lucky. These boys came charging down, intent on some kind of badinage with Miss Snowberry, and eventually spotted, um, Mrs. James."

"Did you find the weapon?" said Harry with gentle malice. "I suppose it might have been around the premises."

"Lead piping is for the taking around those old buildings," said Porterman, "the basement in fact is littered with old lengths from seventy years ago. We're testing them all, but in these days the chances are zero."

Harry rather agreed with Hawker that crime writers, who had taught the working class so many criminal techniques, should be placed in a hygienic concentration camp on the Isle of Skye and be brainwashed by visiting politicians. But Porter-

* Author's note. This is so. One hopes that it does not put ideas into anybody's head. The Publisher disclaims responsibility in the event.

man, who took things literally, was a bore on the subject, so the Inspector returned the drink and got a taxi to the hospital.

Honeybody lounged in the anteroom amid an aroma of tinned salmon and vinegar, tinctured by some vague alcoholic background. He scrambled to his feet. "All serene, Mr. James, and your missus like a little lamb although nurse says resentful that she can't get out of bed until tomorrow. Her Aunty was here for two hours and," Honeybody whispered, "I gather that Amanda benefits under the Will. I was listening in execution of my dooty."

The Inspector found Elizabeth listening to a transistor and looking very well. "Aunty brought it," she said smugly.

"I gather Amanda has got it," said the Inspector, kissing her.

"Honeybody, I suppose. I could hear his bronchial wheeze through the keyhole. A good thing the Aunt is deaf. She's even cut out the Vicar because of his remarks about Social Justice—two thousand quid the poor man loses. Amanda will have a large dowry. I thought it would only complicate matters to tell her about little Cedric, but being a man he can always make money somehow."

"She'll change the will half a dozen times a year."

"But I am her only flesh and blood, about which she has strong views. And while I'm on the subject have you arrested the fellow who banged my sconce; a bit of lead piping Honeybody said when we were having tea?"

"I'm off the case," said Harry. "Personal feelings have nothing to do with police work."

Elizabeth said something rude before adding, "I have been in this bloody bed thinking and I cannot remember a thing."

"Don't try," the Inspector held her hand and spent an hour listening to the future glories of little Cedric, via the Bar to the Judiciary. The smallest—and most intimidating—nurse entered, restraining the grin that some sally of Sergeant Honeybody had produced. "That's enough until tomorrow, Inspector. Now we have our Bengers' and a little sleepy-bye."

"Aunty was telling me about Jamaican food," said Elizabeth, but the Inspector disappeared behind a smile.

"I do wish you would catch whoever it was," said the scrubbed consultant, bearding Harry at the end of the corridor, "and get your Mr. Honeybody out of the place. He is becoming a legend and an institution. Little probationers make excuses to peer in and giggle. And the general smell of alcoholic beverages seems to be seeping out. Matron is not, but definitely not, amused."

The Inspector whispered that an arrest was imminent, winced at the sceptical look, and made the best of his way home.

The two ladies were admiring Amanda who, by some inbuilt female instinct of knowing upon which side her bread was buttered, was ogling Aunty with the same kind of look which Harry remembered his elder sister wearing just before she succeeded in locking him in a spider-webbed outside lavatory when aged seven. Mr. Bones swished his tail regularly at the Jamaican lady and ignored Harry.

"Have you got him?" demanded the Aunt.

"No, but we shall."

"Hm." Fortunately food, never far from her mind, saved him a nasty corner. "We waited lunch. Mrs. Smith cooked a wonderful and exotic dish; I never knew coloured people ate so well."

There was a faint flicker of a smile in Mrs. Smith's eyes as she said softly, "Like Mr. Bones we do the best we can."

"And very good it was," said Aunty, "not like some poor people near me who you always see buying tough steak when they could get nourishment out of trotters or Argentine frozen ground."

"I had to see my superior officer," said Harry, not quite lying, but throwing Aunty, who whilst being kind to lesser breeds within the law never fundamentally regarded them as human, off the scent.

"I suppose if you are respectful you might get a raise," said Aunty, soberly. "In business I always let it be known that cap-in-hand would be treated liberally, but above-their-station certainly not."

When she started talking rationally he'd have to have a quiet word with Amanda, Harry thought, making an excuse to go to his bedroom which seemed strangely lonely. He peered around and looked into the tiny offshoot, a cubicle with shelves which Elizabeth grandly referred to as the 'dressing-room' but in which only a pygmy could have donned a very primitive garment with ease. "Damn," he tripped over something which he recognised as Elizabeth's favourite but most battered suitcase. He might as well empty it as she could hardly have had time. He put it on the bed and found the spare key neatly labelled on its hook behind the dressing-table; she was infallible and meticulous in such matters. He put away the drip-dries, piled Amanda's clothes to one side—how the devil could one so small need so many garments?—and removed the newspaper with which Elizabeth had lined the suitcase. With a wry twist to his mind he saw it was the *Daily Bulletin*. Almost automatically he leafed it through; the big, black headlines beating at his eyes. The day after Percy Button had died. The lead on page one was 'John Jolly Demands a Stop to All This'. There was the Button demise in red in the stop-press. 'At about 3.30 p.m. yesterday Percy Button of *The Bulletin* was found dead in his room. Murder is suspected of the astrologer, 52.'

He threw it to one side and went into the living-room. A familiar odour assailed his nostrils. Amanda's nappies, on the stainless steel clothes-horse, were brewing before the gas-fire. Aunty was powdering his daughter and Mrs. Smith was saying there was nothing like children in the house. The Inspector gloomily remembered that somebody had once told him that boys were worse.

Aunty's Christian name was a monstrous one culled from the Old Testament, against which the Inspector had an inbuilt block, settling for 'my dear', which he used on this occasion. "I didn't know you took the old *Bully*?"

"That rag!"

"Only that I unpacked Liz's case and it was lined with it."

Aunty snapped Amanda's pants in place. She was not a woman to abandon an unexplained factor. "When I had my illness and phoned Elizabeth I had been staying in Cornwall. I

179

bought a bundle of papers on the station; they always come in for fires and the dustbin after all. I suppose it was one of those."

The Inspector opted for scrambled eggs, avoided conversation, and finally took a markedly subdued Mr. Bones to the statue of Thomas Carlyle. It was early to bed with a sleeping pill and a curiously persistent dream that he was bathing within the confines of a large steak and mushroom pie.

9

PAINFULLY CRANING HIS neck round the Inspector saw it was six a.m. His head felt heavy and he was reluctant to move. He lay there in the unpleasant state between sleeping and waking while something niggled at his mind. At seven he forced himself to take a luke-warm shower. Aunty, proclaiming breakfast the best meal of the day, her inevitable comment about any meal, was already hoeing into ham and eggs served by Mrs. Smith, but had the virtue of not talking while she ate it. He refused ham and ate a piece of toast without appetite. He excused himself and telephoned the hospital, finally being switched through to a sleepy Elizabeth who announced that Little Cedric was fine and that nurse said that, if weather smiled, she could sit on the balcony. If Aunty came could she bring The Knitting, a pullover for Harry commenced three years previously. Perhaps she could transfer him to Honeybody, suggested the Inspector.

"It's his day off. There is a very tough young Sergeant with a cauliflower ear outside. I must say that on balance I have faith in Honeybody. I mean he knows all the filthy tricks like biting people and gouging at their eyes. The Sergeant looks the clean type that thinks anything low is low," she giggled. "Honeybody made the most outrageous remarks to nurse and, man, can she Quell at a Glance."

"I may not be in to see you this morning," said Harry.

"Are you taking the man who hit me?"

It crystallised in the Inspector's mind. "Yes," he said.

He dialled Honeybody, who having wangled a Council-owned flat had installed all manner of expensive refinements including a bidet, the latter with some vague idea of keeping live trout for the gentry. "Ar," said the Sergeant, "morning, sir. There are times when a man gets sick of the left-over fish; kind of greasy and sickly after the night before."

There was a kind of shrill screeching in the background which Harry attributed to the Sergeant's Dodo in defence of old fried fish. "Sergeant," he said, "a caper up Fleet Street on your day off, no names and no pack drill."

"Indeed, sir, I was about to collect the fish, but my Dodo can make other arrangements. Sorry, my love, but my guv requires me in the line of dooty! Where and when, sir?"

The Inspector had a momentary vision of Honeybody in the long, yellowish combinations in which he slept, on the occasions upon which he remembered to remove his outer garments, and frankly wished he had not eaten the toast. "At the Falstaff at noon."

"Right, guv'nor."

The Inspector sat on the inadequate stool and wondered who he could trust. Peter Leeming was the obvious choice, but the lined, grey man had such ingrained loyalty that he would scarcely avoid the impulse to consult Sir Peregrine and the company lawyers. And Harry, despite his words to Elizabeth, was not certain *who*. Finally he decided upon Archer McClout, the girl Mabel Snowberry being too young to be involved with homicidal maniacs. He peered into the Directory.

McClout lived at Brixton and was enjoying a fried egg seated on a lamb chop. He was not at all pleased at being interrupted.

"For Christ's sake," he gravelled, "when I wake up the wife is bad enough insisting on reading out letters from the in-laws."

"I cannot guarantee it, Archer, but there might be a story. Will you listen? World rights!" The Inspector talked for ten minutes.

"Why pick me?" said McClout suspiciously.

"I would stand out like a sort thumb; whoever it is would be out of the building in no time. I don't want a killer on the run."

"Let's have a think," McClout cogitated for several minutes. "All right, I'll go through the motions. When do I see you?"

"The Falstaff at twelve."

In spite of his previous resolution the Inspector found himself patting Aunty before going down and hailing a taxi. In his room sat a substitute looking gloomily at the 'in' pile. He brightened as he saw Harry.

"Thanks be that you are back. The old effer," he jerked his thumb at the ceiling, "told me to add your load to mine. Eleven thirty I got home last night and the wife so irate—it was the pictures night—she'd got her mother round, both tight on a bottle of gin and calling me for everything. The old lady said if she could have got out of her chair she'd have hit me with the bottle and not used the labelled side."

"Sorry, Ted," said the Inspector, "but I'm off today. Tomorrow I'll get in early. Do you know anybody who pinches smoked salmon?"

"Look, Harry, last week I nicked a man who specialises in flutes and piccolos—sneaks up at concerts when the long-haired chaps are having their break and stuffs them down his trouser leg—but smoked salmon, Gawd, ask the old bleeder up there," he jerked his thumb at the ceiling, "and let me get on with this bumf."

As usual Superintendent Hawker looked as though he was graven into his office. The American exercising chair was gone and, to get in with a slow curve, the Inspector enquired after it.

"I gave it to a Home for Old Ladies," snarled Hawker, "it'll shake them up a bit. The Matron says they demand nylon stockings these days. After ten minutes in that chair they'll settle for sensible black wool ones." He surveyed Harry sourly. "What do you mean by hanging about Fleet Street? Porterman was very cross."

"I got a lift with a fence," said Harry. "I got tired of him in Fleet Street. In exchange he'll give us a lead on the smashing of sub-post-offices if we'll tip him off about a reliable source of smoked salmon—he's opening a restaurant for the stockbrokers and advertising."

"Old Spoon?"

"The same, bent on catering for the aristocracy."

Hawker rubbed his chin. "After all we are here to help the workings of capitalism! It's a challenge."

The aged Superintendent had over the years secreted a vast filing system in tin cabinets, quite apart from his own monumental archives in 'Records'. Any personalised query, thought Harry, gave the old man a kind of sexual thrill.

"Fishing rods and flies," mused the Super, "I remember they got from two to seven in 1948, then on to shop breaking. Bombay Duck out of an Indian caff, Royal Swans, though hardly fish, but here we are. 'Salmon, Smoked'. He used to work in an Irish factory producing Scotch salmon. It's done in 'sides' but he's got big feet and each night he could put two pounds in each sock. Every month his old mum used to secrete it about her person and take it over on the ferry, flogging it around the Liverpool clubs while they were listening to the music. Gave them an appetite, she said when they pinched her, thinking it was 'pot' she was peddling. Eighteen months and her son now in a tourist agency. Take the card! Mind, I won't have you messing about the *Bulletin*, so get along with you."

The Inspector found a colleague who was looking lugubriously at a map which had sub-post-offices marked upon it. There seemed a hell of a lot of them.

"Can I use your phone?"

"Sure."

Greasy Spoon was at home in his luxurious flat. He listened to Harry carefully and said, "Given up his bat has he?"

"In a travel agency."

"I'll talk him back, but four pounds a day ain't enough. I've been watching the advertising. I seen two of 'em put four pounds away, cut thin, before tackling the turbot without raising an *eyelid*, although I must admit that it *was* Friday. I'll have to talk to this fellow; straps round the chest like they use in the butter factories, a pound under your hat and what you can attach to the calves, giving your mind to it, is nobody's business. I wish he was a woman, they can stow away so much more without nobody noticing it. My daughter Ethel, who is on the skinny side, once walked thirty pounds of coffee beans all the way from Wapping to her caff in Brixton. Though of course what with short shifts and Twiggy looks it's getting difficult. They say the shoplifters are goin' on National Assistance. When my good wife was at the hoisting you'd be surprised 'ow much she could stuff away, but now...!"

Once a week Mr. Spoon devoted a day to his bottles, being a connoisseur of French brandy, and evidently this was the day.

"You have got the address?" asked the Inspector.

"Drunk or sober, sir, I never lose nothing important. It's written down and drunk or sober I write the same."

"You've got my quid, now your pro."

"Nah, listen," said Spoon and Harry's pen glided over the page of his unofficial notebook.

"Only puzzler, Mr. Spoon," he said when the fence had finished, "is why are you grassing?"

"The bastard used to be a jump-up man* and las' year he sold me a good load of Danish pork meat. So it was, the top layer, but underneath the cheapest quality corned beef. I 'ad to sell at a loss—me at a loss!—to a cove who runs fake homes for underprivileged kids."

"Goodbye, Mr. Spoon!" The Inspector replaced the handset.

The Inspector told his colleague who looked sceptical as he heard the name. "I can't see it, he's a jump-up."

"Has changed to greener pastures," said Harry, "the grass" —you always kept the name to yourself—"says instead of only thieving the cash he can't resist postal orders, stamps and savings books in for interest adjustment. He keeps them under the floor of his larder. It's tiled and one lifts up. Take your time and raid him."

"I can't thank you too much," said the colleague. "If this comes off I owe you a favour any time."

It was always this way, thought Harry, as he caught his bus to Fleet Street, you exchanged one favour against another, like some kind of unpleasant Stock Exchange, except that the divi-

* A citizen who steals cargo from trucks.

dends were gaol sentences. In the saloon of the Falstaff he found Honeybody, who had slightly jumped the gun as he could be relied upon to do on any alcoholic occasion, meditatively drinking gin and eating excellent beef sandwiches. "Just sandwiches for me," said Harry, "and plenty of mustard."

When Archer McClout came in he had two youngish men with him who proved to be linotype operators. Harry lined up drinks, noting that McClout's face was hardly pleasant.

"He never comes in here, but keep your voices down and try to smile. I doubt that I'll do so for some time. Now the Cornish edition is 'put to bed' at three forty-five, that is before Button's body was discovered."

"Is the time standard practice?"

"Yes," said McClout, "the old *Bully* is rather London and Home Counties. Too much replating sucks off the profit and Sir P. sold the Manchester works to a marmalade maker. However, we have to go through the motions as we sell space on a national basis. And nobody reads the bloody thing for hard, up-to-the-minute news. So at four forty-five the vans take off from the loading bay, to the railway station. Thence to the wholesalers, the retailers and the poor bugger who cycles through the snow at five in the morning delivering them. I'll buy another round. Drink up!"

McClout was postponing an evil hour, Harry realised.

"Wonderful advertising," grated McClout, "the Advertising Manager turned down two full pages for cheap cigars only this morning, nearly curdling his blood, but the P.M. had been warned by the U.S. Ambassador that once you start the working classes on cigars anything might happen, he mentioned Cuba as an example. Pot, the Liverpool Beat, and long hair keeps them quiet, but cigars they can't have, so Sir P., patriotic as he is, turned it down."

"If you want to do a comic act canvass the nightclub circuit." Harry gave look for look.

"It's divided loyalties," said McClout, "but I liked Wasey Tump. It was his big mistake to do that. On the other hand..."

"It's too late, McClout," said Harry.

"Yair! Now look, Sir P. flogs the used copy to one of the dead paper merchants as quick as possible so that you could not subpoena it. The reporters' notebooks are kept for six months in a store he's got on the Thames. Come libel he looks at them and if it's okay the book is produced in Court. If not it goes into the water." McClout ordered another round.

"Who?"

"Tell him what you told me, Walter," said McClout.

"It was in thick, subbing pencil," said the operator. "Stop press for the far-west edition. You work fast at that, but when I'd finished, being on the number fourteen machine, I turned to Harry here on my left and showed him the copy."

"Did you recognise the writing?"

"Mr. Leeming, sir," they chorused, miserably.

"You would swear?"

"Yes."

"Right, gentlemen, you'd help us most if you got back to work and kept silent. Mr. McClout, perhaps you'd stay here."

He turned to Honeybody only to find the big Sergeant gone, he supposed to the men's room.

"He's a newspaper man all through," sighed the Australian. "Couldn't resist doing his duty. I dunno but that he did Tump in I'd have come clean with you. There aren't many newspaper men like that left; when I was apprenticed in Sydney we had an old editor who, if there was no news, ran a story about finding his wife in bed with the milkman, sometimes varying it with the night-soil collector—it was primitive in those days —or the bloke who delivered the bread. The breed is dying out."

"Does he always do the stop press?"

"When he's on duty. He works like five of the youngsters put together and has this anxiety complex; always peering over people's shoulders. When he pushed Tump over the platform it was his early night off. He quit at eightish."

"What's his domestic background?"

"Widower, no kids, lives in some rather good private hotel around Mayfair. Can afford to do himself well. Holiday abroad; he's a fair linguist."

"He said something once that niggled in my mind about liking foreign food," said Harry, looking up to see Honeybody returned and ordering drinks, "but it's tenuous; the opinion of two linotype operators. Imagine what good counsel could do. I suppose there's no chance of retrieving the copy?"

"They macerate the stuff within twenty-four hours," said McClout, "there was something important once which got into the sack by mistake and Jolly tried to get it back, but with no luck."

"Hang on, Sergeant," said the Inspector, "I'm going to arrest Mr. Leeming on suspicion of causing grievous bodily harm. My wife must have picked up your far-west edition—her Aunt had bought it—and become curious. So she came into the *Bulletin* office and asked questions. You said, Mr. McClout, that she asked factual questions, but that Leeming stuck to pious generalities. But he saw a very large rat and while she was speaking to the girl Snowberry he possessed himself of a piece of lead piping and...thank God...."

"You'd better brief me!" It was Superintendent Porterman standing behind him.

"Sorry, Harry," said Sergeant Honeybody, "but it was the topmost brass. Hawker tipped that you'd get him, but you have to keep out of the actual arrest."

"The cap-feathers are yours," said Porterman, "but you'd do yourself no good making the arrest."

The Inspector gave Honeybody his hardest look. The Sergeant engaged McClout in discussion concerning the rival merit of draught and bottled beer. Discipline above all, thought Harry sourly as he talked to Porterman in low tones, but he wondered whether it would ever be quite the same between him and Honeybody.

"Very thin," eventually commented Porterman, "ingenious but very thin. He's only got to sit there and tell us to get to buggery...then what?" The big Superintendent was incapable of keeping his voice down and a barmaid glanced curiously towards them.

"Leave it to me, sir," said Honeybody. "My Dodo is bringing in Daft Ted."

"Daft Ted!" Porterman was aghast. Knowing the Sergeant, Harry fiddled with his drink.

"They can't afford to cook, sir. Lord, the local London Authorities, now they're Tory, would come on them scone-hot, so they buy their grub, healthy fish and chippers, from, well, a relative...."

"I am a permanent member of the Disciplinary Board, Sergeant," Porterman showed his teeth, "and some things we overlook if not tried too far!"

"He can't read or write, Mr. Porterman," said Honeybody stolidly. "It's his day off."

"Are there people who can't read?" Porterman was astounded and Harry remembered that for quite a few years the Superintendent had been rather removed from the working class, bullying them, as it were, through capable intermediaries.

"Ah, sir," sighed Honeybody, who had somehow possessed himself of another pint. "Education has been the ruin of the working class. Daft Ted says that if his pa had been able to read he'd probably have died in Flanders in '17 instead of remaining cosily at home, selling patriotic badges and getting Daft Ted, who would just have been ripe to get picked off at Dunkirk if he could have read, instead of which he was flogging stolen cheese well away from the bombed areas. Thousands of them, sir! Can't read a Summons or a Bill and the Magistrate pats their heads and says, 'My poor underprivileged man, 'ere's something from the Poor Box'. Ted's got fourteen children who can't read."

"Kipling!" said Porterman, like a tethered bull.

"That was different, sir," said Honeybody, wiping froth off his lip, "before we had a social conscience. Today the generals can't get a man shot unless he can read. You used to be able to hang 'em, but today it's life and the Prison Education Officers. Many a man learns to read because otherwise he doesn't get the tobacco allowance."

"What does this man *do*?"

"He used to pinch alarm clocks."

There were little beads of sweat starting on Porterman's scarred, massive brow and although he never drank on duty he rapidly ordered a double Scotch and even succumbed to Honeybody's; "Thanks, I will, sir."

"You see," said Honeybody, "alarm clocks are the most easily disposed of article. If I had twenty taped around my chest I could flog them anywhere in twenty minutes. And easy to pinch. All the prollies have an alarm clock in the kitchen, so he used to prowl round the council flats and if he saw an open door, the lady having nicked out with the washing or to have a gossip, Ted would have the alarm under his heavyweight sweater. But now they're getting on to them electrics and Ted is afraid of them. Fortunately the Coloured Citizens are improving themselves and don't want the menial jobs no more, so such things as sweeping and mopping are open for Ted plus the Public Assistance. With fourteen kids it's amazing the fried fish they get through."

Porterman leaned heavily on the counter and sipped his drink, while Honeybody gustily belched like a man who has done his duty. It was strange, said the thought that popped into the Inspector's head, how his own dyspepsia had improved since Elizabeth had been in hospital.

There presently came a piping and gesturing from the door. Honeybody's Dodo did not frequent licensed premises; there was the momentary glimpse of her raw-boned presence. Daft Ted himself, wearing a uniform provided by the London Passenger Transport Board, had an expression of calculated vagueness and a husky voice which accepted a pint.

"I don't think I like this," muttered Porterman.

"Just leave it to me, sir," said the Sergeant, "me what's got nothing to lose but a skerrick of pension that the revenue would have off me like a pair of drawers. Just get Daft Ted in behind me and the rest I'll do. Drink up gentlemen, and one more round on the old Ser'nt."

"Where does he live?" muttered Harry while he eyed Ted's steadily working Adam's apple.

"Lord, sir, he doesn't have no trouble. That's why he got fourteen kids. Two or three now and the London County Council don't care, but with fourteen they've got to provide a big flat otherwise there's an outcry. It took him sixteen years to do it, but since 1953 'e's had no trouble. He's only got to threaten to get somebody to write to Mr. Hogg and they come runnin' round to repair the toilet; with sixteen it gets a lot of use."

"Let's move," growled Porterman. "The building's surrounded and nobody can leave. I put two men on to that old horror Bocker and there are fellows on the fire escapes. Let's make it quick before Sir P., who is in the place, gets on to the P.M."

In the event Bocker gave a wounded look, reached for the intercom telephone and had his mottled old hand smartly twisted inadvertently by a young constable.

The senior liftman was displaced by Honeybody who gave precedence to Daft Ted who was removing cold potato chips from a hip pocket and munching contentedly. At the third floor he produced a piece of cold hake from his trouser pocket and Porterman recoiled from the offer of even shares like a scalded horse. Archer McClout had no such scruple, "Gather ye taste buds while you may," he muttered, "they atrophy at the rate of a million a day even if those bastards upstairs give you anything to work them on."

In the news room there was a fair amount of activity concerning a libel action lodged by a stout, elderly Chelsea chemist, falsely accused of indecent exposure, but by some mishap publicised. The Editor was standing, short of breath, by the side of a grumpy old solicitor with a skin condition, and Sir Peregrine with his long whey-face seething with alarm, seemed to try to take refuge in the long-suffering bosom of Peter Leeming.

"Now, Sir P.," Leeming was saying, his thick black pencil compulsively running over copy, "there are many chemists in Chelsea and I think there are several precedents that cover us."

"Never say that, never say that!" said the solicitor, nervously plucking at the scabs on his bald head.

"Mr. Leeming," boomed Honeybody's basso, "please look up!

Police here!" Leeming's grey, worried face darted to one side. Daft Ted, his left foot deftly trodden on by Honeybody, extended an accusing finger at Sir Peregrine, veering it back to Leeming at the Sergeant's skilful and painful thumb in the ribs.

"Is that the man, porter?" asked Honeybody, promoting Ted several ranks up the ladder.

Ted was not used to affirmative nodding and it required further pressure on his foot to achieve one.

"Pushing Miss Wasey Tump in the path of a train, causing two hours' delay and a fold-up in Battersea Power Station, let alone Union Trouble," intoned Honeybody. It was not unreasonable, thought Harry. With amateurs, you threw the book; it unnerved them and no appeal court could get you for it.

Still working on proofs, Peter Leeming began to cry, muttering something about the Brighton train case on page six not being to his satisfaction.

"You may as well make a statement for all the editions," said Porterman with surprising subtlety, "the bloke from the *Mirror*"—he lied—"is in the foyer. If you talk this paper will have a beat."

"I took a holiday in Czechoslovakia," said Leeming, "and I had some information, 'D' classified. Damn it, everybody said the Russians should be told in the interests of Peace. Later I wrote the second leader saying so. They insisted on giving me three hundred quid as a gesture of sincerity."

"Not that it was not welcome," said Porterman, "and don't lie. On my way here I briefly telephoned your bank. You always had tastes above your income."

Harry watched Sir Peregrine's creased jowls register horror and Leeming seize the sporting page and scribble.

"Then Percy Button came along," said Leeming, "with his astrology—bunch of balls and why should I care? Jolly spotted the stop press and asked for money, but I was sorry about Tump. She saw me and had to go. Then there was this other woman coming round and asking questions. I don't like this North London story," said Leeming inconsequentially, "It's got a very weak lead-in."

"I think you had better go along," said Porterman, gesturing to the constables who had discreetly arrived. Leeming seized his proofs. "Back by taxi immediately, Sir P.!" he said as he was eased out of the news room.

Porterman tapped his shoulder at the door.

"Why did you do it?"

"He wanted more space. The stars weren't enough for the amount he was getting through, so he wanted the sporting page as well." Leeming's sad gaze flickered around the large room. "I couldn't let him tamper with *news*."

Archer McClout was in Leeming's seat, scribbling and yelling for a boy. "The story of the year," he muttered, "Smith, dig up his biography, we're contempt-free until they charge him. Boy! Boy!"

Sir Peregrine's long nose twitched. "Mr. McClout, I appoint you to Mr. Jolly's seat as from now!"

"Terms?" snapped the Australian without looking up. Sir P. recoiled and said something about the next morning.

"It had better be," said McClout.

"Sir," said Honeybody to Harry, "there's a pub I know...."

The Inspector followed him.

NOW YOU CAN KNOW THE EXERCISE EQUIVALENTS OF EVERY FOOD YOU EAT...

ONE HOT FUDGE SUNDAE = 58 MINUTES
OF RACQUETBALL
(if you weigh 120-139 lbs.)

ONE SLICE OF APPLE PIE = 22 MINUTES OF
FAST CROSS-COUNTRY SKIING
(if you weigh 160-179 lbs.)

ONE CHEESEBURGER = 44 MINUTES OF
LIGHT GYMNASTICS
(if you weigh 100-119 lbs.)

ONE FRIED CHICKEN DRUMSTICK = 11 MINUTES
OF CYCLING (11mph)
(if you weigh 180-199 lbs.)

ONE GLASS OF CHAMPAGNE = 25 MINUTES
OF CALISTHENICS
(if you weigh 140-159 lbs.)

ONE PASTRAMI SANDWICH = 62 MINUTES OF
HEAVY CARPENTRY WORK
(if you weigh over 200 lbs.)

**...WITH THE COMPLETELY
PERSONALIZED GUIDE TO MANAGING
YOUR WEIGHT AND FITNESS**

Calories Burned Per Minute

ATTENTION SCHOOLS AND CORPORATIONS

WARNER books are available at quantity discounts with bulk purchase for educational, business, or sales promotional use. For information, please write to SPECIAL SALES DEPARTMENT, WARNER BOOKS, 666 FIFTH AVENUE, NEW YORK, N.Y. 10103

ARE THERE WARNER BOOKS
YOU WANT BUT CANNOT FIND IN YOUR LOCAL STORES?

You can get any WARNER BOOKS title in print. Simply send title and retail price, plus 50¢ per order and 50¢ per copy to cover mailing and handling costs for each book desired. New York State and California residents add applicable sales tax. Enclose check or money order only, no cash please, to: WARNER BOOKS, P.O. BOX 690, NEW YORK, N.Y. 10019